JOSS PHOENIX

Evernight Teen ®

www.evernightteen.com

JOSS PHOENIX

DEDICATION

No ducks were harmed. Promise.

JOSS PHOENIX

HIDE FROM US

Alchem Academy, 1

Joss Phoenix

Copyright © 2025

PLAYLIST

Neon Lights - Demi Lovato

Sugar, We're Goin Down - Fall Out Boy

Willow - Taylor Swift

Bones - Imagine Dragons

Love Song - Sara Bareilles

Rhythm of Love - Plain White T's

How you remind me - Nickelback

JOSS PHOENIX

I Lived - One Republic

Try - Colbie Caillat

Same Old Love - Selena Gomez

Jar of Hearts - Christina Perri

Downfall - Neoni

Afterlife - Five Finger Death punch

Silent Theory - Fragile Minds

Stranger - Fight the Fade

Make It Out Alive - ONE OK ROCK × Monster Hunter Now

The Thunder Rolls - STATE of MINE (feat. No Resolve) - Garth Brooks METAL cover

Life Goes On - Ed Sheeran

Perfect - Simple plan

Centuries - Fall Out Boy

Terminal - Sleep In Motion

Everything - Bridge To Grace

CONTENT WARNING

HIDE FROM US is a young adult gothic romance/mystery suitable for ages 14+. It includes themes teens deal with often in silence and without support. Below is a list that may affect sensitive readers. Please read safely.

Cutting, self-harm, anxiety, depression, violence, drug use, alcohol, physical assault, recounting of self-harm, suicide romanticism, death off the page, violence, recounting abuse, sexual assault, stalking, and dark themes. This book also includes gay kissing, and polyamorous romantic relationships as well as a semi non-verbal character due to family situationship.

Joss

JOSS PHOENIX

Prologue

Never Break

He's going to break up with you.

I stare at my phone, unsure if it's Zeke or Elen who sent the message. The name on the screen blurs. It doesn't matter either way. The information is true, regardless of who sent those seven little words to me.

The school ski trip has become that much more hazardous.

Thoughtful, or bully?

I've experienced both sides of the Elite from all of them.

Except maybe Zeke. That boy has hated me on sight from the first moment I walked onto Alchem Academy grounds a little over four months ago. Nothing in this world would make him happier than to have his boy squad back the way it was before I crashed into Aster Craven's life and caused a kerfuffle none of them have ever quite recovered from.

My boys have a soft spot for you.

Aster's words from months ago reverberate along my spine as a second message buzzes in my hand.

Ex Aster. Not boyfriend Aster. A new status update is required.

The new message isn't any clearer than the first. I blink a few times until the words blur back into focus.

Get your things. I'll find you.

That's … sweet.

I smirk at my phone, though my stomach roils with a familiar pain lanced by a familiar enemy.

Definitely not Zeke. That boy doesn't have a sweet bone in his body. Elen, then. The K-pop star with the blue hair and the lip piercings who busted me perving on him on my first day at school and didn't call me out like the others would have.

Did.

I wonder if Nyx is with him, or if Elen will find me alone. He's always been there even through the bullying. Sometimes taking part, sometimes watching, but always there.

Always hating the hate.

Aster's words again. The ghost of him haunts me though I knew this was coming. Our slice of peace never could last, has always been fake. A facade. But Elen's voice from my first day at Alchem Prep Academy overrides my soon-to-be-ex.

She's an eleven.

He walked with me to classes morning after morning. Warned me about Aster in his quiet way.

I should've listened.

I shouldn't have fallen for them. Him.

Damnit, they do my head in. All of them.

Then … I fell in love. But so did he. The Idle Prince of Alchem Academy, or at least of his own lunchbox.

No, Aster Craven isn't the scariest thing in my world.

Despite the pain my reply costs, I send back a single word.

Me: **Okay.**

My throat blocks as tears threaten my view of the snowy cabins, the trip that was meant to be a founding stone for all of us.

I won't let Aster break me. He tried that last time … and failed. Part of me takes pleasure in knowing that I broke something in him instead.

No, Aster Craven isn't the scariest thing out there.

I am.

The first tear cascades along my cheek. A single drop of denial to my harder exterior while inside, marshmallow me curls in on herself, willing away the familiar pain that loss brings.

Aster's message pops up, but I black my screen and don't read it.

Abandonment.

They will not break me.

A stupid smile spreads across my face as I pack my snow-damp clothes.

No.

I'll break them, instead.

JOSS PHOENIX

Chapter One

Before My Life Turns to Shit. Again.

Three weeks ago
Roxy

A pair of matching headstones epitomize the lives of two people who, in the end, barely knew each other, and the last twelve weeks of my life that have been utter hell.

Dead parents. Narcissistic, filthy rich aunt who shoved me into a life I never asked for and wish I could leave. A place at the elitist Alchem Academy full of the overindulged, often spoiled, world and business leaders' offspring. Bully boyfriend to top the list.

And four boys who watch every step I take, their eyes filled with a cold fury no one can sate that's not my fault, though they all claim it.

Pain. Rage. Loss.

But Alchem isn't where they wait while I reflect on the mortality that can be stripped away so fast and leave us bereft in an uncaring world, shifted about like chess pawns in someone else's game.

I stand before my parents' side-by-side graves where they lie as they would never have in their divorced lives. They hated each other by the end and were still trying to make amends that couldn't fix their patchwork mess of addiction and lies. The not-quite-as-fresh dirt that mounds their passing is covered by an icy drizzle that ekes bone deep on all sides except for one.

Aster Craven stands off to one side and slightly behind me, holding a ridiculously expensive black and silver umbrella branded with his father's company logo. His warmth leeches into my arm, leaving my other shoulder numb as I stare at the stone etched names, *my* last name that disappears letter by letter as pelting rain obliterates everything.

I know the others wait by the cars behind us in their blue and silver Alchem Academy uniforms, posing unconsciously beside the matching Bugatti Aster prefers, and the blue Lamborghini that fits Elen's personality and piercings. Both are sans drivers today.

Because today is different.

Anyone else might tell me to leave when Aster, refusing the protection of the branded umbrella's girth, says nothing. He watches. Waits.

While I'm supposed to grieve.

I'm not sure what I feel, so I feel nothing but the cold and the singular slice of warmth.

This is a waste of their time.

"I'm sorry," I mumble.

His presence beside me, behind me, never wavers.

I don't know if I'm talking to them, the dead bodies beneath the earth who aren't really my parents now anyway, or to the boy who stands out in the cold with me. The stupid, short hem of my Alchem Academy uniform shrinks on demand. I yank at the patterned material, pulling the hentai-esque box pleats out of shape. The damn thing costs enough for its pathetic length, nothing I could have afforded back at my old school, or house back in Providence, Nevada.

My aunt's voice echoes in my ears, ranting on about uncouth females who don't know how to dress. Alchem has standards and I'm … lacking.

I'd smile at the deficit of sentiment, but my lips have frozen, too.

"She hates me," I say to no one at all, still staring at the place where their names should be on the wavering grave markers invisible behind a sheet of impenetrable water. Maybe no one is listening, but somehow I know he will. "I don't belong there."

Or here. *Anywhere.*

In that house. With my aunt's ostentatious display of her accumulated wealth and her finery. Where she doesn't want me, never did. I don't know why she bothered to claim me when all she seems to want to do with the unwanted orphan who she's taken in is to shunt me off to a school a state away where I can fulfill the old adage of being not seen, and go unheard.

Or at school, with Aster and the boys.

Last semester they—*he*—made my lack of *everything* abundantly clear. The first day I stepped between Alchem's hideous golden gates—*ha, my Aunt must love the display of obsequious power and excess—* Aster started his bullying campaign against me. That fast devolved into a hot mess of twisted secrets, some of which I still don't have the answers to, revenge plots that I fully capitulated on in return, and a whole lot of flirting that, weirdly, ended with us … here.

Now, things have changed. Aster showed me who I am, who he is, and somewhere, somehow, we fell into place next to each other like two reversed puzzle pieces mixed in the middle.

I shiver and take a step back, bumping into the boy who bullied me, and maybe saved me from hurting myself once. Who taught me to how kiss, and held me for a long night.

Who never left.

"Take your time," he murmurs, resting long, cold fingers in the center of my back.

I shake my head, turning away from the names I can't read anyway, toward three other silhouettes. Drenched faces I can almost make out through the sleet that spikes at my desensitized skin, though they might be ghosts.

"No. I don't need to be here anymore."

****

Alchem Academy's lux cafeteria swells with the cacophony of four hundred students talking at once. I swear no one listens to anyone else. That's fine, because lost amongst the white noise I can pretend for once that no one watches me.

Even though I know it's not true.

My hands still ache from the graveyard, the cold that seeps in like so many souls whispering between my bones in search of a forever home. I survived my hour's penance like I survive everything.

The death of absentee parents. The father who gave up a perfectly good career in law to become a prison guard with a dice gambling habit, though no one understands why even after his death.

That was the beginning of the mess my family became if I traced it all back. When my parents fell apart and forgot about the child left in the middle. Bills stopped being paid, and two people fell apart separately.

Absence is meant to make the heart grow fonder, but those are lies we create to fill holes and cracks that grow. My father's absence created an abyss between my parents that sprouted a fondness for hatred of themselves and for each other.

They were meeting to sign divorce papers the day they died. Date night with a fresh twist.

We survived without him before that. Well, I did. Not the mother drugged out of her mind while she was still alive because my father stopped coming home from his new job.

Taking her shift at a burger bar because no work meant no money. Or rent, or food. Working underage and learning how grease sticks to every surface—etching beneath every layer of skin, the stench of gritty, overcooked oil an eternal companion. Dirt clinging to my hair. No electricity when it got cut off. Hot water became a luxury, not a necessity.

None of it compares to the pain that brought me to Alchem Academy beneath a shroud where my name became anathema during my first days at the elite school. The throne of offspring power in the US and other nations that includes a few international students. My introduction to California is complete. If somebody bombs this place, they'll start an all-out war with the world's conglomerate wealthiest.

The student body alone, who pay their tithes from their personal bank accounts, rival the GDP of more than one small nation.

But calamity of that sort never happens because Alchem has a security level nobody sees. Rumored to be deadly, even if they don't care how the students behave toward each other—especially if said student significantly lacks wealth, or there's a power imbalance, like between Aster and me when I first arrived.

Then, it's a free for all at a whole new level.

Which brings me back to four sets of eyes leveled on me as I toy with my food, dirt and grease free. No matter how many weeks and months I sit in this cafeteria, ahem *dining hall*, surrounded by the boys who watch me constantly, I know I'm not completely safe here.

Even my once-bully and now-boyfriend, Aster Craven, keeps his secrets. The father who told him to stay away from me before I was made it onto his radar remains a mystery via the connection to my aunt's pharma company.

"You're thinking again. I did say it was bad for you," Bully/boyfriend—Aster—murmurs as he leans down to brush his lips across my temple.

Warmth sprinkles across my skin in the wake of his brief touch. Long, inked fingers flex at my side. I know he wants me on his lap, but I refuse to move my tush in a cafeteria filled with people.

Especially wearing Alchem's pornographically short—*mandatory, welcome to the twenty-first century and beyond*—skirt that belongs more in anime than reality. I clutch my snobby coffee in its porcelain mug, another remnant of Alchem's unique culture. I requested bamboo cups we could take to class and was glared at until I removed myself from the lunch line.

So here I sit, twirling my sushi rolls about on my plate with a side serve of extra kimchi Elen steals with the hint of a smile tugging at his clear lip piercings.

"Roxy." Aster sighs when I don't reply to his passive-aggressive barb, though I'm not sure if he's amused or exasperated with me, or plain tired. Pale hair flops artistically over his brow as he watches me through dark eyes that never leave my face.

His arm snakes around my shoulder and drops to my waist, drawing me tight to his side in an overt display of ownership that sits both pleasantly over me and that I hate all at the same time.

A girl can have dueling emotions, right?

I don't want to risk knowing my short few months with him are over already—we both know that's coming, thanks to his father's sickening obsession with me—and focus on the three other boys seated around our table, their backs turned to the room. Not that it matters, because their attention is focused singularly on me, and I can't escape.

K-pop star Elen Vash with his Korean characteristics and blue/black streaked hair, plus facial piercings and a gaze to match are courtesy of a custom range of contacts he wields like weapons. His tongue drifts across his bottom lip to toy with an anodized blue ring there as he watches me with lazy eyes that disguise none of the intelligence that lies beneath his easy facade.

Nyx Huxley, our resident starving musician, is covered in green ink he's done himself, tortured leather that covers narrow shoulders, and a fuzzy mass of hair that's recently spouted a few dreads. Like Elen, nothing about him is Alchem Academy issue worthy. A guitar case covered in retro grunge band stickers leans next to his seat, most of his crinkled brown hair pulled back into a manbun. As always, his phone rests in his hands. He taps at the screen absently, a soft melody changing as he works on whatever song currently resides in his head.

Zeke Fallon, I save for last. Our angry boy. If I make a scan around the table starting with Aster as the coldest, through Nyx and Elen getting warmer, Zeke's constant fury blares off the charts at the other extreme of the scale.

The Elite. The crème de la crème of Alchem Academy. Untouchable.

Zeke glares at me over the hamburger he attacks like both of us have personally affronted him, though I bear his residual punishment. Pure rage emanates from him with every heartbeat. I scoot into Astor's side without thinking.

The corners of Zeke's mouth turn up as he places his ragged burger remnants onto his plate, though his eyes never leave me. Not even to blink. Somehow, that makes his anger a darker shade. The emotion emanates across the table, roiling toward me like a palpable thing.

Refusing to give another inch, I stare back, meeting his fury with a hard stare of my own made of too many nights flipping burnt burgers and warding off wandering customer hands.

The sort of labor these boys will never

understand.

I flick imaginary grease remnants from beneath my nails as Aster tightens his hold on my waist, leaning a long leg forward in his tailored, charcoal uniform pants to kick Zeke under the table.

"Stop it." His soft command shouldn't be audible beyond the edges of our table, but everyone outside the tight radius of our social circle listens.

Zeke alone appears unaffected.

"Get fu–"

"Stop." Aster's command rings with power. "Language. You know Roxy doesn't like it."

I actually don't care. This appears to be his hill to die on.

Never shy of sharing his rage, Zeke slams his plate containing his mangled meal against the table and swipes the back of his hand across his face in a grotesque display that goes against everything the Elite and Alchem stand for.

I blink between them. "Don't blame me for this." I wave my hands at Zeke, wanting no part in any responsibility of the fight brewing over my head between the two boys. Aster looks down at me pointedly, and I sigh. *Committed front, and all.* "Fine. Why don't you say … duck." I blink again.

"Duck. Are you F—*ducking sh*—whatever, me?" Zeke snaps, his annoyance and amused irritation vying for prime real estate on his face, his burger and fight forgotten for the moment.

I shake my head and point. "No, *duck*," I enunciate, pointing at the feathered bird that waddles right up to Zeke, coming out of literal nowhere, and quacks.

Loud enough to echo.

Zeke ducks on command, and the entire dining

hall erupts in laughter.

Swearing, he climbs to his feet to shoo the waddling thing away while I giggle, rocking against Aster's side, though he might as well be a statue for all the reaction the odd experience ekes out of him. Zeke keeps flapping and the hall breaks up, though the duck ignores everyone as he plays up to the crowd.

For a moment, I stare at this new side of him exposed for the first time. All I ever see is the furious part of Zeke. Right now, him waddling about with bent knees and quacking, pretending to flap his bent elbows, is too hilarious for words.

Finally, the random duck deigns to move away on its own, but not before leaving a duck-sized present right on the toe of Zeke's boot.

"Ducking fantastic," he mutters, attempting to swipe the sticky stuff off with his heel as he sits his butt back down. Within seconds, his angry facade reclaims its habitual place, and the status quo resumes as though nothing changed at all.

In this strange world of perceived perfection, Zeke seems to be the sole human with a grip on this twisted reality. For me, there's no rabbit hole to climb. Two funerals and an empty mansion armed with a service of ghosts is all that remains of my broken family.

And a narcissistic aunt I'd never heard of before my parents' death who insisted on stuffing me into an Alchem Academy branded uniform a week after I arrived in her home before she dispatched me for my first day at a boarding school I never agreed to attend.

Where I confronted Aster, and the rest of the Elite.

Enter Aster's twisted brand of obsession—bullying, betrayal, and other assorted variants of pain. Plus, my previous roommate who added a decent dollop of deception right into those cracks when I so stupidly handed her my trust without checking her credentials.

Maybe a side dose of self-harm made it in there too. That last seemed to be the pivot point between Aster and me, and some of the bullying factor dropped away.

None of the intensity.

Aster sat on my bed that night after my last roommate—and his ex—picked apart the trust I gave out. While that hurt was still raw, he took some of it back, pulled me into his arms, and taught me how to kiss.

Then he spent the entire night with his back to my wall, letting me cry on his chest and fall asleep there.

Every touch innocent, all aboveboard, fully clothed.

Promise.

Despite all evidence to the contrary these last weeks, I've pretended that the insulated bubble the boys keep me in is perfect, that things will stay this way forever.

I'm getting better at lying to myself each day.

Aster's fingers twitch at my side along the seam of my shirt, pulling the thin material out from where it tucks into my skirt. The concealed touch sends a thrill through me, but I know he won't stop there. What Aster Craven wants, he gets.

He's proven that to me time and again. My knees press together beneath the box pleats that I grip over my thighs with flattened palms to the bench seat beneath us.

"Don't do that." I wiggle a little as he pulls me in closer, still trying to lift me onto his lap. I huff at his tenacity, but that doesn't give him pause.

Resilience, meet resistance.

Motion at the table stills, except for Zeke who lifts his burger and contemplates the mangled remains. "Are you gonna tell her?"

Aster's wandering fingers halt. "Maybe later."

"Tell me what?" I look up, but he resumes his prior activity, tugging another corner of my shirt out as he watches me.

The edge of his mouth curves into a frown, and he shakes his head once. "It's not time yet." His fingers graze my stomach, and my eyes drift shut at the rare contact.

"Stop," I murmur again, but there's no real effort behind the single syllable.

"You've got a new roommate," Elen butts in, putting me out of my misery. The rockstar—not the wannabe sort, the actual rolling-in-millions or billions or whatever type of crazy-duckbutt fan base the K-pop star of boyband *Failure Asylum* fame has—rescues me.

I blow out a breath and glare at Aster like it's his fault. Let's be fair. It probably is, as the boys all seem to know something I don't.

Again.

"I'm happy on my own."

And in isolation.

His mouth curls up in a sinful smile. "Not that I object to that…" He tugs my shirt up at the back an inch and runs cool fingers along my spine. A shiver of the full body type ripples over me as his look turns speculative. "Speaking of, I wouldn't mind using a little of that privacy before—"

"Too late," Nyx chips in with an inordinately happy voice for a male who has been non-verbal for over ninety percent of our interactions so far. "She's already arrived."

Aster huffs, digging his fingers into my ribs in recompense. I try holding back my giggles, failing when his attack doubles. He does his best to look unaffected, but I know the truth.

"Bullshi—ducks. Tell her everything." Zeke eats as he talks. Demolishes, really, but he holds to our earlier quacking accord. "She should know about Rhani."

"Directing, much?" See, there goes my mouth again. "Wait, you can actually talk without swearing?"

Aster's chest rumbles. "Good to see you getting along."

I return Zeke's fresh glare with one of my own, still refusing to back down. It might be my imagination, but I swear the corner of his mouth flickers up.

"Should I get a welcome party out?" I have no idea about Alchem Academy traditions, apart from the Elite who have surrounded me from day one, like an inked, uniformed hamster ball.

While Aster, Zeke, Elen, and Nyx might be considered the Elite of Alchem Academy, there is another group who outranks them, though I suspect Aster is a member. The Eight-ball club. I still have no idea why it's called that, but it seems that every member has a personal bank account with zeroes exceeding the number nine. *After* the decimal point, not before. There are three known members: two boys, and a girl.

Represent.

At least it's not an all-boys club. Maybe someone should earn up and get an invite to even the odds.

"Okay. I'm down to go meet this Rhani person."

"Rhani and Roxy sitting in a tree, *K-I-S-S-I-N-G*." Nyx sings the playground song in an undertone with no emphasis, and perfectly in tune.

I could listen to him for hours.

"Didn't think you were talking today," I murmur, nudging his shoulder as much as Aster's hold on me allows while he still runs his fingers along my ribs in an effort to gain a reaction.

I ignore him as best I can, but he knows every

sensitive spot, damn him.

Despite whatever is supposed to be decorum amongst them, Nyx offers me an impish grin. He wraps one arm around me in a gentle hug, ignoring Aster's mood, though he withdraws the contact almost as soon as he touches me.

"I can't promise anything," Nyx whispers into my hair in his raspy, unused voice, and pulls away to his side of the table.

Aster clears his throat at my side, his nails digging into my skin. "Enough," he says sharply, and I look up at him in surprise.

"I think I'd pay to see Roxy kiss a girl," Elen muses, running his tongue along his bottom lip. He plays with the clear, pointed piercing there next to the blue ring I swear he's not supposed to wear at school.

I remember turning up on the first day at Alchem, watching him change out the blue pointy stud that matched his hair, in his then lime green Lamborghini that he's recently upgraded for the blue-silver one he drives now.

Gotta match the accessories to the drapes, and all.

Picking Aster's fingers from my skin one at a time as he watches me, dark eyes hooding with every touch, I rise and manage to shake him off.

Elen grabs for me as I skirt the table, but I avoid him, too.

This girl isn't without skills.

I blow him a kiss. "Nope. What happens in the dorm room stays in the dorm room."

Elen sends me a winning smile. "Not if I'm there with you, Roxy-Rockgirl."

I shake my head, laughing as I leave the cafeteria, conscious of more than four sets of eyes on my back, though the knowledge of my new roommate eats away my humor with every step.

As it happens, my new roomie isn't there when I get to my room that day, or the one after. I laugh off my trauma-induced anxiety as leftovers from my Aster-bully days, before I understood him better. I know he keeps secrets, but there's plenty he doesn't know about me, too. Things we don't talk about on either side. It hasn't been the right time yet, no matter how much time we get to ourselves.

Still, a new roomie can't be any worse than the last catastrophe. There's simply *no way* she can be as bad as my last dormmate.

Not at all.

Right?

Chapter Two

The Apple and the Tree

Aster

Ash drifts from the tip of my father's cigar to decorate the edge of his French polished desk. Fleshy lips tilt up in a smile that has redefined insanity many times over in my lifetime as he stares at me over the rim of his untouched whiskey.

I recognize that smile; I've never walked away from it unscathed. My facade doesn't crack as I pretend not to care about what sort of torment he's designed for me today.

"It's time." He leans back in his chair and ashes the cigar onto the carpet, forgoing manners like any normal person.

Except my father doesn't bother to hide the monster within, and hasn't for a long ducking time.

I fight to keep my face blank at the ridiculous show of wealth he doesn't need to flaunt around me but displays anyway. His lieutenants flank either side of his throne behind his ebony desk, both inked heavily. One bears snake scales along both arms, the twin heads peeking out the neck of his shirt, the other a full house of cards tattooed across the back of his hand, and a pair of dice, sixes up, on the other. They're a mirror of my single column of support where Zeke stands at my back, his hands clasped behind him, unmoving.

It's the place he has always occupied no matter what my old man throws at me. I know he'll never falter. That knowledge doesn't soften the blow my father strikes with aim perfected over seventeen tortured years.

"It's time to end it."

I recline in the leather chair placed on the other side of his desk rather than the uncomfortable wooden affair that usually sits in its place. That one he uses to torment his business partners, or those unfortunates who were stupid enough to enter into dealings with him and not hold up their end of whatever bargain they struck without understanding the consequences.

Alonso Craven might be the head of the largest pharma corporation in the world, but he runs it like his personal army. Correction—the biggest pharma corporation, apart from the one Roxy is set to inherit. Which is what his obsession, and by default mine, is all about.

I lean back in my comfortable seat and don't prepare to die. Today is not one of those days, though I've sat in that wooden chair many times and learned life lessons across this desk. Often those lessons was at the hands of the men who stare over my head at Zeke now.

Today's lesson is for both of us. That scares the shit out of me.

My father smiles at me, and it doesn't reach his eyes. I can't remember the last time that happened.

"You've had fun. It's time to let her go. Then you can enjoy destroying her again."

Once, that line might have offered the sweetest sort of temptation. Now, those same words fill me with a brand of dread that rocks my soul.

A soul I gave away the moment she stumbled over the threshold to Alchem Academy months before.

The day I fell for her.

I let my lip curl into the same sneer that threatened before, though my heart pounds inside the dead cavity of my chest as I pray to a God who hasn't answered me in over a decade. Roxy is worth whatever torture Alonso Craven has devised, but not this.

Not again.

Zeke, stationed at my back by his own design, manages to control his emotions better than me by his stillness alone. I borrow a portion of his strength to bolster my own.

"I already did that."

"Yes." My father bestows me with a condescending smile.

No.

Prickles creep over my skin. I resist the urge to scrape my nails over the pores and swipe away his invisible reach.

"If you … insist."

"I do." His smile broadens. "Apparently, she thinks you love her. Sickening. Sweet." His words are anything but, dripping with all the accumulated sin of his lifetime.

I do love her. With every inch of my being.

And my father knows it. Dammit. I should've hidden that better, too. But like every student at Alchem Academy, I'm watched. The combined wealth of the student body alone, without their parents' combined income, could form an army to take on the world if they desired.

If they could be bothered.

As I stare at the man who sired me, whom I'd love to plunge a knife through his throat that bobbles like an overfed turkey, I contemplate the thought of raising my own legion. It's not a bad idea. I'm capable of organizing with Zeke's aid, and I have access to more funds than most thanks to the inheritance my mother left me that my father cannot touch.

A happy ten figures sits locked in a trust account accessed by her lawyer's signature and my own, due to turn over upon maturity of my twenty-first birthday.

I'm fairly certain that my life is due to expire on the same day. At my father's hands, of course, or at those of the men who flank him.

Which is one of the reasons Zeke refuses to leave me alone in this room, or Alonso's mansion. My best friend is with me every time I travel to see my father. Not at my command, but at his own behest. He's refused to leave my side since he found himself on the opposite side of the table I sit across from now, his hands locked around mine, with myself stretched across the wooden surface, my shirt torn open at the back awaiting the first blows of my father's whip.

Once, Zeke scoffed at the idea of three against two. Then, when he realized the futility of fighting back, he refused to leave me alone, willing to share my punishment should my sire inflict that upon him, too.

"*Good odds,*" he said, as I gripped his fists to the point that sensation left my whitened knuckles and swallowed the bile that threatened to spew in his face. He held my eyes, not watching the lash my father rained across my back for some imposed slight. Zeke crouched at eye level, holding my gaze. "*Together. They don't know what's coming.*"

So I kept my gaze locked on my best friend and trusted him to have my back, wondering somewhere in the corner of my mind if I will see twenty-two.

This darkness resides inside all of us, and the single joy in my life—in all our lives now—is Roxy.

"Who do I give her away to?" I crack my neck, leaving my bored persona draped over my growing fear. My knees spread wide across the supple leather I know has been doused in as many drugs as it's worn blood over the years.

My father is a formidable businessman who believes in aggressive tactics when negotiations do not flow his way.

He pushes a cheap pack of cigarettes across the glossed wood at me. "Your choice. Him." He shrugs, eyeing Zeke over my shoulder with ill-concealed dislike. "Any one of those friends you collect. The rockstar. That loser kid who hangs around you. Bargain her off to an enemy for a high price. I don't care."

Zeke. Elen. Nyx.

My throat tightens when he mentions them so disparagingly.

"They each bear their scars," I utter, the old marks crisscrossing my lower back itching on command.

Alonso huffs. Sweat gathers beneath his armpits, beading around his neck folds. He'll need to change the shirt soon from a collection hidden beneath the paneled walls in his study before his next meeting. The mansion is situated a two-hour flight from the school by private jet. I'll be back before dinner is served, thankfully.

Before Roxy notices.

My hands flex on my knees though I keep the movement small, irregular. No stimming permitted in this house, certainly not beneath the watchful eyes of my father's men.

Zeke makes a small sound low in his throat. The barb aimed at Nyx isn't missed. I hate the way he's spoken about too, but that's not today's battle.

Alonso leans forward and points his cigar at me, ashing on the French polish. "Stop messing around with her. She's not yours. You have the first pleasure of destroying what you love." His next smile is a genuine thing that decreases the temperature in the room despite the climate control. "Now get out and fix this, like you should have before."

I manage to flick a cigarette from my preferred pack, ignoring the pathetic peace offering, if that's what it is, laid out before me. Zeke snaps his silver lighter open. The wavering flame provides the sole evidence of his concentrated rage.

"How do you want me to do it?"

My father watches me with the same pride one takes in a pup learning a new trick. "That's up to you. You had fun before?"

That I enjoyed bullying the hell out of Roxy when she first arrived at Alchem Academy, tormenting and humiliating her before my friends to earn a few coveted tears, sickens me.

"Yes," I say, stiffly.

My father's gluttonous grin widens. "Of course you did. You're a Craven. It's what we do, son." His smile wavers for a moment before he fixes the facade that he loves me and isn't planning my demise in place over the flaccid monster declining within the meat sack covering his brittle bones. "Perhaps you'll be worthy of the name one day after all."

If I don't die before you do. If I don't fleece your body before it's cold.

I smile back, my dead eyes a mirror of his. "My pleasure, sir." I rise before he gives his permission, sucking on the end of the cigarette and leave the room without looking back.

Zeke holds the door for me, closes it gently, and falls into place at my side. "Sick duck."

I shoot him a look as we parade along the thickly carpeted hall, raising my gaze to the cameras lining each corner. "Careful," I caution. "He's always watching."

Zeke doesn't crack a smile. "You think I care? He's planning to murder you. His own son. It's–"

I catch his arm in a death grip that digs my fingers into hard, corded muscle I know he's worked for and stop short of swinging him into the wall.

Zeke shuts his mouth but looks down at my hand in surprise. Apart from clocking each other on occasion while sparring in the school's boxing ring, I don't think I've ever laid a hand on him in anger before. Nor do I have any intention of losing my best friend to a few loose words when his fury and mine can be better placed elsewhere.

"You heard what he said. There's no choice. I have to ruin her. But you don't."

His teeth grind, the noise matching the sickness swirling in my stomach. "I won't touch her."

"I'd prefer it's someone I understand than … anyone else."

"Give her to Nyx, or Elen."

"I'd prefer to give her to no one," I hiss through a smile I don't feel, baring my teeth. "She's not a toy to be bargained with."

"Isn't she?" Zeke's lopsided grin seems out of place. "You enjoy playing with her. So play. Make her your toy. I'll … watch, and make sure you don't go too far."

"That's not the order I was given."

"When do you ever play by the rules?" he snorts.

"You know what he's capable of. He killed—" I clamp my mouth shut, the memory of walking into my mother's room, finding her splayed out on the floor deluging me in the scent of stale blood.

My father stood over her, sprayed with scarlet as he watched me so calmly, the murder weapon dangling between his fingers like a discarded cigar.

"An intruder, son. He took her life. Why don't you find the man responsible for this?"

Of course, I found no one, because there was no one to find.

"Yeah, he's gonna hurt her if you don't. But he

didn't say kill her, or get her thrown out," Zeke says in a low voice. "You know his rules. Play around them. He told you to break her, not kill her."

"Yet." I stare straight ahead down the carpeted hall with its dark wood panels, the entrance lined with private mercenaries to protect the sole man within when no one else inside the mansion matters.

"So, make it hurt. For both of you. That's the ordeal. You do that, and you stay strong. We'll ... make sure she's okay." His jaw works, and I know he's struggling with this order as much as I am.

At least he's not the one who's been told to rip her heart out of her chest and shred it. That responsibility lies with me alone.

Ruin the girl I love, and enjoy the process.

"You have to do it," he adds softly, whisking away my last sliver of hope in a breath. "For her."

We make it out the front door to the waiting car that will take us back to my father's private jet and the Academy before I speak again, my head whirling as I form the plan I'll have to implement, but not today.

"I know."

****

Roxy flies into my arms and crashes against my chest the moment I step through the gaudily gilt, filigree gates of Alchem Academy. Her body presses to mine as I wind myself tightly around her. Deep, fathomless eyes stare back at me for a single moment, swallowing me whole as I tip her chin up to claim her mouth in a soul-etching kiss.

Zeke makes a disgruntled noise at my side that mingles with the surprised one that emerges from her. His judgment is a palpable thing, but I don't care. If my time with Roxy Quell is limited, I plan on absorbing every inch of her remaining love. The next hours will be spent memorizing her touch. The riot of colors shot through her eyes, the way her skin depresses beneath my fingers.

Everything about her is on offer, because there won't be anything left after I'm done.

Ignoring my best friend's ill-timed grunts, I cling to her as she does to me like she's my last tether to this life, knowing tomorrow those sweet touches will be something else.

Tomorrow, I will ruin her. Destroy her.

When she'll hate me again.

Fear me.

But, tonight, I hold her, pretend she's still mine, that every day she'll still look at me like I'm her whole goddamn world, and not the horror about to tear it down.

"I missed you," she whispers, arching her neck back so her long, dark hair grazes the backs of my wrists. Hair I love to sift my fingers through when she sleeps, bury my hands in and hold her close.

I trace the corners of her eyes with my lips, her temples. The next time she looks at me, tears will fill those fine creases. Will she let me come close enough to taste her fear of me? I hope so, because I'll starve for her fear, any taste she wants to offer.

The dregs of her love I steal away now.

I've held back so far, from the night I stayed in her room kissing her for hours. As far as we went, I know she's a virgin. I was her first kiss. I should be her first everything. Now, I'll claim one of those things.

It will have to be enough.

I catch her chin in my fingertips, cradling her face like she's the most precious thing in my world.

The lie I tell us both, and pray she'll believe me.

"I missed you, too." I kiss her again, gently, cradling her to me.

I love you.

Neither of us say the words, but they don't need to be aired to feel it.

Zeke shifts at my side, swearing.

"What's your problem?" Roxy demands, twisting away from me at the unwelcome distraction.

I instantly hate that he's stolen her attention while I count the seconds until she's not mine any longer. "Ignore him. He's in a mood."

I keep a hand wrapped around her nape, directing her back to me and lose myself in her. My fingers trace her spine, and I'm back to memorizing every inch of her I already know, keeping everything PG, despite wanting so badly to take it further.

Once. I want to for the memory, to savor her, but I won't. It'll be too painful for both of us.

Maybe I'm that selfish.

She lets me lift her off the ground until her toes kiss my shins where she dangles helplessly. I squeeze her a little harder as soft squeals leave her lips. "Did you guys eat?"

"On the plane, but–"

Her brow knits. "Where were you?" Her gaze locks on mine and, when she doesn't find the answer she seeks there, she looks to Zeke. Those eyes that should be on me study him for a long moment, her pretty rosebud mouth turning down in the sweetest moue.

"We were–" he starts, as lost in her as me.

Swearing about ducks he breaks off, raking his knuckles across the back of his inked neck. Zeke storms away, blowing curses out in a long string and muttering at the cloud-covered sky above the school.

She looks up at me. "He's always angry." Her lush bottom lip sinks between her teeth as she watches him stalk off, concern etched in her eyes that should be meant for me, and my blood flows in the wrong direction.

I swallow hard, letting her watch him and pull her back against me. It's all too easy to relish the soft breath that evicts from her lips, knowing I'm too rough with her, and that we're both going to have to get used to it.

All of it.

The memory of how much of a bully I was to her when she first arrived at the school floods me, and what she'll never let me do again after tonight.

Ever.

Dipping my head, I steal her breath and another soft sound because I can. And one more. She should slap my face and skip back to her room after that last kiss. Instead, she leans into me, her resolve and worry for my best friend softening as I distract her.

But even her sweet touch isn't enough to pull me out of my head.

"Where did you go?" she asks again.

I don't answer her question, aiming for a little sleight of hand of my own. "I want to feed you before we crash. I need to sleep next to you." A lump grows in my chest, filling my throat.

It's not her tears I'll taste after all.

Roxy twists, glancing over her shoulder. Both of us face the opposite direction to where we should, though one of us knows what's coming. She turns away from Zeke's shadow as he disappears beneath the admin building's archway, back to me. Her fingers tangle in the chains always wrapped around my neck, each a penance. A delicate, trusting smile parts those pretty lips.

I hate how much I'll enjoy ripping it from her beautiful face.

JOSS PHOENIX

Chapter Three

You Don't Influence Me

Roxy

Falling asleep with Aster is one of my favorite things. He never pushes me for anything, and clothes stay on. No pressure. *Unfortunately*. I get the impression he might want to take things further, but his self-control outweighs mine by a full Craven body weight, and that's no small burden.

Sinking into the warmth of him, my fingers twisted in the chains he never takes off unless he's sparing with Zeke, I listen to him breath or smoke while I drift off. That means I don't have to think about anything.

The home I left, the family I don't have. The new one I don't understand. Two people attended Mom and Dad's funeral: myself and my aunt's driver. She didn't bother to come. It seems she hated my parents as much as she despises me.

I stood by the graves, both freshly dug on an overcast day and tried to cry. Those tears haven't come yet, and I still don't understand why I can't grieve like a normal person. One life was ripped from me and replaced with another I don't want. A shitty substitute. My aunt hates my presence in her life. I'm an imposition to be dressed, primped, and shunted off to a school where she can pay to forget I exist.

Aster and the boys were my bullies for the first weeks at Alchem Academy before all that changed because his ex, my old roommate, made my new life hell. And now … it's not. Sleeping beside Aster is a simple joy that doesn't happen as often as I want.

Being who he is, he doesn't have to creep around half as much as the other boyfriends on Alchem's campus. Not having a roomie helps.

Which is why in being allocated a new one, I'm far from impressed. Maybe I'm ready to slip on my diva shoes and strap myself in. Being Aster Craven's girlfriend comes with benefits, and I'm not prepared to give those up yet, let alone the man himself.

My previous roomie was a bitch. Aster's ex, who orchestrated the whole bullying–Aster–hates–me Alchem initiation experience. Two strikes that slammed me into the reality of the Elite lifestyle when she tried to ruin my entry into the school I didn't want to attend in the first place.

Now that I've found Aster and the boys, I can't imagine living anywhere else. Thus, my rising nausea as I approach my dorm. Situated at the end of the long corridor after the elevator bank that mostly works, it's been my haven away from the rest of the student populace, where the boys make no secret of visiting on a regular basis.

Room 308.

In a horror-esque flick trope, the lights blink above me as I reach my door the day after Aster and Zeke returned from their un-named, destination-unknown trip. I hate the secrets, and both of them have been absent all day. Nyx and Elen shared lunch with me, watching to make sure I ate as always, even though I threatened them with the fruit salad bowl, the same one I once upended over Aster's head.

My happy thought dies as the lights flicker again. It's only once, but it's enough to highlight that my previously locked door now stands ajar.

"Hello?" I tap the space with my foot, my satchel held before me like a pathetic shield ready to halt an oncoming attack of absolutely nothing at all.

"Come in!" a cheery voice yells.

In a breath, I'm weeks back to bullying land and the moment I found a dark-haired girl sitting on the bed in the middle of the room on my first day at Alchem Academy after my parents died. The girl who lost all my emails and cost me the last fragments of fragile trust.

Trust Aster and I spent weeks rebuilding afterward to get to this point, right now.

When the door opens fully at my foot's behest, the beds aren't pushed together, though the black and red hideous mess that Saskia and I painted across the entire back wall of the room in a drunken non-party rage one night remains the sole physical reminder of her abrupt departure after our confrontation.

On the bed on the right-hand side of the room sits a curvy girl with blonde hair curled into pin-up, Marilyn Monroe-esque waves. Massive boobs are barely contained by her white tee and denim, rainbow painted suspenders fixed with jewels that look real.

She's at Alchem Academy. Let's be honest. They probably are.

I gawk for a second, and then resolutely focus on her face. "I'm–"

"Roxanna Quell. Deceased father. Your Aunt, Willa Sloan, owns Pyric Pharma, a long-term enemy of Craven Enterprises." She smiles at me, flicking her hair over her shoulder. A swath of boobage is exposed. "And the current heir apparent. Unlike the last one you unseated, even if it was unintentional."

"Rhani, right?" I throw out my own scant info that stops right there, not that she needs to know it, and try not to respond to the Saskia-level jibe. "How do you know that if you arrived today?" *Two days later than Zeke said.* My eyes narrow. "What sort of spy are you?"

She releases a beautiful, musical sound that belongs to some angelic choir or other, and wiggles her assets. "The one who leads boys around by their nipples, lovely." Rhani snorts at me. "I arrived last night."

"What, you–" *Slept out in the cold?* I clamp my mouth shut, remembering how much trouble it nearly got me into at lunch when Elen made watching me devour my sashimi a new religion.

She pauses and tips her head to the side with all the grace of an angel. "I stayed with Zeke."

I swallow hard, unsure why this matters, though the penny finally drops for me. So *that's* why he asked days ago, pushed for the boys to tell me about her. Why didn't he fess up?

Answer: Because Zeke and I don't have a working relationship, or any sort of relationship other than glaring at each other over mangled burger remnants.

"Is Zeke your ex?" I raise both eyebrows and kick the door to my pre-solo dorm room shut behind me. For a moment, I contemplate flicking the lock, but, somehow, I think this girl will see that as a threat. I leave the door unlocked and traipse across to my own bed, kicking my shoes off at the end, tossing my keys on my pillow where they bounce and topple to the mattress with its plain but heavy, weighted quilt. Another present from Aster, one I adore. "Or are you his long-lost sister, or something?"

"He wishes I was his ex." She rolls her eyes and throws a quick grin my way.

A smile spreads over my face, tentative, but it's there. "This isn't an all-out Craven war, then?" I shrug the remnants of my misgivings away. "There's a history."

"With the psycho ex. I know." Rhani nods. "But you hadn't met me, then." She shimmies again, and all the assets move with her.

I clap my hand over my eyes. "Please stop doing that. I need my vision for life."

She laughs at me. "Zeke's my brother. Foster

brother. As in I belong nowhere, live everywhere, and know everything. Influencer. I'd say *in the making*, but hey, I've already made it on my own. I don't take his family's money, and I pay my own way."

I lower my hand slowly, unable to fight the grin spreading across my face. *There's hope.* "I think I like you already." I wave a finger in her direction. "Don't photograph me, or put me on your socials."

"Hmm. The influencer, and the displaced hermit. I think I like it." She lies back on her bed and tosses her phone in the air, catching it over her face. I watch with interest, wondering how many times it will take before her reflexes fail, but that doesn't happen.

"What's fun around here? Oh, that's right," she says, answering her own question. "You don't know, because you're the hermit."

I rifle through my drawers for the books for my next classes. "Got it in one. Calc is next. What's on your schedule?"

"Don't know. Don't care. Unless it's *who's* on my schedule." Without turning to face her, I can almost *see* her eyebrows wiggle. "So what's this I don't hear from my big foster bro about a school ski trip?"

I groan. "I've *still* forgotten to order stuff."

I'm fast running out of time. Thanks to the ex-roomie who deleted all my emails, I found out about the upcoming ski trip a few weeks back and the still new-to-me aunt who gave permission for the school to do basically whatever they want, making me their happy little guinea pig. Or not so happy, and not so permission granting. Being sixteen years old makes no difference to the mostly absent authoritarian dystopia-esque the school created like it is its own living entity.

I keep half expecting floating heads and Oz-like facades to give us orders, but the teachers are real, though

I still haven't met the principal in person.

Maybe there's hope for my Oz fantasy after all.

"We should go shopping." Rhani perks up impossibly more than she already is. "Zeke can take us if you don't have access to a car."

Something twinges my gut that feels like a combination of guilt and hope. *He's not your boyfriend. He hates you, and wants to see you gone.* Oh, and she's his sister.

But the way he reacted yesterday, stalking away, seemed weirdly possessive, a memory I can't shake.

"What was he like to grow up around?" I can't keep the curiosity out of my voice and bite my lip the moment the words leave my mouth.

"You mean, was he born angry?"

I straighten, gripping my textbooks and holding them like a shield to my chest in defense. "You mean he wasn't?" I try to imagine Zeke as a bawling newborn sans ink. All I get is a mind full of man flesh definitely *with* ink.

Inappropriate timing, thank you hormones.

"Oh, I'm sure he was a sweet little boy in some previous life, but he's always been an asshole of the highest order." Rhani rolls her eyes dramatically and swings her legs over the edge of the bed.

"You mean he never helped Mommy make cupcakes or bandage your boo-boos?" I tease.

Rhani's face stills. "Actually, he did do all those things. He also tipped the icing over my head later, or caused the boo-boos." Her shoulders go back and everything on the front thrusts forward. I keep my eyes locked on her face. "Yes. They're fake. I paid for them myself, and I love them. Want to feel?"

I shake my head and back into my bed, bumping my calves. "Um, no thanks. There's a song about us already." My eyes squint shut at the blatant admission.

"There is?" A bright smile lights her face when I risk a look. Cue hair toss. "What about?"

I shrug, unable to help the blush that heats my cheeks. "Oh, you know, the one about sitting in a tree..."

She whoops, tossing her phone into the air again, catching its glittery case, and spinning it between deft fingers. "I bet the boys loved that."

My eyebrows rise. "You know them all?"

"I've *heard* about them all," she corrects me. "And maybe talked to some of them online when I stalked their socials profiles." She shrugs. "Craven doesn't talk. Nyx ghosts. Elen is full of himself, and Zeke is..." She flips the bird to her imaginary foster brother.

"He's an alphahole." Crap. That slipped out too.

She grins. "You spelled dick wrong."

"Whatever." I shove back the mantle of her stare and start for the door. "What have you got next? Or first? If you haven't been to classes today, this week—whatever." I stumble over myself verbally and try to make my way out of my dorm without falling on my face to tie the whole shemozzle off.

"Calc."

I grimace on her behalf. "Let me introduce you to the most hellish class Alchem Academy has to offer."

****

I do end up getting my shopping for the school ski trip done, thanks to Rhani's incessant needling which I kinda don't mind that much—we gelled as soon as she showed up in my bedroom. It turns out my new roomie is actually worse at calc and math in general than me, which is an achievement in itself.

While Aster and the boys flourish in math, I suck big hairy lemon balls, and now I have company.

The tag along on our shopping trip and chauffeur

for the day is the part that has me on edge, where I've been since Zeke picked us up in his Jeep AEV. The letters decorate the back of the vehicle, the sidesteps, and pretty much everywhere. I get that it's an expensive toy, but he drives it like it's his favorite one and I'm not worthy of tarnishing its polished surfaces with my tainted presence.

Once we hit our destination store, Rhani is in her element.

"What about this one?" She holds up a lurid yellow ski jacket and matching boots. "At least you won't lose me when I tumble down the hill. Make sure you film it." She points over my shoulder at Zeke.

He raises both hands in surrender. "I'm at your service as per ducking always," he mutters with no short supply of venom, glaring around the exclusive snow kit shop we drove over two hours to visit.

The two female sales assistants cringe away from his attention, though the sole male in the shop apart from him crosses his arms over his chest and watches us with a small smile.

Or more to the point, he watches Rhani, and he doesn't seem to give a shit about the foster brother attempting to ash him with a single furious glare.

"Adam. Heel, boy," Rhani calls, ignoring the testosterone fest surrounding her. "My girl says yellow doesn't work. You're the expert. What's your choice?"

The manager/owner grins as he steps forward, unfolding his arms as he crosses the cavernous store. Taller than Zeke by a head, which is no small feat as he must top out at over six feet in height, his loping step is easy, and his gaze never leaves her.

By the time he reaches her, his arms are full of a bespoke aqua and white bundle, and he holds dueling beanies in his hands. The white one he passes to Rhani who coos all over it, and the gray he tosses to me.

"Go with this," Adam says to me. "It'll offset your colors. The boys…" He shoots a smirk at Zeke. "They won't be able to keep their eyes off you."

I squeeze the soft knit in my hands, its luxurious texture telling me it's mine from this moment. "Oh, he's not—I mean, my boyfriend isn't here," I stutter, unsure why I'm justifying myself to the tall shop owner-cum-ski instructor.

We all know who he is because he rattled off his qualifications while he flirted with Rhani from the moment we set foot in his shop.

"It's a good color for you," Zeke murmurs right in my ear, his gravelly voice that matches his attitude to perfection rippling along my spine. "You should get it."

"See? You even have my brother's approval," Rhani pipes up, emphasizing *brother* as she smiles fresh-powder bright at Adam. "I like your taste, honey. Take them into the dressing room for me?" She wiggles her shoulders.

It's a miracle the poor man manages to maintain his attention on her face, or maybe it's more admirable.

"You got it," he says softly.

Zeke growls low at my side. "Hands to yourself, as—quackhole."

Adam risks his life flipping Zeke off.

I gawk while Rhani laughs, that musical note a siren song to the man who follows her into the dressing rooms like a trained puppy.

"I better make sure she behaves." He sighs and steps back, his abrupt absence leaving me with the ability to breathe again.

"You know she can look after herself," I mutter, a little awed by his brotherly attention. "But it's cute, you know."

He's a handful of steps in front of me before he swings around, his face darkening. "What's. Cute?" He spits the singular syllable sentences in my direction, his customary glare locked in place and laser focused on me, and we're back to square one.

"You." I stand my ground, refusing to back down despite the sense of impending anything.

Doom. Death. Something worse.

He's your roommate's brother, and your boyfriend's best friend. He won't hurt you.

But as he stalks back in my direction, I know full well that if Zeke wants to tear me limb from limb that no social convention will prevent him from doing exactly what he intends.

When he's within an inch of my nose, he stops, sharing the air I exhale—if I can breathe.

His face transforms as he offers me a slightly lopsided grin. "I don't think I've ever been called *cute* before."

"First time for everything." I try not to stare as the distance between us diminishes. My mind goes blank. "Uh, thank you for driving us today," I say lamely. "It's not like I can drive." Or have a license.

Because before this year, I never had the money for either. A bus trip was outside the realm of the expense tin most days. Walking was my preferred mode of transport if I wanted to also eat, before I lost both my parents.

That time seems like a past life now, a shadow of this incredible world I've been immersed in that also comes under the *overwhelming* category. I never would have been able to walk into a shop like this, let alone ask about the price tag I knew I couldn't afford before we started browsing.

"Aster would have made time for you. Or either

of the boys," Zeke says slowly, his eyes narrowing a fraction.

"Probably," I murmur, retreating a step for each one he takes in my direction in an endless dance between the racks.

A giggle reaches us from the dressing room.

The easy expression on his face dissolves, returning to his usual fenced fury. Inked knuckles rake through his hair, leaving the spiked ends standing straight up. "Duck me. I can't take her anywhere."

"I wouldn't go in there—" I start, but it's too late.

Zeke storms away, throwing me a glare over his shoulder like the interruption is my fault, and that window into a different side of him never happened, as with the duck scenario in the dining hall that day that he seems to have taken seriously. Like that part of him is closed off forever. "Pick what you want, and make sure it fits. I'm not sure how long we'll be here."

Or how long Adam will survive. He doesn't have to say the words out loud for the entire shop to pick up on his meaning.

I sigh and select the gray and white things I need, sliding the bulky pants and jacket on over my skinny dark jeans and black tee depicting a certain goblin king. Everything feels huge and too airy, but Adam told us we needed the sizes to be bigger so I figure it works.

Folding everything, I make a small pile at the desk where one of the sales girls starts to ring up my selections. A stack of holographic stickers and cheap beaded jewelry decorates a stand beside the register. I finger a crystal snowflake necklace, its beveled edges shattering white light into a rainbow kaleidoscope across the counter.

"You don't need crap like that," Zeke snaps over my shoulder.

I jump. "You're a creeper," I retort, wrapping my arms around myself like it will ward off the heat rolling from his massive frame. "You know I'm going to get a ton of plastic stuff because I know it'll annoy you now."

"If you say so." He passes a silver card over my head to Adam who appears beside the girl. She disappears and he takes over with a curt nod. "Everything goes on there. No snowflake," he adds, flicking my ear with a spare, calloused finger.

"I'll pay for myself," I protest, fumbling for my purse, unprepared.

"Not today, Roxy," Zeke growls. The low timbre in his voice stills me like prey, but that's not the way he means it. I think. Maybe. He huffs when I protest, one hand pressing into my lower back for a moment before the apologetic contact disappears. "Let's get out of here before I kill this motherducker for touching my sister. I'm sorry your shopping trip got cut short."

"Oh." I blink at Adam, who gives me a tight smile before his aqua eyes that match the colors he picked out for Rhani flick back to meet Zeke's stare. "*Oh.*" I take my bags, mumble my thanks, and turn back to Zeke. "I told you not to go back there."

Rhani preens at his side, and I get the impression that not only has she gotten exactly what she wants from today's trip, but also that this fling with Adam isn't over. I groan internally, knowing Zeke can't see his sister's planning.

Or maybe he can, and knows well enough to ignore her.

"True. Maybe I should have listened to you." He ushers us out of the store, ignoring my shocked look, and hauls me toward his Jeep where I pause, staring at his back.

"Did you just apologize? To *me?*" I mutter to his

jacket.

Zeke stiffens but doesn't break his stride. "Not the time, Roxy." He directs me to the front seat and shakes his head when Rhani beelines for the passenger door.

"I called shotgun," she pouts.

"And then you tried to screw a *salesboy* in a *ski shop*, Sis," he sneers back. "That relegates you to the backseat. Spread out all you like back there on your own."

She flips him off as he holds the door for me.

"Uh, thanks?" I frown at him. "I *did* tell you—"

"Don't get used to it." He cuts me off before I can do both that and babble uselessly at him.

Rhani cackles from the backseat, enjoying her joyride and inciting her brother.

"Give me your phone." Zeke opens the back door and holds out his hand.

Her mouth gapes. "Like hell. You don't own me, and I bought it myself," she snaps when he lunges for her bag.

"My car, my rules."

Silence holds for a whole second before Rhani tosses her hair. "Fine. We'll walk. Or hitchhike." She winks at me.

"Yep. I'm good for it." I stick out a leg and wiggle it. "Got the goods." I might have seen a nicer side of Zeke today, one I kind of like, but that doesn't mean I'm about to leave my girl out in the cold.

"I really like you," Rhani tells me seriously. "Maybe we should do a party thing and try that kiss they were singing about for real."

Zeke groans and covers his eyes with his hands, letting his forehead thump onto the top of the Jeep. "*Lalalalala.* Do whatever you want, Rhani. Not like you'll listen."

"Must run in the family then," I snark at him, tucking my hitchhiking leg away as he capitulates on the phone and climbs in the driver's leather bucket seat.

Zeke gives me the faintest hint of a smile that transforms his face to the version of himself who spoke softly to me back in the store.

Rhani groans and flings her head back, waving one slim arm out the window and calling out to Adam who emerges from the store to watch us leave from the alpine shop. The strange smile from before decorates his face as he watches us drive away, though he doesn't return Rhani's wave.

Strange, because that same smile is echoed on Zeke's fury-lined mouth.

Chapter Four

Defrosting My Heart

Roxy

Snow sucks.

I mean, it's really pretty, but it also sucks. After my first three runs on skis—the boys opted for boards while Rhani and I chose the alternative—my thighs ache and I've lost all feeling in both my pinkie fingers. The insides of my cuffs and the zippered neckline of my ski jacket, the gray one that Zeke liked so much, quickly develops minuscule ice crystals for the amount of time I've rolled in the cold, crisp stuff already.

The longer I stay on the baby slope, the surer I become that I'll be a walking snow person by the time I hit the bottom of the hill. And man, am I determined to conquer all, despite the light dusting of fresh snowflakes that begins to obscure my vision.

Plenty of those have found their way into the inside of my undershirt earlier, leaving me damp both inside and out. Not that my body temperature has changed that much, basically leaving the inside of my jacket gooey enough for me to resemble a melting snowflake all over.

I grimace as I position myself at the top of the baby run that's become my nemesis. It's a straight slope with a gentle gradient and a few remaining cute, snow-covered trees planted straight through the center. They look pretty, but from where I stand, they're the world's biggest hazard. I line myself up so I won't hit them and tip my skis over the ice encrusted edge that looks like a ninety degree drop several feet straight down, even though in reality it's less than a third of that.

"You've got this," Rhani cheers from her safe

place off to one side of the run where she's created figure eights like a pro, despite proclaiming that she's never skied before.

I force a grin and wave my pole, attempting not to wobble on the spot.

Rhani breaks into giggles, raising her phone to film me.

I realize there's little more to see from the outside of my self-imposed fluffy enclosure except the tip of my nose that protrudes from the balaclava and goggles combo on my head.

Paired with a matching soft gray scarf wrapped over my mouth and my hood up over the whole thing, I probably look like a snow bunny prepared for the end.

Still, the tiny falling flakes manage to push their way along my cheeks, leaving my skin burning.

Yup.

Snow. Sucks.

Where I come from, I never got to see snow. In Providence, I never had a chance to play in it like this. Do I feel guilty? No, ma'am, I do not. Which is why I'm intent on conquering this hill, baby slope be it, or not.

Determination is not in short supply today. Eyeballing the trees, I lean forward. My gaze drops to the precipice of death that yawns beneath me. Blowing out, my breath fogs the bottom half of my goggles as I push off and sail along the slope, crossing my skis the way the instructor showed me in order to control my descent.

The moment I get on that first little patch of snow, it feels like the blackest, slipperiest ice. Everything goes haywire. One ski spins backward while the other crosses over and somehow underneath the other. In seconds, I'm less snow plowing than I am hurtling straight toward the first previously cute tree, and—

Thunk.

My entire front is snow bunnied face down, tush propped in the air and ski poles sticking out at all angles. As I try to right myself, hands and knees sinking deeper into the otherwise undisturbed powder, I'm amazed to discover my skis are still attached to my boots and hang in the correct direction.

Hoisting myself the right way up, I blink. Everything whites out until I tap my goggles, dispelling some of the snow crusted there. My cheeks are on fire, and not the good sort. Cold ripples down my body and ice filters through *everywhere* inside my jacket.

"I thought this stuff was supposed to stay on the outside," I mumble, spitting out a mouthful of stubborn snowflakes that refuse to melt.

Rhani breaks into fresh peals of laughter as she twists around, passing my prostrate form, filming me the whole time.

I try sticking my middle finger up, but my hands are stuffed inside my gloves and nothing works the way it should. All I manage to do is whack at her retreating form uselessly with the ski pole that dangles from my wrist.

Her laughter increases with my pathetic attempts.

"Stop that," I grumble, though I'm not really angry. Damnit, I wanted to ride the slope once.

She snaps a few pictures and manages to complete a little pirouette on her skis that I envy instantly.

"Oh, my God." Rhani sounds like she's crying inside her aqua and white ski suit as she clutches her sides and snowplows simultaneously. "Oh, Roxy. That was beautiful. Do it again," she begs.

I shake my head, push myself up, and manage to sink lower into my personal snow pit. "This isn't fair."

A giant, gloved hand curls around my shoulder. Before its owner spins me around, a mammoth shower of ice arcs up in a stunning display that hovers above the world for an instant before it tumbles to the frozen vista below and sprays Rhani head to toe.

My mouth hangs open as I stare. I know from my own fall how cold that stuff is, but she still looks stunning despite what happened to her and who did it.

Zeke rotates me on the spot, skis and all, in a feat of coordination I envy, and takes me in, his brow creasing as he surveys the mess of me. Certainly not a hot one as I shiver within my melty-snowflake persona. His goggles perch on top of his head and his jacket is unzipped to display a t-shirt while I freeze my tush off.

A freaking t-shirt.

"Why aren't you wearing more clothes?" I stare, trying not to study the way his mouth *almost* pulls up at one side.

Zeke cocks his head. "Girl, I can't even see you. Give me a second." He reaches out with his gloves and hesitates. The black, thick fingers retract from my vision as he pulls the gloves off, stuffing them into a jacket pocket, and reaches out again. The hood is removed first, then he flips my goggles on top of my beanie.

He ruffles the pom-pom on top, showering me with a fresh layer of snow I don't need. I'm so numb that I don't even wince, just stand there while he fixes me like a shivering doll. He pushes my scarf down without further incident to expose my face.

I suck in a breath of cold mountain air and know I'll associate pine scents with him forever.

Warm fingers brush along my cold neck, stalling on the silver chain that remained hidden until now. A tiny snowflake that is not crystal hangs from it, nor did I buy it for myself. That package arrived shortly after our catastrophic shopping trip. I opened the tiny, unexpected box, gaping at the delicate jewel. Then I read the card.

Don't buy plastic crap.

At least I knew who sent it.

I tried returning the gift, unsure of his motives, but Zeke shook his head and turned away. *"Keep it, Roxy. It's my fault your day was ruined."*

That wasn't true in its entirety, but I understood his meaning. And I ... liked the snowflake. When we left campus, I put it on beneath my clothes, next to my skin, and hadn't shown anyone.

Now, out in the real snow where the gem reflects the glittering landscape, his fingertips trail the chain, lifting the pendant to study it. Something possessive flashes in his coal black gaze, and he makes an approving sound in his chest. That's the single point of acknowledgement I receive, though at least feeling has returned to the numbed area.

"You've got more snow on the inside than the outside. Why are you such a mess?" he says in exasperation, breaking the moment as he tucks the necklace away, hiding the softer part of him I don't understand at all.

I shrug, concealing my unease at his closeness. "It's a talent?" Even I hear the weakness in that excuse.

He makes a very Zeke sound as he pats at my cheeks. "Can you feel anything?"

"A bit?" I wrap my arms around myself, unsure if it's to keep the cold in or ward him away.

His hands cup my cheeks as he holds my face. "Ducks, Q," he mutters. "Come on." Giant arms engulf me as he depresses my face into his dry t-shirt.

A giggle erupts from my lips as I imagine a Roxy-shaped face impression left on the center of his t-shirt.

"What are you on about? Hell, girl." His tone warms me like his body heat and I forget all about soaking his shirt. A single, solid heart thud later his arms stiffen. Then, he steps back, and I'm left cold and exposed again. "She was covered in snow."

I glance around, disconcerted by the change in temperature from Sahara to subarctic again. Aster and Zeke stare at each other over my head, neither saying a word despite their obvious communication I'm not privy to.

Rhani is still filming and offers a pinkie wave in a delicious show of coordination. "It was hilarious. They say so."

Zeke throws up a hand in her direction and flips the bird for me. I'm grateful. He swears at her, no ducks present, as I wind my way over to Aster.

"You are a mess." Aster stared down at me, something indecipherable flickering in the backs of his eyes.

I flounder. "What?" Am I really that much of a mess? I bite my lip as I get a little lost gazing back at him, all blond hair tousled sexily like a poster boy for some expensive alpine brand. "I want to try again."

Arched eyebrows rise. "You are crazy."

"Never said I wasn't." I tromp the last few feet along the hill. Apparently, I slid a whole lot farther than I thought. Staring back up at the baby slope, I imagine myself skiing successfully down the hill.

Crash. Crash. Crash.

"I can do this thing," I mutter. *I will. I will. I will.*

I don't care how many times I eat snow. Even if it is the baby hill, I will conquer it. This is my first time seeing snow and it might be my last, but I will enjoy this trip.

Nothing can ruin it for me.

Aster clicks his tongue behind me. "Okay, princess. Whatever you need. But right now, let's dry you up and get you something warm."

Zeke storms past us. "Won't argue with that.

Girl's gonna get frostbite."

I roll my eyes at his back. *So much for nice Zeke.* "What snow bunny bit you?"

A one-fingered salute over his shoulders is the reply he offers.

"Classy," I call to his retreating shadow.

"Ignore him." Aster stands on my skis so I can liberate my boots and slides his gloved hands around my waist to pull me into a hug. He's already off his board that's lined up against a shed nearby on a rack with everyone else's discarded gear.

I wrinkle my nose. "Why are you so graceful?"

"Natural habit."

"Arrogant, too—"

His fingers press over my lips, warming me, before he replaces them with his mouth and snow no longer sucks so bad. I sigh into his embrace as we stand in the snow, kissing until the wind ruffles my beanie and fresh flakes kiss my cheeks.

Aster thumbs a snowflake from my eyelashes. I blink away the residual moisture. "Go inside, Roxy. I'm not doing it right if I don't keep you warm this trip."

I let him lead me inside the chalet where the bar has been transformed into something more student friendly. Hot chocolates and spiced lattes line the bar top along with bowls of pumpkin and parsnip soup. Baskets of steaming, hot bread rolls fill the remaining spaces and short tables closer to the giant fire. One entire wall is glassed floor to ceiling that overlooks the ski fields to give the perfect view to the milling students who warm themselves telling wipeout stories.

Aster leads me to a table and plants me in a seat near the fire once he's divested me of all my excess, damp clothing. Left in my long-sleeved black tee, beanie, ski pants and soft booties, all dried out after I got rid of my ski boots, I curl into the chair and clutch the mug of chai Aster places in my hand.

He flicks the top of my beanie. "Cute."

"Glad you think so." I pull it down over my ears before he can snatch that away, too. "I'm keeping it."

He offers an apathetic shrug. "Whatever."

I watch him walk away, his usually lazy gait too abrupt. He stops beside Zeke, his shoulders stiff as they talk with their backs turned to me.

Elen crouches next to my recliner. "Stop trying to analyze him. You'll go mad. Greater minds than yours have attempted. Trust me." His tongue flicks out to toy with his blue lip ring he put back in for the trip.

"Aren't you supposed to not trust anyone who says that?" I watch the hypnotic motion. "That doesn't mean I should stop trying," I offer.

His easy smile leaves me feeling slightly ticklish inside. "No, but you might go insane in the interim."

"Are you sure that hasn't already happened?" I smile as Nyx places a bowl of soup and fresh, crusty bread in front of me with butter melted into a small cob. "You're my favorite right now."

He flashes me a quick grin, reappearing with a bowl of roasted chestnuts.

"I think I love you."

"I aim to please." His soft voice is rough-edged, though I hear the smile in it.

"That's a hard line to follow, you know." Elen stretches and heads off to collect his own food while Nyx settles into the chair beside me, making eye contact and foregoing his phone for once.

"Don't wear yourself out," I murmur, engrossed in my soup, though the chestnuts smell divine.

"Doing…?" He watches me attempt to crack open a stubborn chestnut and liberates it, peeling the crosshatched shell away and popping the roasted nut in my palm.

"Being a people pleaser." I tap his knuckles in thanks when he offers another nut up. "You're looking at one. It took me a long time to learn to say no. I still get stuck trying to fix everyone sometimes, so I get it." I wave an index finger back-and-forth between us. "People like us." Wow, that got serious fast. I shrug my mood off. "Or something like that."

Nyx smiles faintly at our stunted conversation, digging into his soup. He mightn't talk much, but his company is the quiet sort, and it's enough.

****

Steam clouds the hot tub that's the best luxury I've ever experienced. The baby slope did in fact defeat me, but the tiny hot tub we all stuffed ourselves into afterward made the hours of frustration, giggles, and being filmed by Rhani worth it, though I covered my face.

Until a few seconds before Nyx and Elen crowded us. The conversation is good and my sore muscles enjoy the soak, but once they get out in search of alcohol I sink into the hot water, leaning my head back against Aster's arm.

He shifts behind me, letting my hair trail around us. I tug on the straps of the one piece I borrowed from Rhani that's a tiny bit loose in the top but otherwise fits okay.

Everything still aches. Tomorrow will hurt, but right now I want to drift. More ice—it would be an insult to call that stuff snow—made it inside my ski suit than stayed on the outside throughout the day. Although I did manage to conquer a portion of the baby hill one time, my efforts hurt me more than it.

Aster traces his fingers along my shoulders then

digs in with a full-blown massage.

I close my eyes and make happy llama noises. "That feels good." My head reels as I spread my fingers out in the water, enjoying the odd sensation of pins and needles fizzing like sherbet in my fingertips. It's nice to have feeling back in them at all.

"Does it?" His voice comes from above me, distant and far away.

Smooth and spiced like a good dirty chai.

I crack open one eyelid and smile at him. I'm pretty sure it's not a sexy smile. More in the realm of pure sleepy. Or maybe dopey with a side serve of *ouch*. I don't realize I've said that out loud until he laughs down at me.

Oops.

"Cute, Roxy." The tip of his finger presses over my nose.

I'm being cuddled by an alpine ski model lookalike in a hot tub. It still feels surreal. I shiver despite myself and before I put too much thought into the action, I swing one leg around to straddle him.

His eyes flare wide, and part of me registers the panic written there before his hands clamp down on my hips and slide me backward. "What are you doing?" Aster's jaw sets in a hard line, unforgiving.

My fingers link behind his neck, refusing to be deterred. "Is it bad that I want some alone time with my boyfriend?" Both of us know full well I'm pushing for more, and that he's pushing me away, but I pray he won't call me out on it. It's how we've been for weeks now.

He sets the limits. I try to break them. That's how we always play.

Recently, those limits feel like hard lines he pushes out every day, and I'm chasing something unachievable. Like intimacy.

My heart cinches, but I push the emotion aside, covering my rising fear by tossing my wet hair over my shoulder.

"Alone time. With my boyfriend." I repeat my statement, waggling my eyebrows.

Aster's smug grin is cute and relaxing as I lean in to kiss him, thankful of the steam that keeps my exposed shoulders warm and covers a little of my insta-insecurity—

"What the duck am I?" Zeke snaps at my back. Water sloshes against my back as he climbs out of the tub and stalks away.

Guilt roils in my stomach. I forgot he was there.

"Oops?" I answer too late, keeping my voice low, and lean my forehead against Aster's.

A deep rumble echoes in his chest. "Apparently so." He laughs at me, giving my thighs a squeeze, and lifts me off his lap.

"Spoil sport," I grumble.

Still laughing softly at me, Aster climbs out of the tub.

I twist as he steps out, and garner a whole eyeful of bare butt.

He isn't wearing bathers at all.

Squawking and covering my eyes as I mime about blindness, Aster finds my hand and leads me from the tub into the chill air where he wraps me in a heated robe— heated, can this place get any better?—wrapping his arms around me from the outside.

"Are you safe?" I mumble from between my fingers.

Warmth permeates me from all angles as he rests his chin on the top of my head. "It's safe. You can look, Roxy." There's a trace of laughter in his voice, and something else.

I press my cheek to his chest and encounter bare skin. "Aren't you freezing?"

He shakes his head. "Not with you here."

Aww.

"Sweetie." I butt his chin with the top of my head.

"Smoothie," Zeke snarks as he stalks past wearing a towel draped low around his waist that exposes the deep vee at his hips, a ton of ink, and the top of his ass crack as he passes by.

"Why would you put anything on?" I shake my head and avert my eyes. "Show off."

"Don't give him attention." Aster nudges me, drawing me back to him. "Let's get some clothes on before you get sick."

"I won't. Herd immunity and all." I shrug his protest off. "But you, on the other hand … what was that?" I tip my head back to stare up at him.

No wonder he didn't want me coming closer if he was in the buff. And here I thought I was underdressed for the occasion. All the other boys wore board shorts in the tub.

"What was what?" he asks easily, avoiding my question.

I roll my lips together and wrinkle my nose. "Fine, be like that."

He watches me for a long moment while I hold his gaze, albeit upside down. His lips move on a silent phrase, three small words neither of us have uttered yet. Three tiny words that make me freeze up every time I think of them. We've been together for months, but ours has never been a traditional relationship.

When I first arrived at Alchem, Aster bullied me. Then I repaid the favor. After that we sort of … fell into each other. It doesn't stop me craving what I really want from him.

Craving Aster Craven.

Snickering at my sad joke and waving away his confused expression, I give him a little shove toward the sauna where the other boys are hiding. "Go cool down. Or warm up, or whatever. I'm gonna get changed."

The look he gives me tingles my insides. He lowers his mouth to mine in a gentle kiss, his hand lingering at my waist. I wait for more, but the light touch is gone too soon.

When I open my eyes, I stand alone in the steaming room, a chill drifting over my exposed skin as snow falls outside.

JOSS PHOENIX

Chapter Five

RADU-- Roxy All D*cked Up

Zeke

I watch my best friend stick his tongue down his girlfriend's throat, knowing full well he'll break her heart by the end of the day. Armed with that information, I still wish it's me she makes those small, addictive sounds for, and I can't help staring at them like a creeper in training.

They stand in the swirling snow, the perfect billionaire couple that should be featured on a postcard or in one of my sister's stupid videos. I don't think Roxy even knows what she's worth, or will be the day her aunt finally kicks the bucket. Something tells me that day isn't too far away.

One day in on the ski trip everyone beleaguered her about, and already it's about to be shot to duck sh—eets.

I rub a hand over my mouth to hide my smile. She's right; I can't think—or talk—without swearing. Her ban has done weird things to my head, and it's not all about ducks, though the damn birds are starting to feature in my dreams.

The smile drops right off my face when Aster pulls back from their kiss, and she doesn't. My best friend leaves her standing on her toes, her head tipped back, lips parted while he stares down at her like he's trying to memorize every contour of her perfect face.

Because we all know he won't have the right to stare at her like that after today. But he will anyway. Like me.

Or any of us.

Roxy Quell is the centrifugal force we all orbit around, out of control while we crash into each other and occasionally her. I relish the moment it's my turn to ground myself with her and find out what she feels like in my arms.

If she ever gives me that chance. It's no secret we hate each other, though for different reasons. After today, the likelihood of her wanting me anywhere near her is debatable. Unlikely at absolute best, and absolutes is what I'm built on.

I scuff my foot in the snow that's turning fast to sludge as I decimate it, making swirls in the slush with the toe of my boot. By the time I look up at them, she's gone. Headed back to her hut with Rhani or wherever. I tried to warn her, but as per ducking usual, no one listens.

She looks so pretty, all snow bunnied up like I knew she would. Her soft gray beanie and matching jacket obscures almost everything but the slightest hint of pink in her cheeks. Those thick lashes as she stares out at the fresh powder like it can't hide the wonder in her eyes, like it's the first time she's ever seen snow outside of a video.

It took me too long to realize it was her first time. I want to be present for a whole lot more of those.

The way she bent down, scooped up a handful of flakes, and tossed the tiny cache of white glitter at Aster left us all in gales of laughter, especially when her face crumpled and she stared at the drifting, scattered heap in utter confusion.

Then, he showed her how to make her first snow ball, his gloved hands curved around hers, pulling her into his body as he aimed their payload at Elen who stood with his arms stretched out like a motherducking starfish.

"*Hit me, baby,*" he crowed.

"*Ready, aim...*" Aster raised their hands, but it was Roxy who pushed the envelope.

"*Fire!*" she cried, flinging her shoulder back hard

enough that the snowball tumbled out of her outstretched arm and straight down the front of Aster's jacket.

His face turned white while he patted frantically at the snow contacting bare skin beneath while hers turned the prettiest shade of red I've ever seen.

Elen opened one eye, managing to look disappointed she missed him and offered a second freebie before the morning devolved into a free-for-all.

This was the way the ski trip was supposed to be, not the duckfight it's fast deteriorating into.

"How long are you gonna hold off before your father cracks his lid?" Elen asks, his face closed.

Nyx doesn't look up from his phone, but his stiff stance screams volumes over his usual slouch. I know he's out of his head and listening in.

"I'll do it. Give me time." Aster's voice is tight.

"You had no problem bullying the duck outta her, and now you struggle to break up? Some double standards there, my friend." I slap his shoulder a whole lot harder than I should, and he glares at me.

"Duck. Off." He enunciates clearly, spitting the words out with enough undiluted venom to murder a flock of the feathery creatures. "It's bad enough it'll hurt her to rip off the Band-Aid to our world this early. Don't heap the crap on," he adds his warning.

A warning I don't have any ducks left to give.

"Then maybe you shouldn't have gotten involved with her in the first place. You knew better then."

You know better now.

My unspoken words hang in the air between us all.

Aster pushes his hair back from his face. "I don't have the brain space for this," he mutters.

"Of course not. What sort of Alchem royalty would you be if you didn't play pass the buck with your girlfriend every time daddy comes calling," I scoff.

"Maybe you should take up the reins if you're so interested," Aster fires back.

I smirk, the image of her body folding beneath mine, her lips soft and pliant as I devour her to taste her soul with my personal brand of violence is all too tempting.

"Maybe I will."

Aster's face darkens as he rakes his hands through his hair and storms away. I give it a full minute's grace in which no one speaks before I turn to Elen.

"Message her. This is going to motherducking sting."

"Aw, man." He clasps his heart and flutters his blue and gray dyed eyelashes at me for some album cover he shot for before we left that are longer than they have any right to be. "I didn't think you cared."

"I don't." *I do.* "Get her out of here before she breaks in front of everyone. It won't be pretty."

"You're a sweetie, bro." He gives me a one-armed hug and flashes me a Korean finger heart.

"Weirdo."

"The best of them," he agrees.

Elen sketches a salute, pivoting on his heel with the sort of grace Aster wishes he was born with and pulls out his phone. His fingers are a blur over the screen as Nyx falls into step beside him, both lost in their heads, or hers, away from this world.

I storm to the ski racks, grab the board I chose back at the shop with Roxy, and hit the slopes. Maybe I can find a cliff to sail off no one's gone down yet and break something.

Yeah. A really steep ducking cliff, see how far I can fly.

Cause I don't wanna witness my best friend's girl

cry.

JOSS PHOENIX

Chapter Six

Heartbreak Without the Hotel

Roxy

"*Ducking Aster.*"

Elen curses, crossing the room to kneel before me where I crouch in the empty cabin I share with Rhani, staring at the message my boyfriend—ex—sent through with no explanation whatsoever, other than a simple and crushing *it's over.*

Or close enough, but that's the general gist. Blessedly, my head remains blank. I have no real idea what the message does actually say because my vision is so obscured by tears that I can't read it. And I'm glad I don't have other company, because this sort of heartbreak is limited to a party of one.

"Or for two," Elen murmurs, his hands cupping my shoulders and I realize I've spoken aloud.

"Sorry," I sniffle, attempting to swipe away my tears. All I can see of him is a blurry black and blue shadow with a gentle touch. "What are you doing here?"

"It's okay," he mutters. "I wanted to make sure you were all right."

"No one is okay after this." I wave my phone at him, though talking helps still the tears. "Wait, he told you?"

"He was grumpier than usual. We dug it out of him."

They all know. Not that it surprises me. I nod at his admission, swiping my hands across my face with better results than before. Deep blue eyes that aren't his natural color stare back at me from his contacts, so pretty as they bore into me, his brow dipped in a mirror of my frown.

Those arched lips form a hard line that draws his mouth down. Bright blue streaks fan out against the black strands in his razored fringe. A cool sort of anger—a dichotomy, like him, but so different to Zeke's brand of searing rage—rolls off him in waves.

At the moment, I don't even care if his rage is directed at me. My heart hurts at the overload of everything, while my chest collapses at Aster's cruel words that he couldn't even bring himself to say to me directly.

Coward.

But the Aster Craven I know—that I *thought* I knew—is anything but a coward.

He's your bully. What did you expect?

The logical part of my brain calls it like it should be while my heart is stuck in the way he kissed me in front of everyone this morning, laughing and joking with the boys like … normal. Our normal. Playing, touching, kissing.

And I had no idea this was coming. Or how good an actor he's become. Or perhaps how good he's always been. Not that I knew him for more than a few months, but this is the first boy I trusted at all, the same one who taught me to kiss. I'll never forget him sitting in my dorm room, showing me the even lines carved beneath his perfectly crisp, buttoned shirt, his personal torment locked away from everyone, but that he shared with me.

He'd trusted me with his secret.

Now, that trust is gone.

Instead of thinking about words coming from Aster's cruel, clever mouth, a calm drops over me like an out of time hyperfocus. My hands cup Elen's cheeks, tracing his porcelain skin when he won't make eye contact, breaking the barrier.

"I want to see what your eyes look like without

the contacts," I tell him seriously.

He chuckles in my hands but doesn't pull away. A sense of wildness enters his deep azure gaze, and his hands close around my arms in a decision that doesn't seem to be ours to make. Elen brings me to my feet, squeezing my shoulders in a rhythm only he can hear as his jaw sets.

"I'm gonna take you home. Are you okay with that?" His voice is clear and sweet as he asks for my consent, like when he sings with his band, Failure Asylum, but his chin drops and his gaze is pure venom.

Wrath—no, intensity is what exudes from him, but then it isn't. I study him with the same sense of displaced calm as before.

"Are you angry with me?" I tilt my head to one side, noting the difference to his usual M.O. "I thought you guys did everything together."

A rumble emanates from his chest that he cuts off before it grows any louder. "Had to come get my Roxy girl," he says in that same quiet voice that threatens danger, like the moments before the worst of the storm breaks. "I knew what he was gonna do, but it shouldn't have been like that." Elen shakes his head as if to negate everything that happened in this room, but all that proves is that my heart hurts.

Quiet falls between us as I stare at the floor and will the tears not to drip from my cheeks. "I'm pathetic."

Elen's teeth grind. "Ducking Aster. That wasn't well done."

"You're not pathetic." Nyx appears by my side, his voice a mere whisper.

Surprised at his ghost-like appearance, I drink him in. His hands are tucked into his pockets, and his hair is wild, a little like him today.

"So you do travel in pairs." I return Nyx's small

smile and some of the pain in my chest eases, making way for brain processing space. Weird how the two are connected. Rather than get the answers I need, all it seems I can do is come up with more questions. "Why would he date me if he planned on doing this?"

Why break up with me like this?

The boys shift on their feet, saying nothing as an uncomfortable silence fills the room. But they don't need to speak. I get it.

"It was all fake," I say, making my first statement to the room at large. No one fights me on that point. "It doesn't matter what it was." I gaze at the large, empty doorway. "What matters is what he did. And you're right. That wasn't well done."

Elen makes a harsh noise in the back of his throat I want him to take back. His sounds are always so smooth, and I don't want him to damage his vocal chords over something as pithy as my break up. A fake up.

A sob breaks free from my chest that I can't contain. Both boys converge on me, a hand taken on each side. Each squeeze provides a constant pressure that eases the ache inside my heart for a moment.

A phone buzzes at the same time as someone knocks. My attention is torn in two directions at once. I can't focus as Elen rubs circles on my palm with his thumb as he works his phone with his other hand. Too many stimuli, and my concentration is blown.

"That was the door, right? And you two, did he send you...? Duck it, I don't want to be back to asking questions."

I can't trust them. They're his best friends. *But they're also mine.* Should I trust them? Because I want to, so, so bad.

Questions, questions, questions.

"You need to be away from him for self-care right

now. For a while," Elen says in a low voice.

Nyx nods along.

I twist to look at him, gripping both boys as my lifelines. I expect to be abandoned at any point after what happened with my boy—with Aster.

Just Aster. He doesn't get a title anymore. A sliver of my heart drops and shatters.

"What do you sound like when you sing?"

I stare at our joined fingers as Nyx interlaces our knuckles and presses inward. The sensation is unusual, but I like it. It's grounding.

Elen's multitasking increases as he sends off a flurry of messages and makes a handful of super brief calls. Most don't pick up, but the ones that do involve a plethora of rapid-fire chatter that has to be swearing in Korean. He hangs up and changes the direction we're headed.

"This way, Roxy girl."

I glance over my shoulder toward my cabin where the door stands ajar. "All my things are in there."

"Everything of yours is this way," Elen corrects, tugging on my hand to bring me a side step closer as the three of us fall into stride together. "And anything that isn't in my car will be shipped back tomorrow."

I bite my lip on every objection that tumbles forward and let them lead me away from my cabin, away from where I last saw Aster. Cowardly Aster. My stomach gripes at the reminder, and I clamp a hand over my belly button.

"I feel as though getting in a car is not a safe option," I warn them, but when they don't fight me on it, I keep walking.

I'm that desperate for friendship right now.

My chest aches and my vision blurs at the edges more than a little.

"It's fine, Roxy. Puke if you need. We got you." Elen extracts his hands from mine to run his fingers through his hair, until the razored ends all stand on end. Blue spikes stick up between the black like craggy mountains against the snowy landscape.

Nyx plays with my fingers, twisting and knotting them to undo the pattern and start all over again. Now that we had physical contact, he's not laying off any time soon. "Not alone." He talks over my head, holding a silent conversation with Elen.

When the K-pop star's gaze links back to mine, there's a decent dose of determination in there, and maybe a little of the crazy that makes him so popular. His eyes are unwavering as he stands his ground as though sensing my indecision.

"Roxy, I walked you to class every day for weeks, months, and I never hurt you," he says as though gauging the measure of trust we have, whatever that's supposed to feel like. "You didn't cringe away from who he was when he did those things," he murmurs, and I know he hasn't forgiven Aster any more than I have for his offenses.

My panties stuck on my face in the gymnasium when Aster dropped them there in front of everyone when I first arrived at the height of his bullying campaign. Saying nothing when Aster broke up with me because I couldn't. The cafeteria incident at the height of my own bullying, when I upended a tub of fruit salad on Aster's head and made a neat fruit pyramid by accident.

Though to be fair, that last is my fault. Elen did try to vote my number higher on that first day when they were grading everyone as they passed.

Am I justifying their toxic behavior in the name of the hike? I shake my head in desperation, tears tracking my face as my hair flicks across my vision.

Cool fingers graze my jaw and tighten for a second. He sighs, and the contact gentles. "Trust us, please. We're not here to hurt you. I will take you home. Then, if you wish, you can get away from us as far as you need…" Elen lips tighten, and his tongue makes a bubble in his cheek while he forgets to play with his lip rings.

I wish he would.

"Promise." Nyx says his one word for the half hour and steps a little closer. "We promise you won't be hurt, Roxy."

I look up at him, dwarfed by his tall, hulking frame he always tries to hide, bowing his shoulders like his bulk is something to be ashamed of. Those liquid hazel eyes bore into mine, a keeper of secrets. But his gaze is steady, and I believe him.

Elen sucks in a long breath. "I'll let you out once we reach your place," he says in a low voice. "If that's what you want when we get there. Or…" He doesn't finish that sentence, playing with his lip rings, drifting off.

I don't need any more convincing.

"Okay."

****

Two hours later, I know I've made the right choice. Seated in the back of Elen's Lambo, the blue one that matches his hair with the silver, chrome, and blue interior, all custom made, I'm sure of the K-pop star.

More than that, I'm sure of Nyx. The strange musician slid into the backseat where the boys made a nest for me out of the surprising amount of crocheted rugs and pillows that were jammed into the tiny boot. It never occurred to me that billionaire rockstar boys might camp out in their billionaire car toys.

Nyx tucked me into my nest while Elen collected the things that were delivered to his car. In a rare moment of privacy, Nyx slipped in beside me, stripping off his jacket and wrapping me in that, too. Before he departed for the passenger seat up front, he leaned in and covered my mouth with his in a gentle, full contact kiss that lasted less than a second, and a full eternity all at once.

I'm still not sure if Elen knows what his friend did while I sat stock still, frozen the entire time, unable to respond. I keep playing the moment over and over in my head. My hands ache to touch him, but Nyx seems to like brief moments of contact, and I know that kiss won't be repeated any time soon.

I treasure that interlude and snuggle amongst the blankets and the pillow, resting my head on Nyx's leather jacket. I've sunk down so far I doubt I'm much more than eyes and a nose visible from the front.

"Cozy back there?" Elen called from the driver's seat.

"Pretty warm." I wiggle three fingers free from my layers and give a wave. Then on impulse, I make a finger heart I ensure is visible in the rearview mirror.

Elen's eyes light up, and he's recharged full of sass. "That's my personal pillow you're hugging, Roxy. If you drool over it, be ready for the consequences."

Topped up and mischievous after their overdose of TLC now that the pain of Aster's cruelty has waned a fraction, I turn my head enough to face the pillow in question. Holding Elen's gaze in the mirror I stick my tongue out, make sure he's watching, and press the tip to the pillow.

Nyx's wolf whistle surprises me again. I hadn't registered him listening in on our flirting. Is that what we're doing? I broke up with one boy, bawled my eyes out, and now I'm flirting with his friends?

Whatever. It lessens the sting somewhat.

Elen fakes outrage, shaking his head at me.

I smirk and refuse to relinquish my hostage. Another few minutes into the drive back and my stomach aches, then rumbles. Loudly.

"I didn't grab food." Elen meets my gaze in the mirror. "Sorry, Roxy."

I curl deeper into the blanket, jacket, and pillow bundle. "I'm a pest."

"You're not." This comes from the passenger seat.

I close my eyes and pretend the boys aren't there. "I'm fine."

Expecting someone to say *you're not* I wait a second, and then crack an eye in time to catch Elen pass Nyx a hundred dollar note.

"What was that?"

The boys exchange a glance. Elen's nose twitches before he fesses up. "I bet you could hold up for the trip without stopping." He snorts at me. "Looks like I was wrong."

"Yeah, I'm sure that sucks." I shake my head as my stomach drops in a low swoop.

My vision blurs, and my pillow shifts. I clutch everything as Elen pulls up to the curb, grating something beneath the low-slung sports car. He hosts a brief conversation with Nyx and climbs out, pulling his seat forward and hopping in the back.

His long legs fold up high as Nyx climbs into the driver seat, pulling his seatbelt across his chest. He then heads for drive-thru.

I stare at Elen, who shouldn't ever fit in the back seat, but he doesn't fit because it's already occupied by a person. This car wasn't built for three, let alone ... whatever this is.

"What are you doing?"

"So many questions."

"You have no idea."

He pulls his seatbelt across himself, and then reaches under my blanket to grab my thigh. "Are you attached to anything?"

"Like a seat belt?"

Elen's eyes narrow. "Have you been unattached this whole time? Naughty girl." His growl is something that's so far from flirting it's well on the other side of the *inappropriate* line.

His fingers find their way beneath my shirt and press to my stomach, skin finding skin.

I gasp at the contact wherever he touches me. "Don't do that."

"Why not?" Elen tugs on my blanket pile, rearranging me so my back faces his arms where they wind around me. He plays with my over-the-shoulder length hair, and loops a seatbelt around my waist. "Safety conscious, beautiful."

"Doesn't help when your heart's breaking and you're suicidal," I mutter into his pillow.

"That's not what I want to hear from you, Roxy girl. But it's my turn, okay?" He tilts his head up, and before I can think or protest, he glides his mouth across mine in an easy, open-mouthed kiss.

Oh, he knows about Nyx's kiss.

My breath stalls. This time, I refuse to be frozen, a non-participant. I lean up, pressing my mouth back against his.

That's it. That's all it is. Elen keeps me safe in the circle of his arms, offering comfort and affection in one as he has every day since he started walking me to class. I sigh as I sink back to my blanket nest while Elen hums a song I don't know but like all the same.

Somehow, that's his other arm around my waist holding on tight. Elen tucks the blanket in over my fingers so I can clutch it and him at the same time, his long arm bending to encompass all of me.

I try to wrap my hand around his wrist, but he's more muscular than I expected. My fingertips trace up and down the corded surface, the ink there, and I enjoy being able to discover what he feels like without using my eyes.

"Having fun?" Elen breathes out in measured heartbeats.

My answer is to mumble something that even I don't understand in reply. "Tell me about this one." I manage to enunciate a full sentence. *Proud Roxy moment.*

"Nyx did it. Can you read it?" he asks in a soft voice that lulls me to a peaceful, safe place away from the hurts of today.

"Not with my eyes shut. Keep talking?"

Above me, Elen presses his lips to the top of my head in a chaste kiss. "Sleep, Roxy. We'll figure it out when we get home."

I fall asleep breathing in Nyx's leather jacket still tucked around me, mixing with Elen's cool, watery clean scent.

The last time I drifted off this fast was in Aster's arms. But I'm too tired, and the heartbreak that should come with that thought eludes me.

For now.

JOSS PHOENIX

Chapter Seven

Watch Your Back

Aster

There's a line in an old movie, a satire where the good guy tells his friend to watch his back. The friend watches him get beaten to a pulp and gives a good commentary on the whole scene, play by play. That's how I feel right now.

But Zeke isn't talking, and there's no satire or bad guys beating me up.

Just my best friend, and I'm the one about to become the pulp.

His wrapped fist—who has time for gloves—flies at my face. I dodge his personal weapon by a hair's breadth to find my knee kicked out from beneath me. The next blow comes to my shoulder and I raise my hands in surrender. We've been going at it for over half an hour and by the looks of it, Zeke has more rage stored than usual to throw my way.

"Hands up," he snaps. "If you're fighting for your life against your father or his minions, is this how you're giving up? On your goddamn knees? Get up, Craven."

I spit on the ground, and there's the faintest taint of blood in it. *Good.* I watch the red mingle with my saliva and the sight surges fresh energy through my veins. I shove upward, my knuckles tight, and clock Zeke in the chin.

Textbook uppercut, my friend.

He stumbles back, rubbing his face and glaring at me. "Better. Now do it again."

"That would have knocked anyone else on their duckbutt," I mutter.

Damnit. I broke up with the girl, and she's still

haunting me.

"You won't knock down an old biddy on a windy day. Get moving. Feet. If you give up, I'm cracking ribs with my toes." He dangles a steel capped boot in my field of vision in demonstration.

"When did you get all serious?" I huff, my thighs straining as I duck—quack—his next blows.

"When did you turn into a duckhole?"

"I was born this way," I seethe.

"Nah. Stop hiding and show me what you can do, Craven," Zeke taunts, dancing around me the way a man of his weight and muscle bulk has no right in doing.

Fine. You wanna play? Let's play.

I swipe blood from the corner of my mouth, staining the wrapping on my own hands—gloves are for duckers, Zeke's new mantra—and bounce forward.

I mistime my second bounce and catch his incoming fist with the corner of my eye. The fresh cut opens over my brow and blood drips into it. I'm not sure which is injured more; my body or my pride.

Zeke seems to want to beat me to a pulp, and I have no one to watch my back. Maybe this is his method of doing it in his own twisted way.

"Feel better?" I pant.

He glares at the floor. "You shouldn't have done it."

Blood drips onto my fingers and I make no effort to swipe it away. "There wasn't a choice."

"Ever think of fighting back?"

Too many times to count.

The scars on my back tighten where I rub my shoulder blades against the boxing ring's ropes despite that the injuries are years old.

"I understand the cost of fighting back." I tip my head up to stare up at the high vaulted ceiling of the warehouse with its giant fan that chops the still air above us. Warm currents cake sweat to my overheated skin. "I won't have my failings revisited on her because of mistakes that could have been avoided."

"Doesn't stop you being a duckhole. And you still can't punch for shit."

I bring my eyes back to his. "I'll take what gifts I've been granted."

"You're in a mood."

Huffing, I pick at the wrappings around my fist with numb fingers, mangling the job before I start.

Zeke clicks his tongue and grabs my fist, peeling the tape away. He's on my second hand when they walk in.

Elen, Roxy, and Nyx. They stand on either side of her like guardians, each touching her somehow. Elen's hand is slung across her back, his fingers tangling in her hair where he gives it a little pull. Nyx bumps shoulders with her in almost constant contact while he plays on his phone.

It's the first time I've seen her since I sent the message that still burns its way across my retinas. For all the things we've done to each other, this seems the most permanent, the least retractable.

Not once does she look up to acknowledge either of us, never catches my eye when I give Elen and Nyx a murderous glare I might've borrowed from Zeke.

"What are they doing here?" My words come out harsh.

Zeke nods his agreement, folding his arms at my side. "Who knows."

"Still think you should do it," Elen mutters, but the empty warehouse picks up his clear voice and throws it.

"Never gonna happen." Nyx's negative comes

next.

"Sign. Please." Two slim hands rise in a prayer position. "Pick the simple path." Elen hosts a one-way conversation over Roxy's head while Nyx talks to his phone.

Good to know they're as dysfunctional as us.

I frown at the pop star as Zeke flicks a towel out of nowhere to drape around my shoulders, concealing everything no one else should see. I nod my thanks, my attention still zeroed in on the Korean singer. He hasn't spoken to me since the snow trip—not that I blame him. They collected Roxy and took her home, and I'm grateful for that. She didn't need more attention once the damage required was done.

What annoys me is how she's shifted into their orbit, settling between them like they had a ready-made space carved out for her. It's what I wanted in theory, but in reality … I need her to hurt as much as I do. Petty, but true.

Her gaze lifts from her concentrated study of the warehouse floor to where I slump against the side of the boxing ring. A few seconds earlier, and all my scars would have been on display. She's seen most of it before. Hell, she's one of two people I've let touch my marks. That doesn't make me wanna cover up any less. I slip my arms deeper into the cover the towel provides, meeting her gaze before hers drops away, her cheeks flushing.

Pleasure spikes through my chest at her flustered stance, the way she twists her hands together. Maybe she didn't expect to find me here. Maybe she thought I'd come crawling to her.

My lips twitch at that last. No, she knows me better.

The others' reaction is far less satisfying. Nyx, as always, ignores the world at large, but Elen's sharp gaze misses nothing. If he ever parts company with the band he carries, he'll make a formidable business adversary.

"What are we signing?" Grabbing my water bottle, I flex the hand that Zeke freed. The knuckles are already stiff from trading blows and the cut over my eye aches.

In my periphery, he grabs the rubbish we've created and stalks towards the change rooms at the back of the sparring area, leaving me alone with at least one person who hates me and two who are more than borderline.

Three to one. Still good odds for me.

One on one with Roxy? I'm screwed.

Elen's face remains a blank mask as he surveys me for a fraction of a second before the moment passes and his expression dissolves into a crooked smile. He reaches out and ruffles Nyx's man bun. "Just trying to get my boy here a career in music. Money he deserves."

I upgrade my previous assessment of the rockstar a notch. Formidable is an understatement.

Roxy shifts at his side, her fingertips dragging through his and the room darkens for me. I ache for a smoke, but Zeke's taken everything I brought with me and locked it all away with a *no distractions* clause while we fought.

"Not everyone wants the same things." I talk to Elen, but I'm looking at her.

She sighs and lifts her head to stare back, unflinching.

If I thought she'd back down after I pulled her apart and ripped her heart out of her chest, then I'm disappointed.

But it's Roxy Quell. Nothing about her is disappointing. Maybe the heart broken here is mine.

The thought that the breakup didn't hurt her

leaves a bruising sensation deep in my chest. I don't know whether I want to kiss her or make her crumble at my feet.

Maybe a bit of both.

Her other hand reaches for the muso on her opposite side, her gaze all defiance as she fortifies her position, but like with Elen's attempt nothing quite goes her way. Nyx slides from her touch, stopping a few steps back from them both.

It breaks her attention from me, and she looks after him, longing written in the curve of her thick lashes.

My heart takes a dive.

Give her to a friend. My father's words slam back at me. *That loser friend.*

Mission achieved.

If Zeke were here to see me now. A large part of me is glad that he's not.

My pride and winded body coil on the cold cement the floor, blood dripping from my eyebrow into the corner of my eye. My vision turns red, but it's not with rage.

I still love her.

Her head jerks, and I shut my mouth. I can't keep anything together around this girl.

I clamber to my feet that don't work the way they should, my vision swimming. "Need to shower." *I need to escape.*

Uncaring that she'll see me run from her, I stride across the open room on unsteady legs, willing my body to hold out for a few seconds longer. I pass Zeke on the way through, fist bumping him as he hands me a tray with my chains laid out across it.

Usually, he waits until I've showered to put them back on, but this time I clip them up one at a time, thinking of the heavy weights wrapping around my neck when they sit at the top of my scars, the towel still covering the ink around my chest. The pack of cigarettes beside them and lighter finish the mini ceremony he refuses to drop. I leave Zeke, shirtless in his gray sweats, his hair ruffled and covered in water droplets like he rushed his shower to look after me.

Is that what I am, damaged goods they all need to be wary of? I'm supposed to be the one dealing out hell, and here he is, my goddamn nursemaid.

I need to be harder than this. I need to break her, even if I break myself in the process.

Maybe that's my new goal. Shatter and splinter to reform into the monster she needs me to be. The one she already hates. Fears.

I stop at the doorway to the shower block and look back to find Zeke gazing after her, his shoulders set in a hard line. Beyond him is the flash of color where Roxy disappears out of the warehouse before I can catch her eye, Elen following her in an unhurried stride.

Nyx stares at the floor, studying nothing at all.

Cursing way too loud, I head away from them all, unwilling to let more of my sweat and blood seep into the cracks and stain the cement beneath my feet.

There's no point when she's not watching.

JOSS PHOENIX

Chapter Eight

Whispers in the Walls

Roxy

Calc is my least favorite class. Rhani is no help as she glides through the problems despite her claim that she sucked at math, leaving me with my substandard Providence, poor-girl education that lacks in every area as a stand out failure. Her talents she didn't disclose on the first day in class are slowly exposed until I'm left as the lone straggler.

Mary Rector, our drawn, angular teacher who needs a good meal and maybe a surgical procedure knows it, opting to pick on me *every single time*.

"How do I calculate the hypotenuse, Miss Quell?"

I jerk in my seat, and my pencil rolls off the end of my desk, clattering to the floor. Cursing about wayward ducks, I lunge after it and head butt the desk.

A snicker rolls around the classroom, but the male laugh that slices through me comes from the desk behind mine.

Aster's laugh screws with my day in ways I didn't think possible.

"I don't know." I clamp my mouth shut, retrieving my pencil, twisting it between my fingers. The fragile thing, already cracked from the fall it sustained, falls apart the moment I place it back on my desk.

Aster's still laughing at me, and I still don't have an answer.

"Shut up," Zeke snaps on my other side.

He's angry again. Big surprise. I don't think he has any other expression at this point.

I frown at my desk and risk sneaking a peek at him from the corner of my eye. But he's glaring at Aster this time, not me.

"Mister Fallon." Miss Rector clicks her heels toward our desks one harsh beat at a time. "If you could please try to solve the equation rather than evaluate another student's mental state?"

She glances sideways at me to make her point, and heat stains my cheeks in an instant reaction.

"It's fine," I mutter, as he opens his mouth to rip her a new one. I suck at math. Bald facts, but it's true. I never had time to study when I worked Mom's job as well as going to school. Back before—

A lump wells in my throat and I stare hard at the fractured pieces of my pencil.

"Roxy," Zeke mumbles out of the side of his mouth, reaching for me.

I shake my head, unable to focus on anything, unwilling to deal with his attitude along with the teacher's.

"Maybe you can have lunch with us." Amelia Hart leans diagonally across the desks and taps my shoulder with her branded red lollipop that matches pretty much everything in her possession including her clothing and her sports car.

"Um, thanks?" I shoot her a confused smile, still trying to work out the math problem.

"Work on your social life in your own time, Miss Hart," Mary Rector snaps.

Amelia smiles. "Sure, Miss. How 'bout it, Roxy? I've got an invitation for you."

I don't get to answer.

"She's got a lunch date," Rhani steps in.

"Girls!" Miss Rector shouts, losing all her ducks at once.

Zeke snorts into his braced arms, dipping his head.

"It's a simple fix." Aster strides between our desks, catching Miss Rector's elbow and towing her about in a semicircle, though he sends Amelia an indecipherable glance.

The teacher stumbles on her heels, but he shows her as much mercy as he does anyone once he's set on a specific path. His voice rings out as he takes on the class solving the problem she gave me and the next one on the smart board.

I sigh and sink lower in my seat, rolling the pieces of my pencil and praying for the class to end. I haven't been able to concentrate since the day I came back to school after the ski trip. Nyx and Elen kept me in an insulated bubble for as long as possible, but that slice of pretend peace had to end.

But the clock ticks backward I swear, as Aster waltzes back to his desk, trailing his fingertips along mine and swiping everything off it.

Miss Rector doesn't say a word, ignoring his attitude as always.

Zeke sits stiff in his chair as I duck beneath my desk with a sigh and collect my things. Usually, I'd throw out a foot to try to trip him or snark back, but I've already run out of energy.

He's stolen it from me. I sink back in my chair and hate that today I'm accepting defeat.

****

I sit alone in a dim corner of Alchem's luxurious library well after most people have left for the night, unable to face Rhani's happy chatter. My mood from earlier persists, dampening me as I lean across the desk, staring down at the calc textbook that makes no more sense than it did in class.

A tingle starts beneath the heel of my hand where I rub my thumb across the inside of my wrist, searching for the two crisscrossing lines there that I gave myself last night. Uneven, shameful. My shirt sleeve is pulled down over the marks I scratched into my skin with the edge of my paintbrush while I was creating a nice little black canvas that suited my mood. Not that there's anyone here to see, but these are for me alone.

Like the artwork I can't forget. A new distraction.

The project was supposed to be a portrait in pale colors, reflections of light on a grayscale canvas, but no matter what I did, everything turned dark. I threw reds at the black background, but the darkness absorbed those, too. A sliver of charcoal gray, and a flash of electric blue emerged off center, decorating the otherwise austere landscape.

In my mind's eye, I stare at Elen's colors spread across my canvas, nothing like what I intended to paint if I had a plan at all beyond the brief we were given in class. His brightness highlights the darkness of my other two bullies. I have no idea why Astor and Zeke take it upon themselves to torment me. I have no idea why calc isn't segregated by ability, because those two float at genius level, and I'm the total opposite.

Scraping the bottom of the barrel? I'm the stuff left behind underneath all that. Aster and Zeke must be the cream of the cream, and once they're through their work, which takes a glorious five minutes to complete, they target me, though half the time Miss Rector does the work for them.

I get my own little snicker in when I see her eyeballing either boy like they're some tasty treat, then am sickened with myself for the amount of Alchem entitlement rubbing off on my uniform-covered butt.

Which brings me back to my dark little corner of the library on my own on a Friday night when everyone else is out at a bonfire behind the gym getting drunk and dancing while I hide and ruminate on why the boy I still love hates me so much.

And why I still care.

A pair of soft footsteps announces the other presence in this part of the library. I don't have to turn around to know who found me. Part of me doesn't even care why.

Aster leans over me from behind and places his palms flat on the desk, framing my text book. His breath huffs against my cheek. "It'll help if you actually do the work," he snaps out of the corner of his mouth, breaking the intimacy of the moment he created. "Do you care about anything, Roxy? It's pathetic watching you fail again and again."

Depression bears down on me, its familiar tendrils sinking into my arms and legs egged on by his toxic words that hit their targets with perfect aim. The weight is too much, and I slide lower in my seat, unable to gesture at the open text in front of me. He's right. I am pathetic.

"It's all I've got."

He stares at me. "I don't remember you giving up so fast."

I ignore him, rubbing my thumb over the corner of the page my text is open at until it curls, like his lip.

The disparaging noise that comes from his mouth should hurt me, but doesn't. "Do the work, Roxy."

That earns him the rise he's standing there, begging me for. I glare back at him. "Yes, sir."

Aster smirks. "Too easy, Roxy." His steady footsteps fade as he leaves me to myself, though my torment doesn't end there.

The echo of his soft, derisive laugh at my back haunts me through the next hour of enforced study until I give up on calc that didn't make any more sense than it did during the previous hour and exchange my text book for my sketch pad and my pen for a pouch of charcoal stubs I brought with me from my previous life.

The moment I swipe my mark across the clean A4 sheet my mind clears. I work in silence, no distractions, without fear of who watches me. I forget he's there at all. By the time I've finished my piece the library feels closer, and the soft murmur of my hidden neighbors is absent.

It's been an age since I worked anywhere except for the art studios or my own room because I'm exhausted between the boys harassing me and my classes. The grief, I've covered up, ignored, same as the changes in my life. The break up and all that's come with it, as well as moving across to Alchem Academy and hating every step except for those few weeks with Aster before it all went to shit again. The deluge alone should knock me flat. But, in this moment, I'm free of those pressures and weights alternating on slamming me into the floor.

Even so, the reprieve is short lived. Once the strange sketch of shadows and light surrounding a staircase that plummets down and down and down is done, I'm left with a stark return to reality. Ignoring the uncomfortable pin point between my shoulder blades where Aster stares my way, I flick through my portfolio, swallowing back the fresh wave of discomfort that threatens to overwhelm me.

Instead of giving him the satisfaction of reacting, I bury myself in touching up old projects. The concept of heading back to my dorm doesn't stick with me as I roll through the images I drew after my parents' death.

Shattered glass, though I never saw the site of the car crash that killed them.

The jail cells where Dad worked, though I never visited those, either. Two dice bearing double sixes on their upturned faces, because that's what he bet on in his new job at the jail, before he lost Mom, me, and himself.

The canopy of black umbrellas at the funeral, because it rained that day.

I choke on a laugh at that. The umbrellas were from a different funeral held on the same day, adjacent to the one I attended alone. No one attended from my hometown of Providence, Nevada, which scraped together enough money to put up a pair of matching headstones, even though that's not where they're buried.

Tears for the pity they felt for me when I ran out of my own.

More umbrellas.

I'm calm and aware at the same time. It's the same way I always filter when my head is in my art. Lost in it, but not. I put those emotions on the page and they leave me for a short period, freeing up enough space to allow me to think.

Feel.

Anything but numb.

I rub the welts on my wrists from where the edge of the paint brush scratched me by accident last night. At least, the first one was by accident.

The four times after? Not so much.

"I told you not to do that." Aster's sharp voice slices through my serenity on one side.

I drop my wrist to my knee.

He scoops it up in white knuckled fingers, though he doesn't mark me.

I yank my hand back. "You shouldn't touch me at all." I glare at him and don't say the words I want to allow to tumble free.

You gave up that right when you pulled my heart out and stomped on it.

That's too poetic for the hurt that shattered me

when he threw me aside. But he's Aster Craven. Why should I expect any less from him? I know what happened to his last ex, after all.

I expect him to snark back at me in defiance, or show some display of power to prove I'm weaker than him, or proof that I can't control my emotions as well as he does.

heartless heartless heartless

And yet as I stare up at Aster, something about the way his lips part on a whisper of a breath as though he might say something nice, I find myself crazy craving those words, needing more.

broken broken broken

I trace my fingers along my wrist beneath my shirt to the fading welt and find the original one. The memory of being back in my room when he showed me his scars and told me about the cutting, letting out his pain, floods me.

I understood that. But I'm not brave enough to put the blade to my own skin. Yet. Which is what he was always afraid of, and why he was always there to stop me. I think we might be back in that place where he'll soften and give me some wise words because he's taken so much more than I have and *survived*.

"But you're still telling me what to do," I mumble to the desk's surface.

"Because you're not listening," he snaps, his hand hovering over my wrist, though he doesn't touch me, as I commanded.

We're like two repellent ends of a magnet, each pushing the other away despite some unseen force drawing us together.

"I'm listening to you," I whisper, fighting the dual rise of bile and tears that threaten.

Leave me alone.

Don't go.

I'm not sure whether he sees the conflict within me or not, because his blank face is too practiced to show emotion, if he feels anything at all.

"You don't belong here, Roxy. No matter what you do, you'll never be more than a moment's curiosity for any of us." His parting blow leaves me hollow inside.

Aster halts at the corner of my desk when I think he will leave me alone, and *stop*. Of course, he doesn't. Cool fingers wrap around my wrist, find the welt I made by accident, and squeeze. Hard. His smirk turns cruel, his voice soft and intimate.

"You can't even do that right."

By the time he leaves the library floor, I'm shuddering in my seat, gripping the wrist he held. My nails dig into the welt, waiting until I can't feel anything anymore.

But I fail at that, too.

JOSS PHOENIX

Chapter Nine

What They Won't Give

Roxy

The deadly weight sits heavy in my palm. I take one glance at Zeke and hand the throwing knife back. "No way. I can't do this. I don't want to do this." I don't even know why I'm here, with him.

I cast a look sideways at Elen, but the K–pop star sits with his back to the hard wall, frowning at his phone while his fingers move at lightspeed.

"Focus, duck girl. Pay attention." Zeke flicks my ear with two calloused fingers.

I twist my head and snap my teeth, missing his skin by mere millimeters, and he *laughs* at me. "Something's wrong with you," I mutter.

"So many things." Zeke grins, and the expression changes his whole face. When his anger drops away, he's almost … normal.

A shiver works its way along my spine. "Don't do that."

His eyes revert to their usual state. "Do what?" he snaps, pushing the cold blade into my palm that refuses to warm up regardless how long I cling to the stupid thing. "Now, throw. Like I showed you."

"No." I plant my hands on my hips like a toddler about to have a hissy fit. Not so far from the truth. "I don't want to—"

"Roxy girl." Elen looks up from his phone where he pauses in his frantic tapping. Unusual lines frame his pretty eyes. Dark shadows beneath highlight the fact that Aster and me aren't our only group insomniacs. "Do this for me? Please?"

I roll my bottom lip inward. "I have to?"

"Yeah. You can, 'kay?" He offers me an exhausted smile before his attention drops back to his phone.

All the moment's forced happiness slides from his face, stealing my resolve with it.

And Zeke capitalizes on that. Duckhat.

"Come on, Roxy," he goads, juggling the freaking larger blades in his giant mitts. "Show me what you got."

Something snaps inside me. "Fine," I mutter, dragging up every inch of the girl from Providence who never let anyone touch her without permission.

Which meant never. Not until Aster. That stings, so I take Zeke's advice, and Elen's, and I use it.

"Tell me why I'm here," I snap as I raise the first blade and hurl it at the target set up opposite the boxing ring at the opposite end of the school to everything else that Zeke and Aster favor.

The building must be the one place on campus that's not outfitted in luxury appointments, or gilt with some sort of gold leaf. The school's crest is absent as though this hideout of sweat and salt isn't worthy to bear its colors.

No breath exits my lungs as the slim blade, unadorned as the boxing gym, leaves my hand as instructed, headed for the target. At least, I think it's done as instructed. But as the small throwing knife—Zeke won't entrust me to the larger, deadlier looking ones he uses—clatters to the floor, not even making the full distance to its mark, I hold up my hands in a preempt.

"Not my fault. Instruction is lacking." *Or the subject, but who would fess up to that?*

Elen snorts from his place at the wall as Zeke's face darkens. He paces around me while I rotate on the spot, refusing to let him out of my sight.

"You lack strength, agility, and aim." He sighs,

sounding too much like Aster for my taste. "Pretty much anything to defend yourself."

"Why do I need this, again? And why you?"

He ignores me and rummages around in his bag, pulling out a different set of blades, and swaps them for the ones I've been holding.

"Oh, good. They're smaller," I say in a dry voice. "I'll be able to pin floating washing with them."

Zeke cracks a second rare smile. His monthly quota must be down. "You know better than to expect these overprivileged kids to do their own chores, Roxy," he murmurs, sliding the flat of one blade along my arm. The edge is sharp enough to shave the fine hairs from my skin. I don't doubt he'll cut me if I let my breath out too fast. "But a girl like you collects enemies. So does Craven."

He steps back, and I breathe without fear of impalement.

"How … sweet," I whisper, trying to conceal my cough.

Zeke shoots me a smirk. "Try it underhand. Same grip. No spin. Opposite foot. Yeah, like that. It's less accurate but for you, let's keep it simple, okay? Aim, and let it go."

"And you think this will help?" I'm still stuck on the enemies and Craven comment when I let the small knife go. It hits the target and bounces off.

My instructor doesn't bother to conceal his groan. "Not like that, it won't. Grip. Show me."

I hold up my hand, my middle finger extended along the blade where he showed me two before. "Like this?" I offer in an innocent tone.

He rolls his eyes. "Cute. But if someone comes for you, that ain't gonna do duck. Here." He rearranges my hand that fits around the slimmer sliver of metal and nods. "Try again. No big shoulder action. Flick your wrist, and…" He demonstrates with his own larger blade that thunks into the middle of the target.

"Fine." I don't look at the target, too busy returning his glare that's reappeared in the last minutes. Shock registers when I earn a *thunk* of my own. "Huh?"

That gets me an arrogant smirk. "Instruction's good. Subject could use work." He claps his hands before I can roast him. "Again."

Sixty-five *agains* later, along with criticism each time and adjustments, my fingers refuse to close around the little knife that fits well in my hand as I sag against the wall next to Elen. He keeps tapping at his screen but the moment I slouch next to him, he blacks the device off and tucks it away.

"You did well." He nudges my shoulder. "Sore yet?"

"I'm sure I will be tomorrow. He's a taskmaster."

"I wouldn't trust you with anyone else."

I watch Zeke pack up, wondering if I'll ever be able to take him on. Not likely. I've seen him and Aster fight. It's brutal. And bloody.

"I'm more worried about whether one of those blades will end up in my back."

Elen's soft laugh ruins my fantasy. "He won't hurt you. Zeke's a bear. A protector, Roxy. That's what he does."

"He's a—" I pause and paste on a sweet smile as a hulking shadow falls over us. "An excellent instructor," I finish, offering up the blades. "Thank you for letting me borrow these."

Zeke stares down at me, a muscle in his jaw flexing before he swipes the knives from my palm with one oversized paw.

"Thank Aster. They're his."

****

My grumpy instructor is nowhere in sight when I emerge from the female showers at the back of the boxing ring. They look like I'm the only person to use them this year. Apparently, this is a male space, and that makes me all the more intent on invading it. Or maybe hiding, because the walls are imbued with Aster's unique tang.

Without Zeke's barrier, my ex's shade follows me through the open building as I shake water droplets from my hair and tug at the uniform intent on sticking to every available patch of damp skin.

"Looking good, Roxy girl." Elen whistles through his teeth.

A grimace turns my mouth down. "Sexist, much? I hate these uniforms." I tug at the hem of my skirt that I swear shrinks every time I take it off.

He links his arm through mine. "Yeah, but you make it pretty." His lips brush my hair as he lowers his voice. "You have no idea how much inspo I get from visuals like that."

"Inspo for what?" I blink up at him as he smiles slow and dark, and it clicks. "Duck. Butt," I enunciate with clarity, in case the message isn't clear when I slap at his arm.

He mimes being wounded, but dodges my next half-hearted blow and slings his arm around my shoulder. "I'll take the hurt for you," he says in a low voice.

Peering up at his gray contacts today, I can't figure out if he's being serious or not. "What color are they?"

"What?" One eyebrow goes up.

"Your eyes."

Elen laughs and pulls me into a one-armed hug. "Only you would ask a Korean boy what color his eyes are, Roxy."

"Oh." Heat suffuses my cheeks. "What were you working on?"

"Band stuff." His abrupt answer gives me pause. Elen clears his throat and nudges my shoulder. "Got a dance I want you to learn." He flips his phone in his hand, bringing up a video of the boys of Failure Asylum apparently filming without him. I stare at the intricate steps and shake my head.

"Nope. No way."

"Aw, come on. I have to do it." He flashes me a Korean finger heart.

I roll my eyes as we walk out of the warehouse, Elen's arm slinging back around me. His company is comfortable, and at this end of campus, we're alone.

Right up until we turn the corner of the building and we're accosted by a swarm of fangirls bearing Failure Asylum merch, wrapped in branded scarves and hoodies, though I took off my borrowed jacket an hour ago.

"Oh, uh—" Elen's arm detangles from my shoulders as he's mobbed in an instant.

The small crowd collects members, growing bigger with him in the middle and me on the outside. All I can see of him is the occasional flash of electric blue as his head bobs around while he signs books, arms, and—*is that a boob?*

"Who knew fan clubs could be so ravenous?" Zeke stands right next to me dressed in his Alchem charcoal pants, white shirt, and tie, his hands fixed in his pockets like he's been there the whole time.

A stunted shriek leaves my mouth as a part-squeak before I shut it down and slap his washboard stomach beneath his shirt. "Duck. That stings. Yeah." I turn back to the conversation when he laughs down at me. "It's madness. Is he okay?" I frown when Elen seems to disappear in the developing mass.

Zeke sighs. "I'll get him out."

"You do this a lot?" I gawk when he rolls up his shirt sleeves—literally rolls them to his elbows.

That earns me a raised eyebrow. "Well, yeah, Roxy. He's one of the highest paid superstars in the world. Just because they sit in class with him and see him in the dining hall doesn't mean the hysteria doesn't afflict them, too."

"Oh. I can help," I offer, sliding my bag to the ground.

He fixes me with a hard stare. "Hell to the no, girl. Stay your duck butt here. I'll get our K-boy." He's already halfway to Elen, determination written in the length of his stride and the hard line of his broad, bulked out shoulders.

But when I expect to laugh at his antics or panic over some girl flashing my guys, the whole situation unravels faster than ducks charging across a pristine pond top for fresh breadcrumbs.

Men in matte black kit carrying weapons I've never seen outside of movies—the world ending ones—put my throwing knife lesson to shame as they swarm over the cluster. Fangirls, and a few boys, are pulled back by their uniforms until Elen is unearthed as though a zombie hoard attacked. In retrospect, I guess that's not so far from the truth. Even with Alchem's hidden security force in play that I've heard the boys whisper about or rumors in class, the fans seem intent on coming back for more.

Moments later, it's over. Combat suited men herd the masses away while Elen sweeps ruffled hair back from his pale face. Zeke's hand is wrapped around his arm as he tows the battered K-pop star toward me.

"Are you okay?"

I reach out, hesitant, taking in the smudges on Elen's half-buttoned shirt that's marked and even torn in places to his face that's whiter than ever. I draw my hand back when he doesn't react, glancing up at Zeke.

Give him a minute, he mouths.

I nod, biting my lip. "Sorry," I whisper, though I don't know why I'm apologizing.

For once, no one tells me not to.

Chapter Ten

Between the Lines

Elen

Ink splotches the page around my fingers where I've scribbled random notes on a scattering of pages that litters the Alchem Academy dorm room issue carpet around me. Humming a few lines out of order, I record the next on my phone, tossing sections of the verse around, but no matter what I do, I still can't get the lyrics to work.

One more breath
One step away
I'm soaring closer to you

The damn song that's haunted me for weeks now is stuck somewhere deep inside my head and refuses to come out. It's nothing that Failure Asylum would play, and not for the first time I wonder that I haven't made the wrong decision signing an eight-year contract with the band on exclusivity.

Sure, it seemed like the right thing to do at the time. Got me out of a village where everyone fought for their next meal, unsure if a mistimed storm or disease would ruin crops and starve half of us out.

Signing on for a multi-million-dollar contract seemed a no brainer. Right up until a simple life isn't so simple at all.

Take me towards, creeping forward
A twisted curveball on this roller coaster with you

That last line brings a smile to my lips because it's so her. Our Roxy all over. And she is ours, no matter what Zeke or even Aster seem to think. The glimmer of her hair that caught me on that first day to her blazing eyes, and the defiance that rolls off her in waves.

And the sadness.

Like everything is broken inside, and nothing can ruin her from here on in. Nothing at all, because it's already happened to her. Maybe that's why I've fallen in love with a girl who lets me walk her to class each day without complaint, and doesn't mind if I put kimchi on her tray when others have shied away from me for less.

Another reason why I can't get enough of her. My Roxy Girl.

I toy with the title, but again, it's nothing Failure Asylum would even consider. Not the lyrics, not the vibe. They're all big beats, K-pop, *bring-the-life-and-happiness-to-the-crowd* boyband type of music. Hell, none of us are supposed to be in relationships.

That's in the damn contract, too.

Less than half of us speak to each other anymore outside the recording studio. Or on tour.

Marketing had a field day with my life years ago. I agreed to everything, heedless of the warnings my agent—a quick sign on and one of the best things that ever happened to me, Roxy aside—offered at the time. Now, all I can see is calculations and the cost of buying myself out of the pit I've signed myself into.

Every single cent will be worth it to have a chance with her.

If she wants me. *If* she'll consider anyone after what Aster did to her.

Watching her shatter anew on the drive back from the ski trip didn't hurt for her alone. Nyx and I were far from unaffected by the numb way she curled into herself. Or the warmth that exuded from her when her mouth opened beneath mine, and his.

Soft, sweet, and brief.

A comfort in a moment. Memory on a joyride home.

This isn't her home. That's as obvious to me as anyone. Roxy doesn't feel she fits in anywhere, and after the way she's been displaced from her own life I don't blame her. Tossed from one house to another to be cast out to a boarding school she'd never heard of that's as far from her frame of reference as the K-pop world ever was from my small village.

Turn me around
Spin me with you

Culture shock doesn't cover it. Not even close.

One more exhale cause I can't breathe

The residual heartbreak-in-readiness lingers in my mind, and that gets scribbled down, too. Over and over, until an uninvited presence in my room creeps in, and I know I'm not alone anymore.

I stare at the pair of white leather loafers polished to a perfect, habitual shine I know he hasn't done himself and tsk. "How long have you been watching me, stalker boy?" I don't need to look at his face.

"Long enough to watch you make an ass of yourself." His voice is coated in a smirk.

I tilt my head back to check on the unofficial prince of Alchem Academy, always wary of his mood. His intent.

Sharp eyes survey me from beneath white blonde hair. An unlit cigarette dangles from relaxed fingers. Charcoal pants fit Aster Craven to perfection. My critical eye is honed after years of understanding what the public eye will and won't accept. A white shirt and white jacket hang open together, unbuttoned to halfway down his chest, displaying more silver chains weighing him down. One for every sin he feels he's ever committed, or so Zeke confessed to me once in a drunken stupor before he passed out in a puddle of his own vomit after they visited his father and Aster came back limping.

I've kept that little slice of information to myself for the past year, knowing full well he doesn't recall a word. Nor does Aster know. I don't know if it's the truth. I may never check. Or maybe I will, and start the rumor mill turning myself for shits and giggles. Nobody but the three of us would know who it was about, though I would earn myself a beating for the privilege, but screw it. It'll be worth it.

Instead of saying any of that, I cant my head at an angle I know looks damn good because my stylist gushes all over me, and put on a show-worthy, vague-as-hell smile.

"She hates you smoking."

He gifts me a malevolent smile, his lips curving around the butt of the cigarette he slips between them. "She loves the smell of it."

A miniscule shake of my head freezes him in place, seeding doubt as intended. "She loves the smell of the unlit cigarettes."

He scoffs. "What is this, *Who Knows Roxy Better?*"

I shrug. "Something like that."

Better than you.

Not that I say it. There's no point. The unsaid words hang between us.

Watching him taking in the tiny details of my room fills out a new song in my head.

The rat and the kings called throwing up arms.

Ripped apart from the inside out.

Sings sins in silver links across the bones around his throat.

Scratch that. It sucks. I scribble in the corner of the paper Roxy's song is taking form on for the sake of it, knowing I can work on it later. Waste not, and all. I don't need to be told my handwriting is a mess and that I've blotted it everywhere again with the side of my palm. The eternal curse of a left hander.

Aster ignores my twitching, crouching to read the words I've added to her song upside down.

I plant my fist straight over the top of the new lyrics, but that isn't what he's reading.

"Apt, isn't it?" His hand whips out, faster than I'd ever give him credit for.

One moment paper is in my hand; the next it's in his. Damn good thing I put my fist on it, but all I manage to achieve is to tear off the bottom corner.

The part I wrote about him.

The rest of the sheet crumples with my heart laid out on the page between his long fingers bearing their nicotine stains.

But Aster Craven has never been regular, or otherwise.

I add a little extra to my notes on the sly while his narrowed eyes scan my lyrics that are more than obviously written about his ex-girlfriend with her name etched at the top of the page.

No more air before I whisper
It never stops Craven for you

Heavy lashes scan the wrinkled page clutched in his hand.

Intuitively, I pass over the fountain pen I used to blot the crap out of the page before he interrupted my lyrical purgatory moments before, a silver one my mother scrimped and saved for when I signed my first record deal. It cost more than a month's wages in my home village. I objected to the outlay then, but she bought it for me anyway.

I returned the favor by providing her with a royalty clause on that same contract that gives her a lifetime earning for the sake of a silver fountain that brings me a singular joy every time I write with it.

It's my favorite.

"You've almost got it," Aster muses. "*One more breath where I can't exhale.*"

I roll my eyes. "Oh, praise the almighty Aster who will parrot and rearrange my words," I utter with no small dose of sarcasm. I finish with air quotes.

Sure, I can be childish, too. Even when he's twisting my words and making them his, because that's what Aster Craven does.

"Of course. You're such a pleb."

I snort at his delusions as I stare at the adjusted lines, reading them over, and add mental lyrics in without raising my fist over the covered words I concealed before the paper tore.

Turn me around
Spin me with you
One more ~~exhale~~ *breath where I can't* ~~breathe~~ *exhale.*

No more air before I whisper
It never stops Craven for you

My tongue in cheek line fit to perfection with his adjustments, as though he saw me write them and tailored my own words for himself on my behalf.

"Dammit," I swear, glancing up into Aster's eyes in time to witness the solace of blank nothingness slide into place there. "Happy, are we?"

Aster rolls his ankles as he stares down at me, devoid of emotion as though every inch of personality has drained from him with those parting lines.

Grinding my teeth, not half as in control as I need to be and hating myself for the lapse, I snap at him for invading my space and disturbing my concentration that shattered well before he slipped into my room.

"Did you come in here to screw with my lyrics?" I

ask, knowing I'll use the ones he wrote and will have to credit him to boot.

What irks me most is that he could see the potential of my unfinished work while I was blocked on the damn verses, stuck on rewriting the same lines over and over. The words I labored over for weeks, he fixed in mere seconds. I'm not sure which part of that veiled insult irritates me most. Having his name on my label, or knowing he got it better than I did.

On her damn song.

"What do you *want*, Aster?" I grouse, letting my tempter stretch out.

Roxy would hate seeing me lose my shit, but Aster knows all my buttons and pushes every single one.

All at once.

My insurgent scratches the back of his neck and shrugs. "Making sure she's looked after."

I stare at him. "In case the king of everything isn't around to protect her? In case you go … where?" I ask with a spurt of sudden clarity. Perhaps that door that allows him to see what I can't with my own music is a two-way event.

"Home." I finish the last word with him in my otherwise silent dorm room.

His chin jerks in acknowledgement. "Bad habits, and all. But that's not the question I asked."

He never asked a question, but I know what he means. Arguing semantics won't get us through this awkward as all hell conversation. That shoulder of his rolls back-and-forth, signaling his antsiness—if that's even a word—but his discomfort delves greater than that. "Something you wanna say?"

"Everything I need to say is on that paper." I don't clamp down on the torn page between us. "I'm not out to compare dick sizes with you."

That earns me the barest lift of his mouth. "Look after her," he repeats and turns away.

I shake my head, silver, black, and blue hair flicking across my vision. He's not walking out with a suicidal attitude like that. Not on my damn watch.

I grab his arm, wrinkling the sleeve of his pristine white jacket, hating the garment the moment I touch it. I know I'll take the design and shred it, remaking it into something I'll wear on stage at some future point heralded with blue and black and silver with his customary white showing through. "If you ever see this on me, you'll know I designed it out of loathing that you're wearing it right now." I keep my voice light, but this is a dance we both know well.

His head whips around, and his eyes narrow.

Those aren't the eyes of a dead man.

I force my hand to relax. "You're not planning anything. It's someone else, isn't it?" I watch him a moment longer, read the telltale flicker behind his eyes and I *know*. "It's not *to her*. You can't stop it," I breathe, panic curling in my lungs, stealing my air, my next exhale. "Who?"

Screaming numb
Orbiting you until eternity
This endless dance

He gazes down at me, the softest laugh leaving his throat. "That threat has always been there. I never cared until I found her."

I don't look away. Understanding what he does, that shared knowledge ... it changes everything. My heart beats hard in my chest as I watch him. "We do everything together. We can conquer this, too."

My words don't receive an answer, or an acknowledgement. The torn page flutters to the floor as he slips out the door, leaving me in a void of shattered lyrics and fresh heartbreak.

I stand alone in my dorm room amongst the pieces, my heart ripped between hand scribbled pages stained with ink blots and crossed out words, wondering if I just saved a friend—

Or if I lost one.

JOSS PHOENIX

Chapter Eleven

Say It to My Face

Roxy

I am a badduck boss bish.

I am a bad d–

–worthless, hopeless, bish who–

I need to curl up and cry–

–will kick Aster Craven's–

He is not the boss of me.

I won't allow it.

But no matter how many times I repeat the naffermations, allowing the negative to roll around inside my head, fighting for supremacy as my mantra of the day, I can't prevent the sense of ultimate doom that hangs over me.

In no way am I ready to be back in class with the rest of our Academy.

With BFF by my side, I stride with false confidence through the hall full of Academy students chattering on, seeing no one and nothing as we pass.

It's better this way.

This way I can pretend the stares, the smirks, the hands cupped around mouths, and the whispers don't happen.

For a few short months, I was immune to Alchem's incessant rumor mongering that seems to self-generate about me and the boys. The Elite. About me and Aster.

Now, I'm subject to the full blast, and turning a blind eye and every other cliche I can garner is the flimsy shield I manage to erect.

"Don't listen, don't listen, don't listen," Rhani chants at my side, her hand wound tight around mine as we swing them between us like five-year-olds. We might as well be skipping through a field of broken hearts.

"Tell me about your last breakup." I fish for a change of subject. Anything for distraction.

"Oh look, the Elite girl. Who's the sob story now?"

"Don't listen to them. And you don't want my sob stories." Rhani rolls her eyes like the drama llama she is.

Any other time I'd giggle. Not today.

"Another sacrifice on an altar for Aster's heartless cause," someone jeers.

I cringe away, even though half the catcalls don't make sense. The entire corridor is overpopulated with more Alchem students than I've ever seen at one time, and they're all staring in at us—well, me—with all the morbidity worthy of the latest streaming gothic trend.

"This is worse than dealing with my brother's annual hangover after Thanksgiving," she mutters.

I freeze up inside, already on emotional overload, but her words throw me back to the last holiday I spent with my family, or tried to. Before Dad took that job at the prison, before Mom fell so deep into her addiction she forgot I existed. But the memory is too painful and I toss it back into the darkest shadows of my mind.

"It's okay, Roxy. We'll figure it out."

—*too close, can't breathe*—

Still stuck somewhere in the past, I twist away from her concerned face to study my scuffed Mary Janes.

When I don't respond she tries again, more than desperate though I know she's trying her best to make me feel better in a shitty situation.

"Maybe I can hitch us a lift into town. We can get ice cream. Girl date!" She's pushing that cheer.

—*why should she smile when I can't*—

My inner dialogue rampages on and something

snaps.

"With the brother who's part of Aster's inner circle. The brother who—" My throat clogs, but I force my mouth to keep moving. "Who was part of what Aster did." My voice flattens, the overwhelm complete.

"Not true." She twitches at my side. "I'm sure I can find someone we can trust, maybe one of my other family–"

I pause in the middle of the hall, something I promised myself I wouldn't do this time amongst potential catastrophe. "You're an orphan, Rhani. No matter who they are, you've never had a real family." *No more than I have.*

Not to lose or cry after. It's an unfair statement, but it tumbles out anyway. And it's irredeemable. Because it falls amongst one of those rare silences that, no matter how soft, is heard by everyone in the vicinity.

The vicinity in this case being the entire corridor that seems to go on and on like some sort of horror movie.

Rhani's eyes flare wide with a sobering mixture of hurt and panic. She takes a step back, disentangling our fingers.

Side to side we were a team. Apart, our joint protection is broken, and every predatory eye turns in our direction, seeking first blood.

"She never was worth it."

"So stupid."

"The poor girl thought she could tame Aster Craven and keep him," the next voice's owner dares, safe within the anonymity of the crowd, and then the mob mentality slams in.

None of the barbs target my center.

I stare at my BFF on an island where she stands alone, her arms wrapped around herself as she peers at me through her glasses.

"I'm sorry," I say, but my words are lost in the deluge of poisoned barbs coming from everyone. "I didn't mean–"

"It's all right." She trips back a step, bumping into the body behind her and disappears between two students.

Two students I know well.

One harboring furious rage directed at me, the other emanating pure, ice-cold hate.

Zeke. Aster.

Oh, duckity.

My day just got a whole lot worse.

The chatter that filled the corridor a second before Rhani made her escape blankets me in the heaviest version of silence. My feet press into the ground, ready to claim their retreat, but I don't move.

I will not run from you.

My new mantra. I stare right at Aster, ignoring Zeke altogether.

His perfect arched lips tilt up. Aster doesn't speak, nor does he need to utter a word. His eyes say everything.

Shouldn't you be running?

I knew how they worked out. I remembered my first weeks at Alchem. How sickening his attacks were, how much I hated him—both of them—then.

Almost as much as he pretended to hate me.

I lift my chin. Is that what we're back to, pretending, or is the loathing real this time?

I don't want to find out.

Zeke stalks past me, slamming my shoulder with his. His bag follows, slapping me with a side serve of basic bully 101. I twist to the side under the weight. That bag feels like he's got a million bowling balls packed into it. I know he doesn't study, so it's not books. Training gear. His conscience. Nah, too heavy for that.

I try to catch myself from toppling sideways and manage to shove my bag back on my shoulder as my hair yanks. A sharp pain snakes across the back of my skull.

"Stop that—" I raise a hand to my head to release the relentless grip, but it's no longer necessary.

The collective gasp in the hallway followed by a soft cry tells me what happened.

Rhani's soft, *"Oh Roxy,"* can't be missed, not with a million held breaths released all at once along Alchem's packed halls.

That exodus didn't get her far.

My hips twist, hand still raised, but I never make it to my destination. Heart pounding, my eyes latch on to the brown, lanky strip of hair held out on display like a trophy, but it's *my* hair fluttering in Aster's hand as he stops halfway down the corridor and pivots. His prize is laid out across his palm, a formidable razor blade twirling between his fingers that vanishes with his next snap.

Aster cut my hair.

He cut my ducking hair. A lot of it. My nape feels bare, a weight I miss lifting from me as I straighten and refuse to touch the spot where my long hair used to hang. Of course, he didn't choose to assault me with scissors like any regular bully.

No, Aster Craven used a razor blade.

Tears threaten at this personal infringement on my liberties, but I refuse flat out to give him the satisfaction he needs for his next hit. I'm grateful my cheeks pale rather than heat, so my body saves me there.

But four breaths in I can't help but lift the hand that acts on its own as it makes its way to my scalp. I can barely feel where he chopped the locks away. Aster must've lifted my hair and taken a chunk from underneath, because there's no big clump missing that I can find. My fingers come away coated in sticky scarlet when I touch my heated skin.

Aster claims first blood. It won't be the last between us.

He doesn't get to turn away, and he doesn't make it to me because somebody else does what I want to do first.

"You asshole."

Elen appears by my side, his face twisted and furious as he stares at me, but his anger isn't directed my way. Cool fingers trace over the cut on the back of my neck, his thumb pressing hard to staunch the flow.

I look back, blank at first then terrified when emotion hits me in a deluge of a massive overwhelm. Tears fill my eyes at his simple kindness. His defense of me.

I never had this last time Aster let out his obsession with me as his prime target. I don't know how to deal with it now.

The warmth of Elen's body beside me changes. I don't understand what's going on when he brushes his fingers through my remaining hair, combing it back from my face and curving his other hand beneath my jaw.

Elen tips my head back. "I'm sorry, Roxy girl. I wasn't here," he says before his mouth presses over mine.

My breath stalls though the kiss is brief and chaste, but it's enough to make his point.

I am not alone.

In my periphery, as I blink in complete shock as phones are raised, I see students film the whole thing. My skin prickles, torn between needing silence I can't claim and aching to hide. Somewhere in the background, there's a frustrated noise I recognize. For a split second, I forget my panic and smile.

Screw Aster Craven and his attitude. He brought this on himself. His ex is videoed while kissing a rockstar instead of the pseudo-billionaire it could have been.

He made his choices. Now I get to make mine.

Elen cradles me like I'm precious to him. His touch doesn't last long, and he isn't overwhelming. When he releases me, I stumble back, my fingers pressed to the warm spot his absent contact leaves at the back of my skull as I stare, locked between him and Aster.

And then my feet are moving like they were before, the better to retreat from the hallway bustling with murmuring Alchem students. Many still film as I sprint past Nyx who looks up from his phone, his brow furrowing as he spots me holding the back of my neck. Tears coat my lashes, obscuring my vision.

When he meets my eyes there's something in his gaze I don't understand any more than I do the touch of Elen's lips on mine a second time. Nyx's mouth opens, but I don't wait to hear what he says as my feet carry me out of the building and across the lawn, into the forest beyond.

I don't stop for a long time, until my legs ache, and the tears that didn't fall in the hallway coat my cheeks.

The emotions that roil through me isn't the rage I've learned from Zeke or the cold, vicious fury, or the injustice of the blade flashing between Aster's fingers.

It's an echo of the agony that sliced through my chest when he rejected me. The numbness that coated me head to toe all the way home in Elen's car. The comfort of the rockstar's mouth over mine. My shoulders vibrate in a constant shiver. *Too much.*

I pull up deep in the woods beyond Alchem's clustered buildings, in a darkest part of the forest by the side of a boulder twice as big as me, and scream my throat raw into my cupped hands.

****

Cold seeps bone deep. Skin that's been covered in goosebumps for however long I've curled under the forest's cool, shadowed canopy isn't anymore. A deep ache sinks through me. It might seem stupid to pine over a boy who already broke my heart, but Aster's actions are the final measure that end our cycle.

Now we're on repeat. It's like we forgot the rinse part.

Tears dried in dirty, salted tracks on my cheeks hours before, but I swipe at them anyway. My fingers come away sticky. Gritty. Swollen lids blink over dry and itchy eyeballs, uncomfortable like everything else as though they no longer fit in my body. And the forest, the forest smells like…

Pot.

I inhale again and sniff at the air like a rabbit. My back straightens against my boulder at the familiarity, the knowing presence I didn't recognize until now. Around the edge of my giant stone barrier between me and the rest of the world, or at least the school at my back, a hand peeks out, covered in tiny, inked flowers and swirls. Short nails offer me a hand-rolled joint.

The offer is so innocuous, so unexpected, that a giggle and a hiccup burst free together. I cup my hand over my mouth and shake my head so he can't see my rejection. Nyx seems to get the point when my cuddle buddy shifts and the hand is withdrawn.

Moments later, he's back for round two. The cloying scent of marijuana doesn't go away, though Nyx's initial offer is replaced with a wireless earbud. Faint notes of his music emanate from the tiny device, and a smile breaks over my face.

Now there's an offer I can take.

My fingers brush his as I liberate the earbud in the sole contact I've had in hours apart from the cold rock at my back that refuses to warm up no matter how much I press my body against it.

Nyx sits on the other side, soaking in the forest in his quiet way.

I have no idea how long he's been there, or if he heard me crying, but for whatever reason his presence doesn't feel invasive. Nyx is like that, being there at the right time, always. Not pushing me, like when I ran through the hall earlier, overwhelmed and away from everyone.

I want to cry again for a different reason, but the tears have run empty. Yet, the fear of Aster Craven remains. Closing my eyes, I press the single earbud in and let Nyx's music wash over me. One of the songs he played in Elen's Lambo as we drove home from the snow filters through the tech, encapsulating me. When the boys kissed me, and Elen showed me the tattoo he and Nyx etched on each other.

The song finishes, and the fade out lasts longer than I expect. Silence fills my mind. Just as I think he's killed the device, a new track plays, one I haven't heard before.

Like all Nyx's music, this one has no lyrics, but there's no need. The music speaks for him. I'm lost in the sense of spacelessness, floating as my eyes drift shut. The unyielding surface behind me disappears.

I close my eyes, reaching out. Knuckles brush the back of my hand, but Nyx doesn't grab for my fingers in desperation like Aster might, angry obsessive like Zeke, or with a sense of possession like Elen, though he'd never admit to it. The backs of our hands rest together, the barest brush of skin on skin.

"You created this," I whisper, though my voice

comes out like a croaking rasp after not speaking for so long, after screaming myself dry before.

It's a brutal contrast to the beautiful sounds that Nyx has made.

With anyone else, embarrassment would eat me away, but with Nyx, it's okay. He's raw. He gets it. I'm not ashamed.

He's silent for so long that I realize he might be.

"It's beautiful. I'm sorry," I add, breaking into the silence, and wish I hadn't spoken.

His hands turn, the tips of his fingers touching my nails before his hand flips back. That's the lone answer I get, and as before, it's enough. It's how he communicates. Like with his music, words are unnecessary. Something has changed in the way we are with that touch that says so much without saying anything at all.

As the shadows around us deepen with the settling evening, Nyx edges around to my side of the boulder, making a nest for himself next to me. Not once does he take the music away that flows like a river into an estuary, melding with something larger than itself.

When he's still for the first time and as I think we've hit an impasse, he breaks into movement again, taking my hand in his. Cupping my pale palm in his inked one, he links our arms together. Light fingers trace along my sleeve.

"He shouldn't have done that," Nyx says in his raspy, unused voice, speaking for the first time since he exposed his presence to me.

My shrug feels too rough for his music that still plays on in my head, uncouth. "Aster Craven does whatever he wants."

There's no recompense, no comeuppance. That's the world of power and wealth he exists in. He let me see inside that part of him once before when I bullied him back. A part of me that, for a brief time, experienced the power rush he must have felt today before it all crashed down on me. All the self-loathing and hatred that came with being the bully.

Maybe it's time for me to pull that persona out again. But I hated being that girl so much, hated myself for reacting and for having to push back against him. I still hate that part of me. I hated who I became around him, the girl who enjoyed the pain he suffered.

Because he hurt me first, and I hurt him back.

Hate, hate, hate.

It's all I knew when I first arrived at Alchem Academy. I hated that my parents died and left me alone. I hated my aunt's place, and that reciprocal emotion landed me here at the school.

I hated that Aster hated me.

Round and round and round we go.

Until I didn't hate him, and that got stripped away. Then we went through it all over again to fear, even, for the power that he wields over me now, for the emotions that tangle somewhere in the middle.

It can all wait until tomorrow because right now Nyx is everything, and with him there isn't room for hate.

He shakes his head and tries again. "No. Elen shouldn't have kissed you like that."

I turn and stare up at him.

His gaze drops to my lips and holds there when I offer a small smile.

"Do you want to kiss me?"

He doesn't answer.

"You're scared of me?"

He continues tracing patterns on the back of my wrist with his pinky finger.

I can't figure out what, though.

"I'm not scared."

A lie, if a small one. My heartbeat ramps up as his lips lift in a smile to match mine under the flickering green in his eyes that won't let me retreat. How he can leapfrog from so calm and distant to close up and intense in a breath is mesmerizing.

He twists his hand over mine, pushing back his hoodie arm to expose a full tattoo sleeve that decorates his skin in a forest scene so similar to where we are now. Trees and rocks and a stream and toadstools. Vines and glowbugs. Moths and butterflies. Everything is drawn in so much detail. Flowers and falling leaves and mist.

I study the artwork in awe, my mind clicking that I'm looking at his non dominant side. "You did this too, didn't you?" I breathe, unwilling to shatter the silence like before. Intrude on it.

"I want to draw like this." His fingers trace the curves and swirls of an intricate vine similar to the patterns he made on the back of my wrist before. "On you."

Nyx shuts his mouth.

He doesn't ask permission, makes it a single statement.

I blow out a captive breath. "Yes, please." My response comes out breathless, a surprise to us both.

He doesn't say anything else as we walk back through the forest to the dorms, though the backs of our hands touch.

The whole way home.

Chapter Twelve

Lies In Ink

Roxy

Toxic Ex: **Nyx. And Elen?**
Toxic Ex: **You get around**
Roxy: **What is wrong with you. It's 3am**
Roxy: **Go to sleep, Aster**
Toxic Ex: **I can't sleep. You're still here.**
Roxy: **Not changing.**
Toxic Ex: **It will**
Roxy: **Shave me. Idgad**
Toxic Ex: **So sweet. Dream of me.**
Roxy: **No pleasure in that.**
Toxic Ex: **There is for me.**

I wake the day after Aster assaulted me and Nyx shared his music with a raging headache and a sleepless, cry-hangover. Both of those are thanks to Aster, who messaged me at some ungodly hour to have a whinge.

So when I crawled out of bed at five in the morning to pee, I sent him a gif of dead roses and hope it woke his insomniac, over-entitled, bullying duckbutt up, knowing full well there's no point reporting his actions because he'll bribe, threaten, or power play his way out of trouble and reverse the course so I'm the one who lands in it. Because that's what a Cowardly Craven does.

I sent my gif, feeling righteous. Now, I wish I never sent anything at all because he'll know he got to me, but it's too late. Those three little dots haunted my last hours of fitful sleep where I tossed and turned, too hot, too cold, too alone…

Puffing my cheeks in the mirror until I resemble a mussed hair, psychotic puffer fish morning monster, I gargle my sleepless night away. Relishing the pain, I throw my phone at my nightstand without looking to aim where it has the audacity to buzz on regardless.

Grabbing the device back a second later, I sneak a guilty look at my roommate's bed, but her back is turned to me. Letting out a minty-fresh sigh, I flip my phone over in my hand.

Toxic Ex: **Aw. I'm your first thought in the morning**

No, my first thought is of my busting bladder. But I can't find a pee gif and also, goober. I don't need to give him extra ideas on how to torture me. My finger hovers over the delete button. Like the expert stalker he is, Aster gets there first.

Toxic Ex: **Don't block me, Roxy. You never know when you might need me.**

Roxy: **I never needed you.**

Toxic Ex: **Not the time my ex hurt you? When you hurt so bad your skin ached on your bones and you wanted to peel it off?**

Roxy: **High expectations of yourself. I could have painted her back to nothing. Clean her away.**

Toxic Ex: **That's right, your mural. But you didn't paint her away. It's still there, isn't it?**

Roxy: **I like to keep a record of my travels**

Toxic Ex: **Where do I feature?**

Roxy: **You get a corner. Behind the bathroom door.**

Toxic Ex: **I'll check for it next time I break in.**
Duckhat.

I throw my phone across the room, the phone he damn well bought for me, and I don't care when the screen cracks. Crawling back into bed is the sole option that works today. *Already.* I pull the covers over my head, intent on ignoring the world.

As usual on days I don't want to talk to anyone,

that doesn't work out so well. Less than five mere minutes into my sulk, my phone buzzes again. Intent on ignoring it, too, I burrow deeper, but the universe refuses to let me play ball my way.

"Roxy. If you don't get that I'm gonna shove it where the sun don't shine, and when you bend over from now on, that glowbug butt will do its *thang*," Rhani threatens in a groggy, albeit cheerful voice. "You already woke me at all freaking hours grunting like a constipated hamster. Aster issues?"

"I don't grunt," I say, indignant.

"Oh, you grunt. Get it." A glittery stiletto is lobbed my way and crashes into the wall a few feet shy of my head.

Taking her point, I scoot out from my nest and grab my cracked phone, regret at my earlier anger and the waste swamping me. Old Roxy would never have dared treat anything the way I just did. The longer I stay at Alchem, the more the princess ways eke deeper into my bones.

I hate that, too.

hate hate hate.

Elen: **Nyx is up. Ready?**

Roxy: **For...?**

Elen: **Your artwork.**

Elen: **I don't think he's slept. Which means I haven't either.**

Roxy: **A bit of that's going around.**

Elen: **I have coffee, a tattoo artist and new music. Come read my words, Roxy Girl.**

Roxy: **Was that a line?**

Elen: **Come over and find out.**

Ten to six in the morning seems an indecent hour for this conversation. Any hour is indecent. But right now, we all are touched by insomnia, and the number on the clock face doesn't matter when all the times merge in a stream of consciousness.

Besides, after listening to Nyx's music yesterday and the way he drew patterns on my skin, I want to see what Elen can do, too. Being around this much talent can spoil a girl. My nose twitches as I dress in jeans and layer on a black, long-sleeved top with a dove gray one over it.

Rhani doesn't budge as I close the door behind me.

****

The tattoo gun edges closer to my skin. I squeak and scoot backward, running into Elen's legs. His thighs flex at the contact where he catches me in the deep vee his long frame makes, corralling me in, but rather than their room shrinking, I feel a whole lot safer.

"Breathe, Roxy girl," he mutters behind me, pressing light fingers to my ribs to keep me in place.

Nyx's hand curls around my palm, tracing over the flower he drew freehand on the inside of my wrist earlier. "It's okay, little mama. It hurts a bit. Right here." He presses his thumb over my pulse point.

I squeeze my eyes shut, more freaked out by the image of the tattoo gun hovering over my skin than the actual pain. Or maybe I *should* look at the faint marks I've made enough times that the welts remain as a sort of strange raised line on my wrist. A declaration of my independence to do what I want to myself without Aster's interference.

This is … better. Intentional. And I like his art. Truth be told, I kind of love that his art is on me.

I pry my eyes open despite my pounding heart and try to breathe like Elen says. After this, I won't be able to see the odd line, not once Nyx fills the shape with ink like he has the other, smaller hand drawn pattern.

He stops and looks up at me with those moss-laced eyes. "I'm not gonna color it in. Like this."

Nyx demonstrates, displaying his own skin where an incomplete, but similar pattern reaches from his ankle to calf, the work a little shaky. There's a clean, shaved patch there. I watch him trace over the tiny, intricate swirls, leaning forward into his vision as he presses the needle to his skin and freehands it.

I swallow but don't stop him, peering over his hand. He makes a throaty sound and bats me away until he's finished. Afterward, he wipes everything off with gel that glistens over ink and reddened skin, and Elen fusses, bandaging him up.

I stare at my names on repeat where it forms an adjoining chain. "That's so pretty. Why did you do that?"

He shrugged. "Because I want your name on me."

"He already did me." Elen reaches around me and pulls up his uniform pants leg up to expose a matching ankle chain to Nyx's that runs around the narrow bone in concentric circles.

I trace my fingers across the links bearing my name, my stomach fluttery when Elen shifts and swears. "Sorry. Ticklish?"

"Something like that," he says in a strangled voice.

"You're crazy."

"I'm still the sanest roomie. Now hold still and let the real mad one work his magic on you."

Gooseflesh erupts where his arms slide around me, his bare feet crinkling over multiple sheets of crumpled paper bearing his scribbled handwriting and crossed out lines. His intimate announcement sinks around me like a veil.

I nod and breathe out, taking all their advice at once. "Okay. I'm ready."

"Yeah?" Elen leans forward, resting his chin on

the crook of my neck, his longer hands clasped loose around my waist. Black and blue leather bracelets, some with glass beads, decorate his wrists.

I study the carvings on each as Nyx cleans my skin again and presses the needle to it.

This time Elen holds me still, his chest pressed to my back while he hums a melody I can't quite place.

"Is that another new song?" I remember the promise he made about showing me new lyrics and twist, taking my arm with me. Nyx grumbles at the movement. "Sorry." I turn back, trying to stay still, and ignore the burning pain in my wrist.

It stops and starts and stops again in a constant rhythmic motion I soon grow used to. Nyx doing freehand is kind of soothing. Much better than slapping the bands against my wrist that I started again last night after Aster's messages when my mind refused to sleep. When those ceased to work as advertised, I tried scratching.

Damn Aster and his understanding eyes.

Banishing his taunting phantom from my mind, I refocus on the boys who sandwich me between them, and the fresh green ink that matches Nyx's etched into my skin. I'm kind of glad now, because I don't want either of them to see the shame of my pain where I started hurting again.

Small, pathetic, and not even cute like what I used to do, nor neat and beautiful like Aster's scars that are close enough to his personal brand of art.

I suck in a breath as Nyx lifts the tattoo gun from my skin, and words fall out. "If I love it, will you do more?"

Smooth fingers flick over my stomach. Elen's possessive grip tightens, but Nyx never responds. My quiet boy continues to concentrate on what he's doing.

"Has he played you his new stuff?" Elen murmurs.

I nod. "It's incredible," I whisper back in a hushed voice, feeling weird as all get out talking about Nyx while he's right in front of me. He seems so lost in his art that he doesn't hear me. I turn my attention back to Elen, my cheek rubbing his, he's cuddling so close. More flutterbys.

Breathe, Roxy girl. Elen's voice invades my brain space.

"I thought you were going to show me something of yours?"

Nyx twists my wrist a little.

I let him, though I don't understand how he can see what he's doing at all with his hair hanging between us and his shadow overlaying everything. Another moment and he stops, flicking on his phone's flashlight app. Then everything is clear again, and I can see the outline of the flower before he goes in for another round.

I let my fingers drop, tracing around where my name is marked on him in perpetuity, on the older part of the tattoo that's unbandaged, not the bit he finished. I want to ask why he did it again, more than the brief answer he gave me before. He's got a lot of ink, and maybe it's something pretty he liked. My heart squeezes tight. I hold off asking in case he says it's less.

"Music." Elen evades me, sinking his chin deeper into the crook of my neck where I'm sensitive.

I refrain from nodding, taking shallow breaths between them as memories come tumbling back. "Yesterday, in the woods. I got to listen to his songs. They're beautiful. Haunting … it's everything. Why isn't he doing what you do?" I still feel weird talking about Nyx like he's not in the room, but he seems to prefer it that way.

141

Elen shrugs against my back. "I've asked him the same thing."

"So why don't you sign him?"

"With who?" Elen's arms stiffen.

"With her, your agent, or whoever?" I look between them.

"Sonia." Elen huffs out a breath that tastes like resignation. "She's not open to randoms, though we've talked about it. I recommended Nyx. She listened and she wants to sign him, but he won't even read the contract."

Nyx looks up, a flare of passion in his eyes that makes me back down.

"Sorry," I mumble, my cheeks burning.

"It's okay." He returns to finishing the tattoo.

I don't speak again. The burning in my wrist continues, but it's not painful. After a while it's kind of soothing, like when I listened to his music yesterday and we walked back touching hands but not holding onto each other.

Nyx is so different from the rest of the boys—from anyone else I've ever met. He redefines peace, serenity.

Elen releases me with one hand to flick his fingers over his phone. The same, haunting sounds that filled my head yesterday drift around us. Tension loosens as I breathe out, and even Elen's frame softens a degree as he leans his head back against the bed behind him.

My eyes drift shut as he takes me with him without moving the arm Nyx works on.

After a time, the needle hovers over my skin, and the rhythm is broken.

I pry my eyes open with the greatest effort. A night of lost sleep weighs on me like the heaviest blanket, or maybe it's Nyx's music.

Clearing my blurry vision, I find brown eyes shot

with mossy shards staring up at me.

"Aster." I shake my head in denial, but Nyx persists, voice rough, though his intent is clear. "Do you want his name here?" he rasps in his harsh voice.

I don't think I've ever heard him speak that loud before.

"He messaged me at three in the morning." *To make me as miserable as him. I can't forgive him, but I still wish he was here after everything.* I stumble over my words. "He doesn't sleep, does he?"

Elen's chest vibrates behind me. "Not often. Sometimes he sits in on our songwriting sessions. If we can't find the words or we're blocked for too long he shuts us down." He smiles against my cheek, pressing his lips there for a brief, hidden moment. A breath, and I could have imagined the contact before he leans back again. "No rush, man. We're good here."

I swallow when those mossy eyes don't release me. "Yes," I whisper.

Nyx's thumb presses over my pulse, the spot he warned me about. He works around it for as long as he can, and then moves aside, leaving bone and pulse point bare, the image he designed for me and traced on my wrist that night complete.

He releases my hand once it's cleaned and wrapped in a clear bandage like his. I study the reddened skin and our tiny names etched in the outline of the incredible layers that form the intricate flower Nyx designed that matches his and Elen's ink.

Now they're embedded in my skin as I am in theirs.

The boys' dorm room flies open without a knock. I find myself craning up at a—as usual—furious Zeke.

"Do you not have another place to be?" Elen flexes his fingers where he holds me, but other than that,

143

he doesn't move.

Zeke's lips rise in a smirk as he surveys the mess of crumpled music scattered about the floor, the tattoo gun and inks spread about the room. All of us knotted together.

"Aster's going to flip when he sees that."

My patience with his attitude after yesterday's fiasco hits a limit. "Why bother stalking me if this is how you are?"

Zeke's glare deserves its own soundtrack. His personality change from the man who saved Elen from fangirls to the duckhat who knocked me over yesterday still blows my mind. My shoulder twinges on cue.

Charcoal eyes flicker as he turns a death stare on me. "Who says anything's about *you*, Roxy Quell?" The way he draws out my name sends a frisson of fear along my spine.

But I'm not the one who's had a gut full.

"She's not his property, or anyone else's," Nyx snaps as he cleans up his gun and his tools.

Zeke freezes as the boy who never raises his voice draws in a shattered breath. That's twice in one day. I'm kinda proud.

Holding his eyes for a long moment before I speak again, I make sure he hears me. "Thank you. I love it."

The ghost of his smile is back, and it's the prettiest thing I've seen all day.

"If he doesn't make it as a musician, he could always be an artist," I mutter, intent on detangling myself from Elen's grasp, though I'm not sure why.

Zeke's eye is a secondary weight that prickles over my semi-bare neck. "Yeah, I'm sure Mommy and Daddy's trust fund will love that career option." His smirk transforms into a sneer. "Almost as good as drawing blood from a stone."

His fingers slicing in an abrupt motion across his wrist isn't missed before he slips back out the door, leaving me pinned between Elen's cool hands and an unusual flash of fiery rage from Nyx. My quiet boy presses down on the clear bandage and tucks my long-sleeved tee back over my wrist, breathing hard.

"We should hide this."

I twist around in a personal pretzel to stare back at him. "Because of Aster?"

Elen catches my jaw in those warm fingers and holds my gaze with his blue and silver contacts. "Because ink is against school rules. And you're still kind of new."

I raise both eyebrows. "You have it. And…" I gesture at Nyx and the doorway to encompass all the Elite, including the two absentee members.

He snorts. "Yeah, and Aster. We get away with a lot."

"You're pushing it," Zeke grumbles from the other side of the door. *He didn't go far.* "So now she's got ink. Gallaway will be ducking ecstatic. Come on."

"Why are we going anywhere with you?" I shake my head at his disembodied voice and visualize sending him far along the hallway and out of the building altogether.

"Why are you still talking?"

Pity my manifesting technique doesn't work. "If you don't wanna be near me, go away." My voice trembles on the last word thanks to a scant hour of sleep fast catching up with me. I sway as I climb to my feet, supported by Elen in a swift grab that stops me from tumbling back down on legs long gone to sleep.

Nyx produces a bottle of orange juice at the same time that Zeke reappears and shoves a chocolate bar in my hand.

"Eat," he growls.

"I need sleep." I cover a yawn, clutching the chocolate bar. No way am I relinquishing that. "You know Aster texted me all night?"

Elen makes a disapproving noise in the back of his throat. "We all have sleep issues, huh?" He nudges Nyx with a bare toe.

Zeke's eyes narrow as he casts their interaction aside. "He messaged you?" Inked fingers flick in my direction.

I swipe through my phone to the right set of messages, clutching my prizes in my bandaged arm. "No take backsies." I cuddle everything and send a grateful smile to Elen who circles my shoulders with a long arm I sink into.

Zeke snatches my cracked phone, frowning at me then the screen as he scrolls through, then shoves the device back into my hand, storming away without another word.

"Bye," I say to the empty doorway that hasn't closed behind him yet.

Nyx sighs and grabs his satchel, tapping the OJ.

I uncap the plastic bottle and send him a shy smile that he returns. We're back on neutral ground I understand as we head to classes, each of us exhausted for various reasons but topped up, too.

****

My sugar high lasts longer than usual on an empty stomach. I can't ignore Zeke because he takes up residence outside the window of my art class right next to where my easel has been set up all semester. The entire time my class runs he loiters with his back to me like he's got nowhere else to be.

What he said about my wrist is so stuck in my head that I'm self-conscious of the throbbing beneath my skin and tug at my sleeve even when the room grows so hot I end up sweltering. My mind is full of forest, inky greens, and the deep brown of Zeke's fury-filled eyes. So that's what I paint, blending hues together until they form something else.

As promised, in the dark and sort of hidden behind a maelstrom of chaos that suits my mood, a pale flicker emerges that's out of place but a focal point nonetheless. My teacher hates it, but I love it. I take the semi-dried canvas back to my room, ignoring my rage-filled stalker who tracks my every step, clutching the corners of the canvas on the inside so I don't smudge anything.

One by one, the boys escort me at a distance until I reach my dorm, and then they leave me alone as I risk the elevator that blessedly works when called upon. The tiny metal box isn't as stifling as usual, and when I step into my cool, empty dorm, I'm able to breathe.

My wrist aches, my head is blank, and as I promised, I place the fresh canvas behind my bathroom door. Then I push the door back and hide the piece from prying eyes.

Including mine.

JOSS PHOENIX

Chapter Thirteen

Secrets We Hide

Roxy

My reflection no longer looks like me.

"Take it off here." I point to a place below my shoulder, where Aster cut my hair. I've waited long enough.

Rhani stares. "Are you sure?" she asks in a hushed voice. "That's a lot."

I stare resolutely back at the girl Aster cut and place the pack of dye on the counter beside the scissors I ordered.

"I'm sure."

My roommate's smile matches my own.

****

Whispers follow me along Alchem's halls post my dorm room cut and dye session. Rhani's results are spectacular if she doesn't say so herself, though she snapped pictures of the back of my head out of respect for our original media ban agreement.

I'm glad no one can see into our shared ensuite that looks like multiple murders took place there overnight. We made an additional order for bleach after attempting to wash the dye from every surface. But after all her efforts, my hair is cherry red, and Rhani perfected a curly cut in short order.

Nope, I'm not done with length-based jokes yet.

She struts by my side, flicking her fingers in my hair that she's stuck a few random little jewels in as well. "Happy birthday to *you*," she mutters under her breath. "Craven can eat duck—"

"Ahem, I know your roomie is about somewhere, but I seem to have lost her. I had a gift and all, but..."

Elen trails off, making a show of peering over my head. He *oofs* as Rhani's elbow catches him in the stomach.

"Don't give my girl a complex." She fixes him with a hard stare and pops a hip.

"Okay," Elen managed in a strangled voice, massaging his sternum.

"Say something nice," Rhani says while I die on the spot.

I find the cafeteria doors and make a beeline.

"You look beautiful." The clarity in his voice is remarkable. And it *carries*. Even without a microphone.

I'm desperate to drop my head and hide, but I know Rhani will never allow it after the hours she put in. Swallowing the embarrassment, I pivot to face Elen.

"Thanks?" I say, and find him right in front of me.

He must have dashed to cover the distance, because I wasn't slow in my escape.

"I mean it." He gives me a once over and leans in to kiss my cheek. "Happy seventeenth birthday, Roxy."

"No Roxy girl?" I tease, but he's not done.

"For you." The tiniest box I've ever seen complete with a teensy, intricate bow presses into my palm.

"Thank you." I stare at it. "How did you find out—" Rhani waltzes past, chattering at her brother she's collected at her side in the meantime who glares our way. "Ah. Doesn't matter."

Undeterred, Elen carries on like he wasn't interrupted. "The red suits you." His knuckles graze my curls, catching one in a quick tug. "Open it?"

"Oh." I fumble with the small box. "I thought this was the pres—oh." I stare at the crystal flower that matches my hair color. Its petals are carved in perfect symmetry. This isn't a trinket. "Elen—" I press my cupped hands toward him, scared to drop the delicate creation.

His palms close over mine. "It's called the eternal bloom that never fades," he murmurs, following up with a name I can't quite catch or repeat. "It's rubellite. I had it made for you." He shrugs like it's a simple gift, though I know it's not.

"Thank you." Heat climbs my throat as he helps me tuck the flower into its home, closing my hand around it. "I can't believe you did that. Thank you. It's stunning."

Blue eyes lift to mine. "Like you."

He squeezes my fingers and with his customary grin in place as he drops into step beside me like nothing important passed between us. His treatment doesn't stop there. Elen refuses to let me handle my own tray in the dining hall, picking out my favorite foods before I can say a word. He makes sure I'm settled at our table before he wanders off to serve himself.

Rhani smirks at me before starting her live, walking out when the hall gets too loud.

I'm left facing Zeke.

His coal dark stare leaves my burning cheeks blazing hotter.

"Got something to say?" I challenge, but I don't have the energy to fight him. The tiny flower in its box is tucked into my hand. I can't let it go. My gaze breaks from Zeke, tracking Elen across the room.

"Getting the full princess treatment today, aren't you?" He taunts, but like me, his hatred is lacking. Maybe we're on a time out.

I shrug, opting to take a leaf out of Nyx's book, and start on my sashimi. Elen sneaked an extra helping of kimchi onto my tray, and I giggle. The sound seems to infuriate Zeke more.

"Getting your true Alchem on for a six-figure gift,

huh?"

My mouth drops open as the implications sink in. I tuck the tiny box into my inner jacket pocket under Zeke's all too watchful eye and zip it up.

"She's worth every minute." Elen swoops in beside me, liberating the extra kimchi with a wink.

I smile back. "This is a lot."

"You'll manage. Girl's gotta have an appetite." He nods at my tray.

"That's not what I meant."

"I know." He flashes me a Korean finger heart. I huff, but I'm not as overwhelmed as I expect with the K-pop star.

Zeke, on the other hand...

"Gonna spoil her for everyone else," he grunts, ignoring his lunch in order to continue staring like a creeper.

"I sure hope so," Elen murmurs, nudging my knee with his.

Zeke mutters something incomprehensible, attacking his steak lunch option with the gusto of a starving bear.

Phone in hand, mouthing words too fast for me to catch, Rhani runs in, grabs her bag, and disappears. I could bet a hundred dollars she made a date with Adam while Zeke occupied himself fighting with me. I grin at her hasty retreat and wish her all the best.

By the time I've finished my meal, Elen's done. He kisses my cheek again, taking his time to fuss over me. Nyx rocks up, running his hands over my hair, humming something soulful. His approval means more than I expect. Simple, facetious even, but it still means something. I smile back, relaxing. My sashimi sits on a bed of sushi I don't need but love anyway.

Trying not to clutch my stomach, I dig about for

my schedule.

Once I've reorganized myself twice, I realize I'm not alone.

"I'll walk you to class if you're done," Zeke mutters, tugging at his overgrown hair so it stands on end.

I shake my head. "We're not headed in the same direction." I know all their schedules by now as well as I know mine. My memory isn't brilliant; I need the visual reminder. But the classes we don't share are at opposite ends of campus.

"I'll walk you," he says, stubborn as always.

I frown. "I'll be fine. You taught me to throw knives, remember?" I toy with an unused butter knife.

"Not well, if you think that will do anything."

"Fine." I don't want to fight. "I'm going to class. Alone." I push up from my seat, my bag looped over my shoulder.

"Roxy…" His hand closes on my wrist, not tight, though his grip prevents me from going anywhere.

I look down at him. It's not a position I'm used to and it feels wrong, like this should be reversed. "What?" I soften my voice, trying not to let my impatience out, but his touch sends fissions of energy buzzing over my skin.

"I didn't—" His mouth snaps shut, and he swallows. "Check your room tonight. Okay?"

"Whatever."

I don't have the brain space for games. That's Aster's domain. I tug at his grip, more than surprised when he lets go. I make it a solid three steps before he brings me to a halt.

"I don't know how to treat a princess," he says in a low voice.

I freeze in place with my back to him. My hand rises on its own to fumble beneath my too-tight collar. I swivel as I flip out the slim chain that bears the pendant

Zeke gave me that I haven't taken off since the snow trip and drop my hand.

His gaze fixes on the crystal snowflake I don't tuck away, then flick to my face. His mouth opens, but no sound emerges. I know how he feels. The room rocks beneath my feet as I turn back to my path and walk away, and leave the pendant he bought me ages ago out all day.

When my tired legs drag me back to my room at night, I find a black, utilitarian case on my pillow. When I raise the lid, I find an identical set of slim throwing knives to the ones I learned to practice with in the boxing gym. There's no name attached to the gift, but I know who sent them.

At least, I think I do.

Chapter Fourteen

My Keeper

Roxy

Two weeks later, my grace period with Zeke has expired. He turns up at every class I'm in that he's not, watching and waiting. I can't get a breath out around him. Now, the day I want to confront him over his favorite new hobby, my stalker boy is nowhere to be found.

I'm over it. Over them all. The constant *fluctuation* from hating each other to friends and back again, the stalking, the intimidation … it messes with my head. Zeke might think he can avoid me, but that's his problem. I already know his best hiding spots on campus.

Which is why I head straight for the boxing gym at the other end of Alchem Academy, away from everything. Everyone. I know I chose well the moment I walk through the open door.

Booming music pounds the cement walls, but it's not loud enough to cover my footsteps that match the rhythmic beats of his fist hammering against the hanging punching bag he tortures.

Lost in himself, he doesn't see me as I lean against the wall beside where he works out his fury, my arms wrapped across my chest as I glare at him, and wait.

Rough chopped hair I suspect he's cut himself at some point hangs over his face. His knuckles are wrapped in the cloth he and Aster use when they fight. Charcoal eyes are laser focused on his target, that unbreakable gaze I know all too well. Sweat drips down his face, running along his bare back that's covered with ink and beaded in spent salt as he pounds the bag with his fists to his own rhythm.

If that dedication isn't enough to convince me of

the depths of his hatred, the flurry of his fists, elbows, and knees as he roars my name at the bag in the next moment is.

It occurs to me that seeking him out in this sort of mood is hellishly dangerous, but I can't make my feet move.

He's beautiful.

The thought slaps me face first, unbidden.

'Break Stuff' by Limp Bizkit blares through the portable Bluetooth speaker that shakes like a bullet at his feet. Tiny little neon lights in blue and black flash across fluids splattered across the floor I don't want to think about.

Zeke doesn't stop between punches, attacking the bag as if it weighs almost nothing. His method is more machine than human, awe inspiring to witness. At times he launches into a flurry of death, fists flying back as far as his shoulders until the bag hangs horizontal in the air before it arcs back, the constant opponent who never says die.

He keeps on attacking, throwing his body weight behind each blow until he slams the bag with the back of his fist. The heavy weight pops off its hinges where it suspends from a rope connected to the ceiling and slams to the floor a good eight feet in front of him, sliding to a halt on the grainy cement.

His shoulders heave, bloodied fists clenched his sides. Thick, inked arms are held apart from his body as though he can't bear to touch himself. Zeke's head turns, but not enough to see me.

"I know you're there."

I don't shrink back or try to hide.

He'll chase me if I run and part of me ... a crazy, mad, sick part, wants to find out what that feels like, what he'll do if he does catch me.

The other half of my brain runs on a repeat emergency siren and tries to mute everything else.

Run, Will Robinson, Run.

Zeke Fallon is all the red flags I never want to incite, but my feet stay planted, and so do I.

"You're a little stalker, aren't you," he mutters, not quite looking at me as he continues his one-sided conversation. A dark smile taints his voice.

I push away from the wall and struts across the room, regardless of how my stomach plummets and swoops with each step. Anything less, and he'll scent my fear.

I'm so freaking broken.

"You're still shit at it." He faces me as his statement makes me smile.

"I'm sure Aster will give me some training if I beg in a nice way." I don't know where that comes from, but it's the first time I've spoken since I walked into his space, taking a page out of Nyx's book for once.

The less I say, the more I see. Is this how his perspective looks all the time? Because if it is, I like it.

"Roxy." Zeke lashes out with one whitened fist like he's aiming for the bag and forgot he blew it off its rope. "Don't say his name."

I blink and a second epiphany slaps me.

He's not mad at me.

For the first time, I see past the blockade of anger and fury that always blares out of him, making his eyes dark. Hooded disdain drips from his chiseled face, arched lips folding in an animalistic smile beneath a layer of unshaven scruff.

"Do you want to run, Roxy?" Zeke growls.

No, not growls. *He purrs.*

We haven't hit the growly stage yet. Somehow, this is worse. Like he wants more.

That's terrifying, because so do I.

One foot skitters back behind me. Before I have a chance to rectify my mistake, he stalks forward, following the movement, tracking each step like a predator and me his prey as he unbinds his hands.

Because that's who he is in this moment.

He's not Zeke, the angry, seventeen-year-old bully. This is the boy who trains his duck butt off, his body covered in scars and ink, who has a singular focus on one thing right now.

Me.

"Go on, run," he whispers as he strides forward and I retreat in a dance we both know the steps to, even though we've never performed together before.

I shake my head, raising my chin to hold his coal gaze alight with eternal embers. "No. I won't play your game."

"But it's my favorite one."

"I'll keep that in mind later." I sass him back with little thought of survival or anything else.

Zeke cracks a smile that lights his formidable face. "Nasty little thing. I see why he likes you."

I raise both eyebrows. "He doesn't even want me—" The admission catches in my throat. I swallow the name I refuse to say. "But we're not talking about him."

"Just the people in this room, right, Roxy?" he goads, his smile dropping away as he shifts to one side. It's a causal move, but in one step he uses his bulk to effectively block the entire exit.

My way out.

Zeke Fallon is a hell of a lot more intelligent than he makes out. Smarter than any of us, maybe.

All the boys are geniuses in their own right. It shouldn't—doesn't—surprise me that Aster's best friend is cut from the same cloth.

Giving up all pretenses, if we ever had any, Zeke stalks forward, stopping when his breath brushes my lips. His chest still heaves, though he caught his breath long ago.

"If you're not going to play games with me, Roxy, why the hell are you in here? I'm not safe."

"For who?"

"Anyone." He rakes a hand through his hair, spraying me with sweat. "You."

"You think a lot of yourself," I scoff, still putting one foot behind the other.

He pauses, and so do I. "I knew you'd be here, Roxy."

That catches my attention. "If you knew I was coming, why didn't you lock the door to keep me out of your space?" I ask, nonplussed.

Zeke smiles at my assumption that jumps a few logical places. "Because I want you here."

He takes another step forward. I continue our parade in reverse that stops as my back hits the cement wall. His arms brace either side of my head, boxing me in, then drop to my waist. My breath comes in sharp, short gasps, hands rising to rest on his forearms to—*push him away, scratch his flesh raw*—but I don't do any of those things.

I wait. Explore. Beneath the unwound wraps, his scarred and tattooed knuckles are torn where they press into my sides. Zeke stretches his thumbs to where they don't quite meet in the middle around my waist, though his fingers do at my spine.

"Glad you've put on some weight. You were all skin and bones from that duckhole you came from," he mutters in a low voice, plucking at the stretchy, gray cotton skirt I chose today over black tights printed with glittery rainbows and crescent moons.

He raises his head as he stops studying his hands joined around my waist and meets my eyes. A shared awareness flares through us. One breath passes in the space between before he leans in and presses his front flush to mine. Muscle ripples beneath hot, sweaty skin against my black tee that dampens the moment he makes contact, resting his body to mine. Our foreheads press together.

"You wanted me here?" I whisper, my mind catching up with our conversation that no longer suits the moment, but my mouth decides to spit it out anyway.

His hands space on my waist, finding the base of my spine, tucking me against his body. All of him. "I want you."

I close my eyes and shake my head, unable to face him. "Zeke—" I utter, confusion shutting me down.

This was a bad, bad idea, coming here, chasing after him. Between Elen and Nyx, I'm collecting a harem of my own. The ski trip back was different, after that message from Aster that ruined my world. Or I thought it did, and then I found something else. A new peace. But Zeke? He's my ex's best friend. Aster will never forgive me.

I know he won't. There's something between the two who are closer than brothers. As much as Aster hates me, and Zeke flicks between tolerating me and loathing me, I also know I loved Aster once— No, despite everything and all the anger I feel too, I still love him. That's why all this hurts so damn much.

I don't want to do anything to break the two friends apart.

Zeke takes the choice out of my hands as he leans into my space and brushes his chin across my cheek, pushing my chin back. Short, sharp, bristles rub across my skin. He gives me a fraction of a second or less to register his terrible eyes boring into me before his mouth slants over mine in an all-consuming kiss that wipes out every conscious thought.

He doesn't ask permission, like Aster did, go slow or easy like Elen or Nyx. His chest expands against mine as he crowds my space. Existence shrinks to just us. I swallow by reflex, pressing up on my toes to meet his force. My hands slide up his arms, dwarfed by his strength, the presence of him at being so close. Zeke covers both of us in his sweat.

My skirt and tights are gathered in his fist and before I can break away from his brutal kiss, my lips tender, his eyes crazed, he tugs at the material. There's a ripping sound and I *shove*.

"Stop." One word.

It's all I get out before he leans forward to— I don't know, but he stalls as my voice seems to register.

"What?" Even his breath is aggressive. "Tell me this isn't as good as you and him."

The hand that bunches my ripped clothes releases a fraction, his thumb grazing bare skin as everything clunks into place for me.

I stare at him, my heart wild. I have no idea what's written across my face, but it must match my panic as he rears back.

"What?" he insists, his brow dipping. "Talk to me, Roxy."

One large hand cradles my jaw, the contact so intimate I want to lean into him and sob. *Protector*, Elen said. Instead, I gulp in much needed air, and fess up.

"We never did … anything." I shut my eyes, unable to deal with his stare, his face closed and granite. "I mean, we kissed, but that's it," I rush on, my insides squeezing. "He never wanted—" My words stall as everything inside me freezes. "I mean, I—" *I wanted to try, but I didn't know what to do.*

Zeke doesn't move, doesn't say a word, not even when I peek up at him. He stares back at me.

I feel so tiny in the circle of his thick arms, like I might disappear against his massive chest. His mouth moves, but my ears are fuzzy and I miss the first bit. All of it.

Something about ducks.

Or not.

Zeke continues swearing, glaring at me with accusing eyes. "You never— With Aster— You know." He gestures to me with a whole-body wave, as unable to put words into a sentence as me. His thumb still rubs the inside of my hip, skin pressing on skin.

"No." Shame floods me, heating my cheeks. I break eye contact with him, pulling my face away and twist out of his hold.

He lets me go, clutching my torn clothing. Breath whooshes from me as I escape out of the large open warehouse doors, my feet carrying me away as fast as I can run. By the time I turn back, Zeke's silhouette is tiny. His arms brace against the wall where we stood, holding himself up, his head bowed as deep breaths wrack his huge body.

Even that wrenching sight doesn't ease my escape. I trip away from the boxing gym and the bigger man, unable to look back at the sight of his vulnerability on display.

Because in hunting him down, I hurt him. Like I ruined things with Aster. Those breaths I know are sobs—

Those are my fault. I did that.

I run and don't stop.

Chapter Fifteen

Where I Hide

Aster

Water laps at my feet, cold and impartial. I stare into the chlorinated petri dish, my knees bent, muscles warmed. The bleachers are filled with supporters and families from several schools, though mine will never be amongst them. A second before the buzzer sets adrenaline coursing through me, I swear a swath of red hair invades my periphery, Roxy's voice taking up all of my available headspace.

It happens right as the buzzer rings, and I'm the slowest off the mark.

It doesn't matter because I churn through the water, choppy in the wake of the other competitors and slice in front, where I'm meant to be. Out of the way of everyone else.

Alone.

Hell, I imagined her being there. After the way I've treated her, there's no way she'll want any part of me which is my father's design, after all. The new color looks good on her, the perfect distraction. But that's not today's challenge.

Muscles burn as self-flagellation of a different sort urges me forward. When my lungs protest and my arms numb, I keep going, hitting the other end of the pool and kicking out swiftly.

My turn isn't neat and tidy; my toes connect with the tile and shriek their agony, but the pain provides an additional incentive. Before I count too long, my hand connects with the cement at the far end of the pool. The crunch is enough to draw a wince across the timer's thin face, though she offers me a wan smile and shows me the stop watch, her other hand shooting into the air.

"Good time, Mister Craven. That might be a record," she mutters out of the corner of her mouth.

The next person comes in beside me. I'm surprised to see Zeke panting in the water, his face red enough I expect him to puke in his next breath.

"Not in the pool," I warn as a neighboring school takes third place.

"Let me the duck out. I'm sick of babysitting your ass," he grunts, swinging himself up on shaking arms.

I smirk, knowing he hates the pool. He swims because I do, but he hates that there's something physical he can't best me at. But the water isn't about being fast or the best. It's about beating myself, not the person who occupies the next lane.

"Wash it off," I murmur, kicking my legs beneath the water. My body cools rapidly, but I'm not willing to get out yet.

Not turn and see my failure, see that she's not in the stands. Or worse, that she came to watch him instead, and no one's here for me.

It's your own fault, Aster. My father's voice invades my mind.

I haul my frozen ass out of the pool and don't look back because I know the phantom who never came to watch me is also right.

Chapter Sixteen
Back To The Start

Roxy

Nyx doodles flowers on the back of my hand in black pen. I let him, listening at a bare minimum during my English class. Miles Salem, our English and Drama teacher, oversells a Shakespearian soliloquy I don't care about. An ancient version of Othello plays on mute on the projector at the front of the room. Somewhere in the back row, Zeke snores.

I wish I could join him. Not in the back row, but snoring.

No matter how droll the lecture seems, I'm sure there's plenty of merit to what I'm supposed to be reading, but for whatever reason the words refuse to make sense in my brain.

Annoyed with myself, I fidget with my nails.

Nyx makes a sound low in his throat from his seat beside me, smoothing my hands out as he sends me a gentle look.

"Sorry," I mumble.

"You worry." His fingers circle my wrist and squeeze, before he returns to decorating the back of my hand in black pen.

Elen doodles on the corner of his paper, his eyes glazed over, and Aster...

I feel Aster's attention lasered on the back of my neck.

This is the one class we have together, all of us at the same time each week. It's awful. Three of us ignoring the other two for a full double period.

Better than calc where Zeke and Aster gang up on me twice a week. At least here I have allies. A buffer between me and them. Not that I need it, per se. But having friends is … nice.

"You know I worry." I bite my lip at the admission and pray Aster hasn't heard my confession, hating that I care.

Nyx watches me. He lifts a hand, his eyes locked with fierce concentration, and tugs my bottom lip free. He offers another brief smile, and the moment is broken. The black pen returns to my hand as he links a row of miniscule flowers that lead into the other in a double row of figure eights that never ends. The moment he lifts the pen, I trail a fingertip above the fresh artwork, unwilling to damage the muted passion he's laid out yet again.

"I love it."

He nudges my shoulder with his but doesn't release my wrist back, rubbing his thumb underneath where no one else can see.

On my other side, Elen offers me a half smile and wiggles his fingers like he might reach for me.

Despite their easy nature, I still have an unbreakable connection to Aster that I hate, though I can't be rid of it. Even Zeke's snores don't annoy me, though Mr. Salem makes a valiant effort to ignore his pupil's insolence.

It feels weird, this pull between us all. Like we shouldn't have to choose one between the other though we're expected to, regardless. Even Rhani shies away from discussing the way my breakup with Aster has become something more with the others. I've never spoken to her about Zeke. I can't. I'm grateful the next connection is a gentle touch and so easy.

Elen has been a constant comfort, one I don't want to do without. The light pressure of our fingertips touching increases as he lines our arms up together on the desk next to mine, resting the heel of our palms together.

His hand is that much larger than mine, and he's painted his nails in blue and silver stripes to match his hair today.

He smiles as he looks down at my chipped nails and clicks his tongue. "When are you going to level up, Roxy?"

"You want me to become a high society girl? Do you think I'd survive ten seconds in that world?" I lift my pinky finger to tap his, not wanting to break the connection with the boy on either side of me while Miles Salem drones on.

Elen huffs as he leans in at my side and brushes his lips against my ear. "No. I think you'll soar above them all."

I stare at the smart board in front of us, reading the line that doubles in size.

"In following him, I follow but myself..." Iago, Act 1, Scene 1

The words make sense. A *clunk* on an empty bank. It took me reading through the play half a dozen times and watching the movie on mute for me to *get it*. Kind of like life, but I don't have the luxury of watching that on replay, or going back to fix things I screwed up in the past.

My back stiffens as Aster coughs behind me, but the villainy in this room is not his alone. We're each guilty, me most of all. I've reciprocated enough times, hurting him back plenty to soothe my own perceived injuries.

As though hearing my thoughts Elen settles back in his seat, but he doesn't remove his touch. I'm stuck between him and Nyx, flanked by a sleeping Zeke and Aster, who is doubtlessly wide awake. There's no place I'd rather be.

That doesn't mean I'm ready to forgive Aster. But ... maybe I understand his motives a little clearer now.

At least, I do today.

A primped student wearing the stiffest Alchem uniform I've ever seen enters the room with an official air. It makes me realize how casual my boys are. His gaze drifts around the room to land on me. I sink low in my seat between the boys, groaning when he calls my name.

"Roxanne Quell."

Full names never mean good things.

"What did I do?" I whisper when Miles Salem repeats my name for the umpteenth time.

"Who else have you been harassing, Roxy girl?" Elen murmurs under his breath, though he doesn't take his eyes off the unfortunate student at the front of the classroom. His lip curls in a sneer, and I know he's not going to have a good day.

The call comes again, but I stay where I am, still not disconnecting from them.

Mr. Salem steps up, the paper flicking against the back of his hand. He stares at me until I shift in my seat.

"What do I need to do?" I ask, aiming not to be a brat and failing in miserable style.

The closer he comes, the more the boys withdraw until I lose Nyx altogether as he falls back into himself as always.

A long arm reaches over my head to pluck the paper from Salem's hand. "It's a who." There's a scowl in Zeke's sleep-roughened voice that I don't need to turn about to see. "The principal, Roxy. I'll come with you."

I shake my head. "No. Whatever I've done, I'll face it alone." Blowing out a breath to conceal my nerves, I push myself up to standing and smear some of the art Nyx drew on my hand. My stomach clenches at the sight. It doesn't seem like a good omen.

Zeke adds his own parting advice. "Open your mouth like that with Gallaway, and you'll earn yourself an invite back." He leans forward on his elbows. "You won't want that."

I turn around to face him, looking down at him for once. "You don't know what I want."

He bares his teeth, and I swear he growls. In. Class.

Elen *tsks* with an excess of decorum and flicks his fingertips across the back of my knees, leaving me off kilter.

It's a great distraction. Almost as much as his parting jibe.

"I'm sure you'll kill it."

How prophetic.

****

The piece of paper with my name on it crumples in my hand as I stare at Mr. Killington, whose severe face matches his name. However I expected to meet the school head, or in this case, the deputy head who stands in as the principal. This was not it.

"Could you repeat that, please?" I manage, gathering the remnants of my manners as the floor fluctuates beneath me.

Alchem's vice principal's mouth flattens. This must not be part of the job he wants today. "Your aunt passed away in her sleep. Last night. Willa Sloan will be missed. Her contribution this year was ... generous. I'll have your things packed and taken home."

That's all he has to say about the woman who announced herself in my life months ago, took me in begrudgingly, and set me free in this gilded cage. She was known for her money and her attitude. I don't have anything to add.

His words register. *Home.* The concept jolts me out of my reverie. "I don't have one of those," I say, dazed.

The gray-haired man surveys me like he's talking to a lesser lifeform. "You'll be wanting to get your affairs in order, Miss Quell. After all, you're now the sole heir—owner—of Pyric Industries."

He closes a folder on his desk bearing my surname across the top in the gilt letters that remind me of that hideous front gate Alchem is so freaking proud to claim.

I stare at my name for a long second, wondering if the tears will come. It's not a spoiler when they don't.

"I think I'd rather stay to finish out the semester." The decision arrives on cue.

His eyes narrow on my face. "You'll travel to Oregon for the funeral?"

Where she insisted my parents were buried, though she never attended their farewell.

Now she'll rest in the same private graveyard near them. They can despise each other in death as they did in life.

I nod. "Yes." I understand how the occasion works. This year I'll claim veteran status.

Killington's shoulders drop in resignation. "I'll make arrangements. I believe Willa's lawyer will be in contact."

I open my mouth to ask what for, then realize what a stupid question that is. *Sole heir.* Owner of one of the biggest pharma companies in the world.

The reason my aunt took me under her unwilling wing when my parents passed. Now, she's gone.

I'm alone. Again.

I blink at Killington when he shoos me from his office without so much as an *I'm sorry*, or any other useless platitude I'd be grateful to hear right now. His office door closes behind me. My body jerks when it shuts with a soft thud that might as well be a cymbal clash for all its silent echo shattering in my ears.

"Look at that. Roxy Quell, stepping up in the world."

My head twists like a bird on a stick to find Aster smirking at me as he emerges from the principal's office. Of course he's the reason my appointment was shunted sideways to the next in line. His twisted smile widens. I swear he was born wearing that thing attached to his face.

His autocratic lips are arched, though the corners turn down. My instinct is to say something to make him laugh, bring him back to a smile or make him kiss me, and I hate how much I'm still programmed to please him. That I still want him to be happy, after everything.

He hasn't earned the right to be happy again. Not yet.

"What are you doing here?"

He slides his hands in his pockets, something silver flickering between his hands that disappears fast.

Not today. My eyes narrow. "Give it over." I hold out my hand.

He shrugs and doesn't deny me. Flipping the locket that's always been a sore point between us into my hands, he dangles the chain a moment before he drops it and retreats. I close my fingers around the piece of jewelry I recognize because of him, turning it over and flicking open the metal catch to expose the picture of me and my mother inside.

I should feel something, but I don't. Like the tears, emotions are absent.

"I still don't understand why you have this."

Aster makes a soft noise.

My eyes raise to meet his colder, emotionless ones.

Well, almost emotionless. Shadows flicker behind pale eyes turned indecipherable, a language I don't understand that he speaks and I don't.

"You never will, Roxy." He swipes for the chain again.

I should have known better than to think he would let me have the silver piece that was never mine in the first place.

"Greedy," I breathe.

The word slips out of my mouth before I can hold it back and shut my lips tight. I wrap my arms around myself, pulling my uniform cardigan across my body. The light knit does nothing to keep out the chill that permeates the icy void I've become.

"What do you need, Roxy?" His voice lowers, along with his brow as though he can sense all the things wrong with me right now.

I've never been able to hide anything from him. Why should this moment be different?

I shake my head, swinging my hands out to push him away.

He sucks in air as I force him to retreat a half step, a surprised laugh leaving his chest. "Well, well. Roxy has bite." He leans into my space, inhaling like the creeper ex he epitomizes. "Going to show me again?"

I draw back and stumble over my own feet. "Did you miss me?" I snap, bereft of words to say without blurting out the truth.

I'm lost. I miss you. Help me.

None of that comes out. I'm relieved, as that would be the ultimate mistake.

His smile widens as he steps forward. "Yes."

My teeth grind. "Do you miss kissing me?" I dare, pushing his boundaries because apparently I'm suicidal on top of everything. Not that I've had the time to process anything I learned thanks to Aster's annoying appearance.

"Yes." His voice hisses out lower, softer this time. I blink. "Why?"

"I want to taste desolation. Is that what you're ready for, Roxy? Can you up and leave everything?"

That smile, the smooth, seductive look in his eyes—it's all fake. My stomach ripples with acid that I try to hold back but can't as today catches up with me. I vomit on Aster's shiny black shoes, splattering his pressed trousers even though Aster Craven never ironed a day in his life.

Before I came to Alchem Academy, neither had I. Because I didn't own an iron back then.

I lunge toward a potted palm for round two as hands that don't belong to me gather what's left of my hair, pulling it back from my face as I empty my Alchem approved luxury breakfast into a palm that's due out for rotation from the torture kids give it, ripping at its leaves, sticking used cigarette butts down the back of its pot.

I cling to the thin terracotta, like I might fall off the earth if I don't. Bile settles back into my stomach where it belongs, leaving an array of bitter seeds on the back of my tongue. That Aster has seen me at my lowest leaves me fumbling on my phone for the first number I can find. I want to slice my nails across his face, rather than confront the boy I still love.

Right now, all I want to do is get out. My thumb throws out a message of less than four words on automatic, like I'm in survival mode. Aster calls out as I run down the hall, my heels not touching the flashy carpet as I sprint away. Pounding my feet against the thick carpet in a muted rhythm, I attempt to escape my future with him—enemies always, more, maybe.

Not that it matters. I'll destroy that future the moment I get a chance.

JOSS PHOENIX

Chapter Seventeen

One Missing

Roxy

I stand outside Alchem's gilded gates where all this started. On the day where four boys sat on the wall beside those hideous golden freaking gates, grading each student as they passed for the beginning of the new school year, including me. My ancient suitcase burst open, littering the Academy's impeccable drive with my undergarments while Aster stared me down and teased me for the first time.

The ghost of my former self haunts me, but that girl isn't here now. Nor are any of the boys. I stand alone, a small, black bag strung across my body, dressed in my Alchem-issue formal uniform because I don't own anything black to wear to a funeral.

My cleanest jeans and a t-shirt were all I had for my parents' funeral, much to my aunt's disgust, and I didn't know her well enough to care about breaking conformity then, or now. Despite what she might've left to me. It doesn't change anything. Even knowing she's gone, I'm still the girl from the wrong side of the family covered in a little too much dirt for her liking.

I'm so lost in my head that when a familiar black Jeep jerks to a stop in front of me, I don't notice, still expecting Lurch, my aunt's grumpy and silent chauffeur, to pick me up in her six-figure classic.

It's not until Zeke glares at me through the windscreen, tapping his fingers on the steering wheel, and Elen kicks the back door open that I jolt out of my daze.

"What are you doing here?"

"We're your ride," Zeke growls in a terse voice. "Get in."

I blink. "I think I have a ride."

"Yeah. This is it."

"No…" I stall, staring down the road, unsure why I'm not getting in the Jeep with people I know. For some reason, my head insists we're facing this alone. "I think…"

"Pretty sure we're it, Roxy girl." Elen leans back and flicks his fingers at me in a universal *bring it* gesture I'm not sure fits the situation, but somehow, it works. He tips his head on the side when I don't budge. "Consider us your security."

My brows shoot for the sky. "Why do I need security?"

Zeke bangs his forehead on the steering wheel.

"You do realize that even if you added up all my assets, everything I've sold, my personal account … and the rest of the band, you're now worth more than all of us together?" Elen suggests with a little more finesse.

"Ah…" I don't have a response to that. Killington's words sink a little deeper into my brain soup.

Elen gestures again and I slide into the backseat beside him.

Nyx, on his other side, offers a small finger wave.

"You thought you were rich before, Roxy? You didn't know nothing then."

I wrap my hand around the back of my neck, tugging at the fine hairs there. It hurts. *Good.* At least something about this whole thing is real. "Why do I feel like you're going to turn this into a song?"

Elen watches me, playing with one of his lip studs. "Could happen."

An uncomfortable tightness wells in the bottom of my stomach. "I don't want any of this," I whisper, as Zeke revs the engine.

No one hears me.

Laughter blooms across the backseat as I shrink into myself, finding Zeke's eyes in the rear vision mirror. He turns around in the front seat to glare at all of us. "You know you're gonna end up with an invitation to the eight ball club, yeah? Aster is gonna f– ducking love that." He clears his throat, but his eyes never leave mine.

For the very first time today, a smile spreads across my lips. "I bet he will."

Zeke's face shutters, and he faces forward. "Of course that's where you go with it," he grumbles.

Hands grasp my waist and lift me. I squeak as I'm airborne for a second before Elen deposits me between himself and Nyx in the middle seat. "Take it easy on him," Elen murmurs. "He's in a mood."

I don't need to ask who *he* is. The moment the Jeep hits the blacktop, Zeke's foot slams down on the gas. The vehicle rockets forward. I cling to both boys, my nails stabbing into the back of their hands as our psychotic driver heads through town at a suicidal speed, the address to my aunt's mansion—my home?—preprogrammed into the Jeep's GPS.

I swear my mouth hangs open in a silent scream the entire ten-hour drive there.

I'd like to think I'm a thrill seeker, but I wanna be honest. I don't wanna die in this Jeep. Not because Zeke is in a ducky mood, and I'm not sure if it's me who put him there, or someone else.

But whatever happened, I'm begging it to stop. When I can catch my breath.

We pull up at the top of the circular drive near the enormous house with a minimum of stops where I'm grateful to still be alive. Pebbles and dust skitter across the ground around the car. Something sharp pings off the underside of the Jeep. I huddle between the two boys still allowing me to clutch their hands in a death grip.

Zeke climbs out of the driver's seat, slamming the door to stalk around and open the back door like the chauffeur he's pretending to be today.

Nyx scoots out. Elen detaches from me, and I slide out too, willing my legs not to turn to jelly as my feet touch the ground. When I look up, I'm facing a row of servants like something out of a period drama with the local minor royalty come to visit.

I reached down and grab a hand for support because the row of silent, staring, blank faced staff freak me out. The callouses that close around my hand do *not* belong to a rockstar or an artist.

That was a mistake.

His hand folds around mine, either by reflex or design, but his grip is unbreakable and I can't take that back.

Zeke keeps a firm hold as he shifts behind me. Speaking so that his words are for me alone, he murmurs instructions into my ear. "Look straight ahead. See through them, Roxy. Ignore their faces. If you feel judged, look around. Meet their eyes if you feel that you can. Otherwise, don't. You don't have to speak. Walk forward."

My mouth barely moves as I reply. "I don't know what to do." I came here expecting to attend a funeral, maybe walk through an empty house and feel guilty for not feeling the way I should. Not this.

"Your aunt died an extremely wealthy woman. The FBI are sniffing around. Know what they found?" I turn my head to him to ask, but his knuckles brush the corner of my jawbone and force my head forward. "Keep your eyes straight ahead. They found nothing, Roxy. They don't like that. Your lawyer is waiting for you in the study. He's a hard man, and you're going to hate him. He's smart, and he knows his sh– stuff. Don't sack him.

Ask him all the questions. You can change anything once all this is over."

My breath stutters as I try to absorb all that. "How do you know that?"

"Because we share a family lawyer."

"And why should I trust you?"

He huffs in my ear. "You shouldn't."

Zeke's touch against my cheek disappears, though his hand around mine remains. He leads our small parade into the house. Terror warps my perception as I walk past the row of housekeepers and staff who hate my presence as much as I'm terrified of them. But I do as Zeke suggests, managing to hold myself together and stare at the stones behind their heads because I know that if I look at them, I'll crumble. For now, it seems to work, and for now, that will do.

Elen pushes open the study door to expose a thin, bald man wearing glasses from at least two centuries ago who looks at me over a stack of papers and says my name without an inkling of a smile on his face.

"Roxy. Why don't you sit down? We have a lot to talk about."

Willa Sloan's passing seems more like a business transaction than an emotional event. I wonder if anyone mentioned that to her before she left this plane. The moment I step across the threshold of the study I leave the security of the boys behind and enter a new world, entirely alone.

****

It turns out that, 'a lot to talk about', means going through account after account and business after business. My aunt didn't own one business; she accrued dozens of them. My thumbs are numb from typing out all the information Albert Whitman deluges me with. An hour later, I've scribbled through half a notepad and run through three pens that maybe started with half a load of ink each, but my fingers are numb at the tips too.

By the end of the next, I return to taking notes on my phone. An hour after that, I give up altogether, and press record.

He nods at my new method with approval. "Your aunt often did that when she couldn't take notes any more. I admire your tenacity in the face of your desolation."

I tilt my head to one side. "Interesting choice of words. Someone else used the same term."

His eyes meet mine across the desk, sharp despite the thick glasses. "Did he?"

Neither of us mention the name. Neither of us have to.

I sigh, having reached my limit some time back. "What happens now?"

Whitman takes off his glasses, rubbing them with a microfiber cloth that has seen as many good days as the suit he wears. "The businesses are yours. The focus is on what you want to do. Your education is funded well and truly. You can pick any college you want to go to. Alchem Academy will see you through to the end of this year, and the next. Your influence over these businesses is an overwhelming majority. You don't need the college degree, but you're welcome to it if that's the path you choose. A regular life is unlikely at this point for you. You can opt to do college courses from home if you want. Online ... we can arrange what you need, and you can pass your degree in solitude."

I look longingly at the closed door as my chest closes up. There isn't enough air in this room for both of us. "If I choose to try to be normal?"

Albert doesn't crack a smile. He hasn't even tried once during our interview. "I'm not even sure if it's possible. I'm going to be honest with you. The FBI are involved. We don't know what happened to your aunt. She was healthy. Raring. She was full of life, if running on spite. She should've kept kicking for another decade or more, at least. And with her money, medicine was never an object."

"She made sure of that."

I think back on the swath of pharma companies in the portfolio he took me through, the new trial drugs that my aunt ensured went on shelves at exorbitant rates. Most were aimed at aging, or rather anti-ageing. Anything that hit her got an answer. That's what money and power did. It helped the person with the most to live forever.

A shiver runs through me. "I'm not sure how much more I can take today. Funeral arrangements?" I learned earlier that I have hours to spare for that event.

Albert passes over a separate folder.

"Thank you." I shuffle through everything that seems more familiar, this being my second time around in recent memory.

Albert pauses. "Would you like me to be present?"

I shrug and shake my head. "You do you, Albert." I have no energy left.

I'm not sure what sort of relationship he and my aunt had, if he liked her or cared. I don't want to force him to waste his time if she treated him as she treated me.

He nods, as though sensing my waning attention span. "Thank you for listening. I understand how much there is to take in."

"What's your advice?" I ask.

He raises both eyebrows. "You're taking this better than I expected."

I wait.

He sighs. "Stay as far away from Craven

Enterprises as possible."

"Why?" My question whiplashes around us.

"Because." He cleans his glasses once again, repeating his stalling tactic on the crystal clean lenses. "They never do business well."

Albert looks straight at me without the glasses in the way.

"And they can't be trusted."

Chapter Eighteen

a Monochromatic Landscape

Roxy

The private graveyard is filled with black umbrellas though a single raindrop is yet to fall. I stare at the white coffin, glazed and covered in all sorts of bright wildflowers. The floral arrangements were handled by someone I don't know. My attention wanders as the priest drones on in Latin about immortal gifts and escaping purgatory. I hope money buys favors in heaven. Otherwise, my aunt is screwed.

My lips quirk up at the inappropriate, uncharitable thought.

At my back, the three boys stand, silent sentinels all. One person is notably absent, the nameless ex. I refuse to think about him, my hands closing on empty air. My smile fades as I step forward.

"Inappropriate, Roxy," Zeke mutters, leaning into my space. Sharp bristles brush my skin. He refused to shave like everyone, and my earrings bob with the contact, a pearl dangling from each delicate stem.

Rhani insisted on them when she turned up at the house earlier. I didn't ask how she got there, but when I peered out my old bedroom window, a blue classic car was parked behind Zeke's Jeep on the drive.

Adam leaned against the driver's door, his back to the house.

Her foster brother had nothing to say about that— at least, not yet.

"*For tears*," she said, pinning them on. "*The ones you won't share.*" The sympathy in her eyes was almost more than I could bear because it didn't feel real.

Because I don't feel. *Anything*. Even while my

aunt's casket is lowered into the ground. I toss my flower at it, the bud disappearing with the last vestiges of a life that only Willa Sloan knows if she was happy with or not.

"What's inappropriate?" I try not to move my mouth, though the priest seems to be used to people talking through his sermon and drones on with the end of his ceremony, undeterred.

Scarred knuckles brush across the back of my hand. "You're not smiling at the old witch's death."

A surprised giggle burst out of me. I choke on it, clamping down on the sound. Tears stream from my eyes as I huff about, swallowing the sound. Curious and sympathetic glances are cast my way from the crescent moon of people surrounding my aunt's grave. No doubt they all assume I'm lost in my grief, the orphan girl left alone in the world.

Nothing could be farther from the truth. At least one person seems to understand that.

Behind me, feet shuffle on the trampled grass. I fight for dominance and something else in the utter silence filling my head.

Okay, so maybe three people get me. Four, if he was here. That turns my thoughts around again, and my tears spiral into something bitter. Smooth hands glide around my waist beneath my Alchem blazer, offering a hint of warmth on my other side.

"Ignore him. I'll get your ice cream later."

I do smile at that.

Nyx hums behind us, some twisted, upbeat version of an old Catholic hymn that scandalizes everyone in the vicinity.

They're perfect. My boys.

I reach back and grab for his hand too, connecting to all three of them. Almost. I'm determined to hold onto that stupid smile for the rest of the day. I don't care what anyone else thinks. Introductions are made, and I don't remember a single name or face except for two suits who look like they represent some secret government organization.

But they don't. It's much scarier than that.

"They're FBI," Zeke mutters. He bends down under the pretense of tying a shoelace.

I perch on the end of the stone bench beneath a weeping angel once the service has concluded, my aunt resting beneath fresh soil while the hoards mingle.

I stare at the shattered stone beside him, then back up at the angel, missing one of her wings. It seems a good reason to cry to me.

"What are they doing here?" I mutter out of the corner of my mouth.

"Roxy, your aunt didn't roll over and die in bed on her own." Zeke is far from discreet.

A woman in a black dress gasps and flutters her hands over her mouth.

I roll my eyes. "You know, if you say it louder, maybe that one will roll over and die."

The woman shoots me a hard look and storms away.

"Good to see you're making friends." A long shadow falls over the grass, dulling the already muted light. Flat metal flickers between long fingers in a shape I recognize before the blades I learned to throw with slide back into the place where he keeps them at his belt.

Zeke straightens, sliding his hands in his pockets and steps forward between us. "Craven."

Standing with his back to the light, his face thrown into sharp relief, I can't see Aster's expression, but I know those perfectly manicured eyebrows are lifted. Instead, I look down rather than into his faceless silhouette, and am treated to a close-up view of his tight charcoal uniform.

If Alchem's female uniforms are borderline pornographic with their Sailor Moon-esque blue and white box-pleated and way too short skirts, the boys' are of the private school style casualty.

In the business world, they're the offspring of royalty. Just not the coronated or titled sort.

While I ruminate on my ex, he hosts a silent stand-off with his best friend. Scooting to the edge of the bench, I brush pretend lint off my skirt, press my knees together, and push up.

A hand lands on my shoulder that encompasses me from my upper arm to the back of my neck plops me right back down again. Zeke gives me a hard squeeze, and leaves his hand there in warning.

I blink as Nyx joins me without a single word, his thigh pressed against mine.

"What are you doing here?" I protest, still fixated on Aster despite Nyx's warming—and somewhat rarer—contact.

He ignores me. *Typical.*

"I don't remember your name being on the guestlist," Zeke mutters, low and quiet.

I've never heard him use that tone. He's always so full of anger, rage, and fury. Even cold, it's all too easy to see the storm brewing within him. Right now, he's nothing like that. We're in the eye, Aster whipping at the edges of his tenuous calm.

I wait for the interruption, but it doesn't come. Somehow, that's so much more terrifying. Despite my reservations of breaking into his foreboding serenity, I pluck at where his fingers rest on my shoulder, but his hand is lodged in place.

"Zeke—" I murmur. My voice strains at the edges, but he's intent on the man across from him.

"I don't require an invitation." On anyone else it would be a boast. On Aster Craven? Those words are a statement of fact.

A breath escapes me in a rush. I've had enough of their combined show ponying. Flicking my hands up and away, *knowing* I'll end up on my rear end, I push up to standing, flaring my defiance. Surprise flickers over me as the captive hand drops away. Within a moment, I miss the contact and glance up at Zeke with a frown.

He shifts on his heels, looking down at me as though checking I'm all right. His fingers twitch at his side, but this one isn't his fight. They can duke it out later, without me around.

"You're not welcome here." I look Aster full in the face for the first time.

His gaze is fathomless as he stares back at me, a shadow of vulnerability flickering behind his usual intensity, but I catch the change. My lips want to turn down, but I resist the urge and raise my chin instead, throwing defiance back in the face of a long-time enemy.

Has it been that long?

What we started as, we have returned. This seems to be our philosophy, what we can't break away from. Our brief interlude as something more than lovers, less than a dream, the remaining fragments fragile and worthless.

My heart lurches into my throat as I open my mouth, but nothing comes out. Tears—*finally*—gather beneath my eyes for all the wrong reasons. I blink, but once they've started, they refuse to stop and fall anyway, as stubborn as any of us.

Because of him.

I can't even twist away from him as he witnesses my final shame. My hands shake at my sides as I tuck them into myself. Grass squeaks beneath my shoes, graves passing in a blur as I run away from the person who broke a heart already ashed.

Short, fast steps carry me across the graveyard. I am conscious of two voices calling my name. I don't stop, can't stop, not until I reach the outer edge of the private cemetery where the black spear-topped fence that surrounds us like a giant mort-safe turns rusty and unloved. My feet stop by a chained kissing gate that looks like it hasn't been opened in over a century.

My unknown family is that old.

Not that I care.

And still, my tears fall.

****

"Miss Quell."

The voice that draws me out of my stupor beneath the drizzling, pearl gray sky isn't the one I need, but I check anyway.

A black suit stands in the place where I thought Aster might follow me.

I shouldn't care, not today. But I do.

"Hi," I respond. It's all the energy I have left.

The tears stopped several minor rain showers ago. I weathered them all together by the older graves, their long-departed souls and unreadable names my sole company.

Mister FBI doesn't require any other response as I run my fingers across the top of the kissing gate beside where I stand, my legs two stiff pegs, the cold etched beneath my skin. One of the rusted edges catches my fingertip, tearing a small hole there. Bright blood wells in the gap that the metal has created, a drop of scarlet on a stark, monochromatic landscape.

The unnamed agent scrounges in his pocket and emerges with a folded tissue offering. "You should get that checked. Have you had a tetanus shot?"

"In my world, I couldn't afford such a thing," I mutter, letting him press the tissue over my cut. It stains fast.

"Don't you own Phyric Pharma?" The frown in his voice is a tangible thing.

"Not yet." I haven't signed anything. Right now, I have no family, no home.

He blows out a breath and seems to realize he's broken the unspoken agent rule everyone knows and made contact with another human. "I'm sorry for your loss."

Robot agent is back. That's nice.

"Who are you?" I don't care.

"Agent Brown."

"Zeke was right."

"About?"

"You don't have personalities." *Or real names.*

He doesn't laugh. My jokes are as crappy today as any other. Who knew?

I stare over the small graveyard, counting the decaying, lichen-covered headstones.

Nyx crouches by one, tracing time-faded letters with his inked fingertip.

Maybe one of these unknown ancestors will make it into a song. I know I'll be scouring his music for months to come because it's him. A smile threatens again, but shuts down fast because in the presence of this agent. It feels like a threat to their safety and mine.

Inappropriate. All the red flags. More than Aster.

I banish his shade from my thoughts, wishing it could last forever.

No, I don't.

liar liar liar.

"Miss Quell?" Agent Brown prompts me, stuck on repeat.

189

My attention flickers back to him. "Have you been talking? I was lost in my … grief."

Liar. Soul on fire.

His face flattens. Maybe he's a human polygraph, and that's how he got his job. I watch as he seems to fold in on himself, an origami agent in a carefully creased suit. When I don't respond, Agent Whoever slides his hands back into his pockets.

I sense movement around me. Though the boys don't come any closer, I know they're there. In my periphery, even Nyx rises from his study of the gravestone, redirecting his vague focus toward us through the ongoing drizzle that leaves us isolated amongst the silent graves.

Mister Agent sighs. "We'll talk soon. If anything happens in the meantime, you can reach me on this number."

He hands me a card—a freaking business card. *Agent Brown* and a phone number is printed on it. Nothing else.

I run my finger across the too-plain cardstock and wonder if he's ever had the Patrick Bateman conversation with his friends, but then I can't imagine him having friends at all. Are agents allowed to socialize with other agents? I look up to ask him the ridiculous question, but he's gone. A disturbed patch of mud and crinkled, bronze leaves decorate the ground to provide evidence he ever stood there at all.

I don't move as Nyx slides into place beside me, pressing an earbud into my ear. Something new of his plays, drowning out my thoughts while my brain registers the new sounds.

"It's what you were humming before. During the … service. You just made this," I accuse him softly.

His eyes light up at the acknowledgement, the

recognition that he doesn't deny with a single bob of his dreads pulled back into a knotted man bun and held in place by sheer will, I swear.

I smile, knowing he isn't going to talk, and my reaction isn't inappropriate at all. "Thank you." I rise up onto my toes and kiss his cheek.

Nyx doesn't speak, staring down at me for a moment before he starts to walk away in slow footfalls, waiting for me to drop into step beside him.

I let the origami agent's card slip from my fingers. It flutters to the ground beside the kissing gate, landing in a small pool of muddled raindrops next to the bloodied tissue he gave me, pink mingling with leaked ink.

I won't be calling him.

JOSS PHOENIX

Chapter Nineteen

Where Shadows Linger

Roxy

I curl on my pristine quilted bed surrounded by a cloud of ruffle. I slept here for a grand total of five nights after my parents' joint funeral before my aunt shipped me off to Alchem Academy. This place will never be my home.

Machine stitched pillows surround me like a mini fort, each bearing my name in a flowing curlicue with a disturbing sort of accuracy that no real person could ever create. The stitching is too even beneath my fingers as I run them across each letter, and my stomach drops. I toss the hideous thing to one side and regret the impulse, gathering the cushion back into place.

Roxanne Cynthia Quell.

"Your middle name is Cynthia?" Elen's lip curls.

I sacrifice one of the soulless pillows to throw at him. "I hate it."

"Good." That comes from Zeke. "I ducking hate it, too."

I laugh at him and feel good about it.

He cracks the rare smile in return, blinding me with a weapon that should be kept under wraps.

My humor dies as we stare at each other in an impasse.

"So, who did it? The Butler, the maid? The chef?" Elen jiggles the plate of kimchi provided by the latter and digs in like he's ravenous. A sound so unlike his music slips from his throat that I raise an eyebrow.

"That good, huh?"

"Oh, Roxy girl." He shakes his head as he transforms my name into something indecipherable in

Korean. "You have no idea. I'm stealing him."

I shrug. "I'm not living here. He's all yours."

Zeke looks me straight in the eye. "You know you can sell the building if you hate the place that much. Once the proverbial dust settles, it's yours."

I shift beneath my pillow fort, but there's a hole. I hold out my hand and Elen places the cushion I threw at him into my palm. I fix the nest I've set around myself and rest my chin on top of the warm pillow that has started to smell like him.

The three boys look ridiculous, crowded in a white room that doesn't suit any of them. Aster's absence is noted in my mental headcount. Of the remainder, each is too bulky to be in here. Except maybe for Nyx, but he's out of place too, all ink and dreads and distressed leather jacket.

White scalloped lace adheres to every freaking available surface—curtains too. Even the desk is painted white with little pink rings around it like it was designed with some sort of perfect, prissy princess in mind.

It's nothing I would've picked for myself, and I know someone ordered the matching set out of a catalogue. It sure as hell wasn't my aunt.

Or the maid who tried to rip my hair out when she brushed it that first night like she resented my presence in the house. I start to giggle, thinking back on Elen's comment.

Colonel Mustard, in the Observatory, with the candlestick.

"Maybe it was Lurch."

It is what I call my aunt's driver, the who dropped me off at Alchem Academy that first day and who prefers to communicate in grunts. I don't think he's ever spoken to me. Yet today I missed him in the household line up when we arrived at the mansion.

Voices exchange plans over my head, none of them being privy to my internal conversation and logic.

"*Now* she loses it." Zeke crosses his arms over his huge chest and glares at me. "Typical."

Nyx surprises me by sliding onto my bed and wedging close enough for his warmth to eke into my nest even though he doesn't touch me. It's the perfect response.

I give him a fleeting smile before Zeke—*typically*—ruins my peace. Addressing the non-elephant in the room, he brings up the one person who should be here, but isn't. Because I pushed him away.

"Could be Aster."

Talk about ending a conversation that's already died.

I swallow back a deluge of nausea that threatens to sink me beneath the impersonal covers. The pillows weigh over me. If I slip beneath them, I might not surface again.

Nyx's fingertips brush mine out of sight of everyone else, and the gesture is *almost* enough.

My voice returns, along with the dose of defiance I need to push the burst of melancholy aside. "That was unnecessary."

Even if it feels like what he said could be true.

I grab another pillow and pull it into my stomach, choosing to do the self-torturing this time around. The delicate cloud crushes in my fists as I prepare to hurl the thing at Zeke. His comment echoes what Albert Whitman suggested back in the office that felt more like his than something I'd ever want to own. Then I change my mind and keep the pillow to myself, crushing the machine-made piece to my chest.

But the thought that Aster hurt the aunt who hated me, even if we weren't at all close, niggles. "It's not possible that she died of natural causes?"

No one makes a sound.

I sigh and pick a thread loose, unraveling the Y in my name. "Guess not."

A timid knock on my door turns heads, but the interrupter doesn't wait to be admitted. "Miss? The detectives want to see you."

That simple pronouncement leaves me devoid of breath.

"S'pose I'll be back." I look around the room and shrug when the boys remain silent. "Destroy whatever you like. It's not like anybody cares about any of this." I gesture at the pristine, sterile room that holds no life whatsoever. At least if they do something it will hold some semblance of a memory.

I make my exit, smiling into the horrified, too-young face of the maid watching mine, and take an unnecessary amount of pleasure at the stifled laugh somewhere at my back.

I know exactly who it belongs to.

****

"You're at Alchem Academy." Detective C of the FBI—no Agent Brown or proffered tissues in sight—checks his handwritten notes for the fiftieth time.

I nod like one of those bobble headed penguins people stuff on their car dashboards that end up half faded and covered in dust. "Yes." They gave us exactly twelve hours—enough time for a meal, sleep, or a nap where we all curled on the floor of my room in a mass of pillow forts and quilts, and another meal—before the suits began their interrogation.

Spoilers: the sleep was shit, and the boys talked all night.

Not that I minded, because my head wouldn't stop turning. No matter how much my exhaustion and the last day weighed on me, I needed white noise to block out the building, constant wave of panic that refused to leave me. And the boys provided exactly what I needed.

What they can't get me out of is FBI hell. I don't know if the agents think I'm an orphan, a grieving princess set to inherit millions, or a criminal they need to reserve a cell for with a nametag just for me.

"And you were with your roommate all that night?" Detective A, the lone female of the group, pipes up.

Round and round in circles we go.

"Yup." I twirl my fingers in my uniform skirt, tugging at the hem. A thread comes loose and I unwind it, watching the loops pull free one at a time.

"Then you attended classes with your roommate, which covers the time period we've discussed," Detective B, in his charcoal suit that matches the other's non-descript attire, closes up the entire interrogation that's taken three hours to go over the same, scant information.

Time after time after time.

If the boys haven't eaten the pantry out or left me here, I'll be shocked.

No, really.

"Yup."

They're so bad at this questioning thing.

I blink at one of their faces, but I don't remember a single name. I'm not sure they remember mine.

"Okay."

And ... we're all wrapped up.

Agent C straightens his jacket and taps his heel on the floor in an FBI version of a secret handshake.

The next one in line takes the bait.

"Thank you, Miss Quell," Agent B says from the pinnacle of their triangle formation, passing over a card, but I'm too tired to be interested in the glossed rectangle.

"We'll be in touch if something comes up."

"Okay." I stand with them as one holds the door. I'm ushered out into my aunt's—*my*—living area. I stumble over feet long gone to sleep, and run nose-first into a bundle of warmth.

Nyx's arms close around me, and I shiver at the temperature change. "Need to eat?" he whispers.

I shake my head.

"Sleep?"

I shrug. One word questions are his thing. Non answers are mine.

"Home?" Knuckles graze beneath my chin, lifting my face enough that he can look down, and I don't have to look up.

I don't even try to respond.

A different sort of blazing heat blankets my back as a pair of rough hands wrap around my hips. Zeke's breath brushes my ear as he whispers the sweetest temptation into my ear. "Wanna burn this abomination to the ground?"

A giggle escapes me. I clamp a hand over my mouth, but it's too late to stop the out of place sound. I jab out with an elbow into his ribs that does nada. "The FBI," I mutter under my breath.

I feel his shrug rather than see it. "Like they care. The case is public, and she was worth a packet. That's their scope. Anyone you want left inside?"

The darkness in his tone slides along my spine, and some twisted part of me likes it.

"Don't," I murmur back, unafraid for the first time.

"Because you think I'll do it?" His fingers dip into my hips, harsh and brief, then his touch disappears.

I know you will.

"Roxy." Elen appears in my periphery. "The cops

are gone."

I bite my lip, but the question bursts out anyway. "Were you hiding?"

His lopsided grin is my answer.

Zeke makes an unrefined noise low in his throat. "We're taking you home."

I don't get a choice, it appears, but neither do I insist on lingering. There's nothing left for me here. Albert Whitman said he would forward paperwork as necessary, and I'll rely on that.

My trust lies in him until he proves me otherwise and for now, the estate will stay as is. I'm torn between wanting to pull the doors and lock the mansion up forever, come back in a decade, and see the overgrown jungle mass it's become. Or do as Zeke suggests, and ash the place to the ground.

His calloused hand rests beneath my elbow as he guides me out of the house and back into his Jeep, holding the passenger door open. No backseat crew for me this trip.

My head turns as I catch movement in my periphery between his arm and the house, a vision of blond hair and the sunlight's sharp reflection flashing off silver that shouldn't be there. I stare until my eyes water, but it doesn't matter. My specter has gone.

Still, the shadows shift around the spot where he stood as the boys shuffle and fight around me. Zeke seems to notice my distraction as I peer into shrubbery. The shape of my phantom is etched into my mind. I could paint him in my sleep.

Maybe I'll bring out the paintings I stored behind the bathroom door. That feels like an age, despite that it's been a few weeks since I hid them there.

"Roxy?" Zeke stares down at me, his brow creased not with anger for once as he reaches out to brush his fingers across my cheek. "Did you get lost in here?" He taps my temple with a gentle touch, understanding breaching his blackened gaze.

The one time he's genuine, and I have to lie to him.

I shake myself out of my stupor, knowing he'll make good on his threat to make a bonfire of the place in an urban sacrifice if I admit to what I thought I saw, real or not.

"I'm tired," I defend, though that part isn't a lie. I did get lost, after all, and I am exhausted. I don't know if he buys it, but he doesn't push me for more.

His touch disappears, leaving me cold and achy, like I've had a sudden hit of the flu. Turning my back to the space that haunts me, I get in the car, but my gaze keeps drifting to the place between the house and the garden. No one emerges from the flittering shadows that move with the sunlight, not even the house staff who are conspicuous in their absence after their silent display of solidarity earlier.

The boys' conversation swells around me on the drive back to Alchem. I'm grateful I'm not required join.

Less than ten minutes into the drive, Zeke snakes his hand out to cover mine, the rough kiss of his callouses against the back of my knuckles a reminder of our different worlds. His hand is that much larger than mine, encompassing my fingers and wrist in its entirety. His thumb presses to my pulse point and rests there. He doesn't try to rub or anything, holding on.

I let him and don't pull away the entire drive back to the academy except for a few minutes where we stop for fuel and supplies, and to swap out drivers or for bathroom breaks. It's close to midnight when we return to Alchem. The boys stay at the bottom of my building, letting me walk up to my room alone when I push for space under the caveat I'd turn on my lights the moment I get there and wave from my window.

They all stand there in the darkness below, illuminated on one side by the coach lamps along the side of the building. There's no path, and beyond their silhouettes the rest of the school grounds provides a muted dark glow all the way to the boundary fence.

Elen lights up his phone, waving it like a fallen star.

Nyx shoves his hands into his pockets and tips his head back to howl at the moon.

Zeke is back to his usual form and glares up at my window with his mouth set in a hard line. His face is set in harsh relief in the limed glow from Elen's phone like he wants to smash the device apart with his bare hands.

And of them all, I feel the absence of the fourth most. When I wave back and blow a kiss on impulse, they drift away with waves or not, and my phone blows up, one by one.

Elen: **Lock your door, Roxy girl. You attract too many stalkers.**

Nyx: **(nightstarMP4)**

I hit the file and music fills the room, a soft lullaby I know he wrote the night we were at the boulder.

Zeke: **Night Roxy. Sleep tight. I'll kill any bed bugs that bite.**

I smile, stripping off my clothes when the edges tighten and nip into my skin, wishing they were bedbugs and Zeke was here to exterminate them all while Nyx's lullaby plays on repeat. I lock the door and send Elen a picture as proof.

He's quick to reply with a blue heart back as a reward.

I save the message along with Nyx's music, though my mind drifts back to Zeke.

The memory of his touch brings on a whole new level of confusion mingled with all the non-emotion and overwhelm of today. I dart into the bathroom and slam the door shut until it rattles in its frame. My foot flings out to catch the canvas tucked behind the door. But there's nothing there, or at least, not enough left to topple.

The painting of Aster that matches the blond specter of him I saw at my Aunt's house as we left, wearing his customary chains that caught my eye, whether by fate or design, is knifed to pieces.

Chapter Twenty

His Master's Dog

Zeke

"I saw you at the property."

I keep my eyes shut, unwilling to stare at my best friend through a cloud of durry and pot smoke, the mix heady enough to leave me wanting to cough up my whiskey. I swallow the need and inhale a lungful, ending up hacking the organ out onto the floor.

Somewhere in the midst of the jumbled haze Aster laughs at me.

"I decided to stalk my ex. Add that to my list of crimes."

Yeah, sure. I'll keep a list.

I take the refreshed glass of whiskey he offers, knowing I'm doing it all in the wrong order and down it anyway. What's one more headache on a hangover of epic proportions waiting for me tomorrow? I'll be in a shit mood and I know in advance who I'll be taking it out on.

A girl with eyes the color of sin and ash. That's what Roxy does for me. She chips away at the world until I focus on one thing.

Managing to catch a breath, I take the joint Aster offers, inhaling a deep draw and finish the damn thing. Why not?

"Why were you there?" I push back the urge to search his room for snacks.

I know he keeps them around just as I know if I eat too much of his junkie shit I'll put on weight that I'll end up working off again. The kind of weight that ends up with me beating on him in the ring and feeling like shit come tomorrow. I glance at my watch, but I can't read the time.

"What do you mean?" Aster's fading on me fast, but it's the one way he can sleep sometimes, damn insomniac ass.

His evasion earns him a glare through the permitting haze filling his dorm room. "You were there. You tell me."

Smoke twists into a tarnished halo over his pale head. "She managed with the lawyer better than I thought. I thought he'd snowball her."

"I assume you're not talking about exchanging sexual favors."

He returns my critical expression. Admirable, when half my face is numb. "Don't be disgusting. He's at least three times her age."

"I don't think dirty old men care." *Your father is a prime example. Like half the staff here.*

"Moving on." He taps his fingers on the arm of his chair, looking more like his father every day.

I bite back that comment, not wanting to wake up dead or with the knife at my throat. My head tips back and my back hits his mattress. The hell did that happen? I stare at the ceiling above the bed draped in navy silk so dark it's almost black. My stomach can't deal with the endless void above that leaves me in an eternal freefall. I clench to hold back bile that coats my pallet as my brain tries returning to the conversation. "Yeah, she took it well. I mean, she lost you, and the aunt she ducking hated. The parents she didn't." My mouth runs on. Is this what being Roxy feels like? Her words fall out all the damn time.

Aster stops stimming on the corner of the bed. His fingers still the moment I mention her. "She didn't want to come here."

"Man, her family is dead." I don't know how to

push this through his head. Just because he'd love it if his remaining parent fell off the face of the earth doesn't mean everyone feels that way. "Have a conversation with ex-girlfriend, for duck's sake."

"She doesn't want me."

I don't need to look at him to know he's shaking his head, his arms wrapped around his bent knees.

"Yeah, well. There's a lot of that going around." Plenty of days Roxy won't talk to me either, though that's for other reasons.

"Did you do it?" The question drops out of my mouth. Roxy's contagious. I roll over to face him, waiting for an answer that's never coming.

Aster ignores me, sliding off the bed. His footsteps cross the room. A cabinet opens, a glass top is pulled off a decanter. Cold glass fills my hand as he folds my fingers around the fresh drink. "Last one," he murmurs. The bed depresses, heat settling beside me.

I prop myself up against his pillow, lean back on my elbows, and consider downing the drink in one. Not that I need anything else. I'll be lucky if I don't hurl everything up in the next hour, considering it's the most expensive liquor he has.

When Aster is in his most morose mood, this is the shit he always drags out. Something about tossing back a two-thousand-dollar glass of whiskey to showcase the waste sits dandy with me tonight, what with funerals and FBI and wondering who killed ducking who. But it would be a waste and he still won't tell me the answer I want to know.

"Why were you there?" I change my question, staring into the bottom of the glass obscured by the golden liquid.

Aster shifts beside me but doesn't drink. "I wanted to make sure she was okay. Isn't that why you follow her around?"

"You told me to."

"Is that all?" He huffs out a breath. "I am not your keeper."

"You could be."

"I'm your brother."

We finish our glasses in silence. Aster rests back against the bed's headboard beside me. Eyes closed, he looks like an angel with his high cheekbones and perfect, blond hair. It's the sort of face anyone would want to be born with. The wealth, the position. All the things on the surface that people crave.

His chest rises and falls in a slower rhythm. I slide the crystal cut from his fingers and place the empty glass on his bedside table, pulling the cover over his clothed body. "Good night," I murmur as I sweep long, pale strands away from his eyes.

His answer is soft snores as I turn my glass in my hands, watching the dregs of the overpriced liquor cling to the edges.

"Did you do it?" I ask the stilled room again, knowing I'll receive the same answer as before.

His breathing deepens as I slide onto the covers next to him, resting my hand against his ribs so I can close my eyes, knowing his heart still beats. Unlike everyone else, I don't need his words to justify his actions.

Roxy is as safe with Aster Craven as she is with me.

Chapter Twenty-One

Cookies + Cream + Desperation

Roxy

Less than forty-eight hours have passed since my aunt was interred and I took on Pyric Industries, though it seems much longer. Rhani chatters away at the back of my head as I unpack the things the boys stopped and got for me on the way back to Alchem Academy. Milk for our small fridge I didn't need, instant coffee I could inhale with a spoon at this point. Nyx provided that, his own hands trembling as he passed the unbranded bag across to the front seat that remained mine for the entire return journey.

Lip gloss in his signature blue/silver is from Elen, and not because he wants us to match. He spent the minutes after we stopped, before I headed up to my room rubbing my knuckles with cream, telling me I needed to look after myself. Not that I have any idea where he pulled moisturizer from on demand, though his jacket must have endless pockets.

A new shirt is my gift from Zeke bearing a slice of dripping watermelon that's … smiling.

I stare at the array of presents, knowing there's no receipt in the bag, and that the boys lifted everything from the small store they stopped at for fuel on the way back to the academy. They went into it one at a time like a cache of thieves with a master plan.

Thus, they did have one, and this was it.

My throat clogs as Rhani stops talking. Silence fills the room. I guess it's my turn, but I haven't been listening and have nothing to say anyway.

"How did it go?" she asks when the silence stretches into infinity.

I shrug, not bothering to open my mouth.

She waits a full second before firing the next comment at me. "Did you see him?"

I swallow the burning answer she craves and toss the things back in the bag, then pull the coffee and the t-shirt back out again. Yeah, the spoon option sounds good. Who needs sleep, anyway? I'm sure there's a canvas about somewhere. Oh wait, that's right. Aster ruined them.

Asshat.

The tears that held back for hours threaten now.

Rhani's arms wrap around my throat, cutting off those, and my air. I'm kinda relieved on both fronts.

"I'm glad he was sweet to you." She grabs the shirt and taps the bleeding watermelon. *Not dripping.* The damn thing is a murder scene. How did I not pick that out the first time? But she's right, it's very Zeke. "You don't need more crap. Up," she commands, grabbing the hem of my shirt and tugging.

That draws a laugh from me as we both know the stupid school issue uniforms don't stretch, lift, or pull, unbuttoning straight down the front. I battle the top for a second and manage until I'm bamboozled by the stupid little tie looped around my neck.

Rhani tuts as she undoes the bow with deft fingers. "There. Now you get to breathe," she proclaims, giving me half a second to take said breath before she stuffs me into the watermelon tee. "You look more like a murder scene happened than what did." She gives me a kind smile that hurts.

It freaking hurts.

No one should be that sweet. Not to me when all day I've been with people who cared and felt ... nothing.

My hair wraps around my face, obscuring the world as my head pops through the hole. I come up gasping for air. "Does everyone know?"

"Know you left today and that all the boys went with you?" Her head tilts to the side.

I breathe out. "Yeah." I manage a smile. "That."

"Or that Aster tore out of here like the devil called him home after you?"

My smile slips. "That."

"Yeah. That." Her expression is laced with pity. "They know, Roxy."

That last burst of sympathy is too much. The boys had it. The freaking lawyer had it. The staff girl I scared the crap out of even looked like she felt sorry for me. But from my roommate, it's one thing too much.

The FBI man with his fake offering and the card I let fall to the graveyard ground and all his fake, fake, fakeness.

The one person who didn't try to offer me sympathy was Aster. I want his brand of anger, hate, and nothingness more than anything. And I'm the one who pushed him away.

Which is why I take out my frustration, fear, and rage on the person who has given me unending support since the day she arrived.

"Is that because you told them?" I snap.

Rhani blows out a long breath and surveys me with her regular face. "No, it's not," she says.

My defenses fold. "I'm sorry," I whisper. "I'm a duckhole."

Stupid, stupid ducks.

Her arms wind around me. "Your family is gone. The last part, whether you loved them or not," she adds, forestalling my argument.

"I didn't get a chance to try to love her."

"But you wouldn't have anyway, cause you know, she was the Angry Aunt."

I grin. "True."

Rhani smiles back. "Good?"

"Yeah. Better." I hold up the coffee. "Spoon?"

She wrinkles her nose. "Uh, sure. If that's what you wanna do. I'll be back. Do *not* start your party without me, 'kay?" She shoots me a hard glance like I'm untrustworthy to the max and dashes out the door.

I stifle a laugh, clutching my glass jar of instant coffee like a prize. It's bigger than I could ever have afforded back at home before Alchem Academy, and would never have considered stealing.

The boys are their own limit.

My phone buzzes. I scrounge beneath the pile of bags, things, and school uniform for the device.

Elen: **Tell me you're wearing my lip balm. Don't wanna kiss cracked lips.**

A little emoji of a volcano accompanies the message in the group chat.

Nyx: **Started on the coffee yet?**

Zeke: **Wearing my shirt? I want a picture.**

Elen: **Me too.**

Zeke: **Copycat.**

I can almost hear the two of them going at it in my head. Elen chattering, Zeke growling. Nyx watching the pair while they fight.

Roxy: **Not yet to the coffee. It's coming. Yes to the shirt. About to do the lip balm.**

I uncap the lip stain, not caring I'm about to paint my lips as blue as my eyes, and toss my hair over my shoulder for a selfie. I smile and take another on a spur of the moment, throw my hair back off my face, bleeding watermelon front and center, and flip the camera off.

Then I hit send before I can have sender's remorse.

Zeke: **Classy.**

Elen: **I think I'm in love.**
Nyx: **(Morningstar MP4)**

I laugh until that last file scrolls up. I hit the clickable link to open it.

The conversation we had the night at the boulder fills my room. But it's not just our conversation. Nyx has taken the night sounds and copied them over the words until they form their own strange melody, almost stream-like. Tantric.

My laugh dies as I listen, remembering. How cold I was sitting there with him. How alone, until I wasn't. Then he was beside me, me hearing him talk. Learning his truth.

Seeing how he views the world.

But I hadn't seen anything. Because this … is something different. Beyond anything I thought I knew. And I'm not the only one who understands.

Zeke: **Holy shit. You ripped that out.**
Elen: **Awe, man.**
Roxy: **Ditto all of the above.**
Roxy: **It's beautiful. Thank you.**
Nyx:**...**
Nyx: **Didn't mean to send that to everyone.**
Nyx: **Soz.**
Nyx has left the chat.
Elen: **Duck. I'll go handle that.**
Zeke: **Probably best if I don't.**

My stomach drops the moment Nyx runs, though I have to laugh at Zeke's comment.

Roxy: **Bang on, dude. Have a good night.**
Zeke: **Yeah, I'll get right on that. (rolling eye emoji)**

I laugh again, knowing they'll both be on Nyx's case, no matter what Zeke says. Elen's silence speaks for itself. I roll over onto my back, close the file, and find

Rhani standing in the middle of the room, her eyes wide.

"What was that?" she whispers, her voice carrying the sort of awe Elen threw up in the chat the moment Nyx told everyone sent the file by mistake.

I bite my lip, knowing how private Nyx is with his work. "You can't tell anyone," I say. "He didn't mean for anyone else to hear it."

"But it's beautiful," she objects, pausing at the foot of my bed with a four-gallon tub of cookies and cream ice cream in her hands. "How can he not share that?"

"You *can't*," I stress, my chest closing as she keeps staring at me. "Tell me you didn't record that."

She shakes her head, bemused. "No. Wish I had. But, no."

"Good." I pull out the coffee. "Forget you heard it, or you don't get any." I wave the crappy instant about like it's millionaire cake.

She manages to hold back her snort and pops the ice cream lid. "Your wish is my command." She sweeps out an arm, producing two mismatched spoons as if by magic and offers me the larger one.

I stare at the big spoon suspiciously. "Why do I get that one?"

"Because you have the greater need." She taps the coffee jar with the back of her spoon. "Bottoms up."

I crack the seal on the jar and stick my nose in. "Oh, my God. That's the best scent in the world."

"Better than cookies and cream?" I raise my eyes to find her nose wrinkled. "I doubt it."

"I have coffee."

"I have ice cream. And parfait glasses." Out of nowhere, like the socials magician she professes to be, Rhani extracts a folding table, a pair of collapsible plastic parfait glasses, and a small bottle of salted caramel whiskey.

I see where she's going with this. "You're a genius."

"Now she realizes." Rhani gives a theatrical groan. "Did someone say sleep?"

"Who needs it?"

Last time I did something like this I ended up rocking a three-day hangover, and painted a wall of this same room a hideous black and red with the previous Rhani tenant who then stabbed me in the back.

But we didn't have crappy coffee.

I dig into the tub of glorious treats and echo her words from before.

"Bottoms up."

****

The coffee does its job to perfection and beyond. Four hours later, Rhani snores with her aqua satin eye mask askew on her face while my hands shake and my stomach aches.

Not in the same way as it did back when I saw Aster at my aunt's house. Or when I found his portrait slashed in my bathroom.

Or when Nyx left the chat that's been silent ever since.

All through our impromptu girls' night while we emptied the coffee jar, whiskey, and ice cream bucket before it could melt, I kept an eye on my phone.

The chat never blew up once. Not a single message.

I figure that means the boys are off consoling Nyx in their own way, which isn't too dissimilar to my and Rhani's anti-celebration, albeit without the ice cream.

Which means they're occupied, Rhani is out, and I'm awake.

And one person is left out of it all.

Aster.

Ex. Bully. Stalker.

He has a hundred poignant titles that run through my mind, and I refuse to give any of them more screen time than they deserve. My hands tremble as I trace his name on my phone. Before I can work through the consequences of what's a stupid, *stupid* decision—I mean, it's prior to midnight after contraband whiskey that leaves my mouth tasting of ash and stale cookies—I slip off my bed and out into the hallway.

The door closes behind me with a soft thud after I flick the lock. No point in rubbing my stupid off on Rhani when all she's done is support me in every step of this venture. The corridor is empty. No one else seems to be awake at this hour and if they are, Alchem's rules keeps them ensconced away behind locked doors. Like I should be.

Shoving my key deep in my pocket, I traipse downstairs, unwilling to call the elevator with its hellish *ding* that's loud enough to rouse several floors. At the bottom level, the dorm building door lets me out with no resistance. I slip into the night air and wrap my arms around myself, my shivers reminiscent of the school snow trip.

For a second, I sink into the memory of hot soup, fireplaces, and talking with the boys. What came after hurts too much to ruminate on. I throw the daydream away, wrapping myself in cold tendrils that slip beneath my watermelon tee and Alchem skirt and etch their mark on my skin.

My trip across campus is silent and unaccosted. I keep expecting Zeke to emerge from the shadows, full of rage as usual, but he's not around, either. Like a normal person, he's locked in bed, snoring as loud as his sister.

The thought gives me the giggles. I'm halfway

through a stand of Sequoias the school has hidden from the rest of the world, lost in my head, before I realize I've missed my mark.

Aster prowls between the shadows like he's a part of them, never stepping into the filtered light that separates Yuleton's glow in the distance to the school's residual light.

None of it seems to stick to him, and it takes me another moment to figure out he's not pacing about in a randomized pattern. He holds his phone to his ear, pressed to the side of his blond head with enough force to push it inside his brain. Each step is harder than the last as he rounds the next formidable tree.

I sink into the building's shade, pressing to the wall, but he's too focused on his conversation that I can't hear to notice me.

When he does speak, my mind almost explodes.

"Dad, I can't keep—" He starts, pauses, and kicks at exposed dirt beneath one of the trees. A clod of soil explodes over the toe of his high gloss, leather shoes that are always pristine. I've never seen them otherwise. "Fine," he snaps in response to whatever his dad must have said on the other end, pushing the single word through gritted teeth. "Alonso. It'll be done, like any of your other lackeys."

He hangs up and slams the device screen first against the tree's thick trunk. The crack reverberates through the night as I slink back toward the corner, my head whirling.

He calls his father by his first name?

The father who hates me. The father who asked him to get me kicked off Alchem premises before I even started here.

Who knew I'd attend the school before I did.

This was a poor choice.

I back up, but it's too late to escape notice of the devil's offspring.

"You're a terrible stalker, Roxy," Aster calls from his place in the shadows.

He leans forward enough for the light to fall on the chains at his neck, crooking a finger in my direction.

Like some pathetic piece of prey drawn to its predator, my feet move without permission.

Toward him.

My mouth dries, and I shake my head. "I wasn't looking for—" The lie sticks in my throat, refusing to budge farther.

Aster surveys me with amusement. "Anything else you want to lie to me about, Roxy?" he breathes when I'm within touching distance.

I shake my head. "Nothing. I couldn't sleep." I shrug the throw away comment off like this always happens.

Fib number two.

We both know I can fall asleep at the drop of a hat. Or hand through my hair. More specifically, *his* hand in my hair.

His lips don't twitch as I lie straight to his face. I miss his easy humor from before. But I'm not scared like I was when he spoke to his father, before he caught my stalker duck butt. Talking with him now is just … Aster.

He closes the distance a fraction, reducing the breathable night air, though the temperature doesn't change at all. "I remember one night when you couldn't sleep." His hand raises and brushes the air beside my face in a ghostish touch. He drops it again before he makes contact, leaving me yearning for something I'd forgotten I missed.

Lie number three.

The skin around his eyes tightens. Perhaps we

share the angst of that one.

Who is the bully here?

But that has always been the question between us. Aster, forced to push me away by his father. Me, retaliating when I refused to be his prey.

His teeth flash pale as he bares them beneath the shadows.

Nothing has changed, then.

"I remember you stayed," I whisper, giving him too much ammunition to hurt me later, but I don't care about anything more than this moment.

How we are right now.

His mouth twists as he leans in. For an insane second, I think he'll kiss me, and I welcome the brush of his cold mouth against mine. But he stops a breath away, and his smile is lit by pure hate.

"Do you still try to hurt yourself, Roxy? Small, pathetic little marks that never help?"

A slight smile accompanies his words, but his breath is the one thing that touches me as I struggle to inhale.

Then he's gone, leaving me in the middle of the shadows and trees, the night air, and my pain as my companions.

JOSS PHOENIX

Chapter Twenty-Two

The Hate We Share

Aster

Hurting Roxy Quell shouldn't feel so good.

But it does, because hurting her stops me from feeling what I've transferred across to her. Bully I was born to be. I revel in the way her eyes widen, an echo of the way my heart shreds before it returns to a dull ache as I drag my sorry ass away from her prettier one without touching her before I do something stupid I can't take back.

Like kiss her, and never let her go.

Fall to my knees and beg for forgiveness for every damn thing I've said and done this year to hurt her.

Tell her how much I love her.

Instead, I force my feet to step one before the next until I lean my palm against the cold surface of my door situated next to Zeke's. Snores reverberate through the cracks around his door that annoy the rest of the dorm floor, though I've always taken comfort in knowing he's there. He'd have a fit if he knew I'd been wandering about campus without him, understanding what he does about my father's not-so future intentions.

Not that I'm close to turning my majority and inheriting my mother's wealth yet. I have a few more years left to enjoy tormenting tiny things and hearing them cry. Part of me wants to taste her tears. The other half needs to run back to her and bury my face in her hair.

A sickened noise rises in my throat. I shove my door open and shut it behind me before anyone else can witness my shame. My hands are on the buttons of my shirt, undoing them in order as I ignore my phone vibrating in my pocket and head for my en suite.

The privacies given to Alchem students is both a boon and a nightmare.

Beneath my mirror sits a neat row of razors, each edge sharp, most used this year. The face that stares back at me in the mirror wears hollow eyes I struggle to recognize for the hatred emanating back at me. Chains glitter around the strange man's neck, hiding the ink I put there when I first learned to tattoo. Hiding scars my father marred my skin with first, covering the person I shouldn't be but am anyway.

My melancholy heightens as I roll back my sleeves to the elbow without taking my shirt off, exposing the neat lines I showed Roxy that night I first came to her room, knowing she'd try to do what I did. One day, if not right then.

Knowing she might not be able to stop.

How addictive each cut can be.

Pain on pain. Numbness that follows.

The precise row of scars she touched that night— the single person I've let touch me like that, hell the lone person who's ever *seen* them apart from Zeke—have additions for every time I've hurt her.

From the day I shredded her heart back at the ski trip.

It seems an age ago, though it's been months. Maybe two? The weeks merge in my head as I collect the last blade and move the next in row along like a silver caterpillar. It should make me sick, but the process is familiar, calming.

Close to the crook of my elbow I depress the skin, keeping the ends of the cut aligned with the rest in the row. As the blood flows, the ache in my heart eases. Lightness settles over me and the need to—*scream my throat raw, rip my skin from my bones, call her, end us both*—settles into something dull and manageable.

It'll be back, that insanity, but for now, it's nothing more than a side worry.

I bind the break in my skin, clean the tool, and erase evidence of everything that happened tonight. Then I lie back on my bed, stare up at the inside of the midnight material that hides the bland ceiling from view, and wait for dawn to come.

My wakeful hours are full of a numbness that's as addictive as the pain. So serene I can almost sleep.

****

A black and blue card marked with Brian Gallaway's title and the hour twirls between my fingers as I approach the principal's door four minutes before I'm due. It's enough time that I know the slovenly Alchem Academy head will still be dressing down his previous appointment. I hasten my step to get this done.

God alone knows what he wants from me, but after a less than insomniac night, I'm prepared for battle. I rap my knuckles once against his door and poke my head in before he has a chance to answer, just to be a dick. It's that sort of mood. I avoided breakfast, preferring my own company before I imploded in public.

Zeke will be more furious than ever by the time he finds me, and I hope Roxy doesn't wear the brunt of his ire as I peer through the dim lighting at the balding principal's desk.

Sitting on Gallaway's desk, side on to me, is a girl I think is Roxy for less than a nanosecond before I realize it can't be her. Dark hair rests across pale skin, too pale, her body too thin. I know what fear looks on Roxy's sweet face, and this girl isn't her.

Roxy is the last thing on my mind.

My breath stalls as I take in the girl's downcast eyes, her pale skin. The way she's motionless to prevent any attention drawn her way. In this cesspit I could have told her it won't work. Her brown hair drapes around her face to disguise her shame, her legs pulled apart over the corner of the desk.

And Gallaway's hand between her thighs leaves me sicker on the inside more than anything that I've done to Roxy myself.

My brain kicks in as I memorize everything I see. "Sorry to disturb you, sir," I murmur, shutting the door to conceal the side profile of what the head of school does to his student, her face unwilling.

Swallowing back disgust and bile, I open a group chat, the one that we use without Roxy when needed.

Right now, it's needed. If she saw what I did, God knows what she'd do. Even I want to slam my fist through the paedo's face, but this has to be dealt with at a higher level.

One post is enough. The photo I send through blows the group chat up, and in seconds my hand vibrates as—*Faith,* I recognize her from my last trip to Gallaway's office—emerges from the principal's office.

I angle my body to side on from Gallaway and turn my head so he can't read my lips as I catch her too-slim elbow in a firm grasp. "How long?"

She doesn't so much as start at the contact, but the terrified eyes raised to mine tells me everything I need to know. Inside my head I'm swearing as she pulls free and trips away down the corridor. One of her friends—Donovan Lytham, I pull the jock's name from the dregs of my memory as we don't reside in the same social circle in the slightest—steps away from the wall farther down and holds his arms out.

My eyes narrow as he cradles her fragile, bird-like frame to him. But instead of being intent on her like he should be, his gaze never leaves mine.

If he knows what the hell is going on, why isn't

he doing anything about it?

Answer: The same reason why I didn't step in and land Principal Gallaway on his ass.

Because student I am. Even with all the money in the world behind me, I don't have that kind of power within these walls.

Built on lies and deception, Gallaway has spent years collecting all sorts of filthy secrets to cover his own ass. We started noticing months ago, Elen and me, and Zeke clued in within days afterward. Who knows how long the principal has been ferreting away information about the world's wealthiest and their conglomerate offspring. Not for the first time I wonder that having us all jam packed into one place isn't a good thing. His is a smart strategy, and I understand now with a flash of clarity why he needs that security protocol.

A second later, my teeth grind as I drop my head, my path unclear. A single misstep here, and Roxy could be his next target. How close in looks she and Faith are doesn't escape my attention. Though my inaction—for this moment, but not in the long term—sickens me. I can't skip the meeting, or me and mine will shoot to the top of the principal's shit list.

Turning my phone off, I shove it deep into my pocket and slip into Gallaway's office, letting the door close behind me. "Sorry for the delay, sir." My voice and face stay emotionless, as always. My mask is handy today in keeping the distance I've always maintained from everyone. If I change anything now, I'll have nothing left when I need to pull out a dire threat.

Besides, a part of me wants to see how this plays out.

The principal's bug eyes follow my path across his office. "Sit down, Mr. Craven," Gallaway says, still fixing his pants, for fuck's sake.

"In here?" I cast a disdainful look around the sparse room, its once richly appointed fixtures showing signs of decay in every corner, now that I take notice. The faded, threadbare drapes pulled tight across the window. Cracked leather of his high-backed chair. The scarred desk that's seen more occupants than the student seat on my side. "I think I'll stand," I say.

"Of course you do," he scoffs, a derogatory smile on his lips. "Don't mind my little indiscretion." He waves a reddened, sweaty looking hand in my direction.

I incline my head as though the entire interaction bores me, willing my heartbeat to slow the hell down, my blood to cool and not shred him on the spot. Thanks to many nights practicing this exact reaction opposite another desk in my father's home, I manage to control my darker needs roiling beneath the surface, keeping them as hidden as the neat row of scars beneath my Alchem blazer.

And that's it.

He moves onto talking about my father's investment in a new well-being center for students. My father, invested in any student's well-being? It's another measure of control in this place where I have another eighteen months to survive. I'm not sure why he's intent on spending here when his business is farther away from the west coast.

I've never quite understood why he sent me to California, but I've always welcomed the break. Until now, when I want to gather the family I've created here and get them the hell away from the pale, self-indulgent demon squished behind his desk. Part of me wants to rip the drapes apart to see if his wormish form will wither and burn under the sun's radiation.

My lips twitch as I banish my violent thoughts from my face. "Why did you want to see me?"

Gallaway fixes red-rimmed eyes on me. A similar colored line runs from beneath his nose to his lip. "I presume your father taught how to run a business, Mister Craven."

I recognize the chastisement as he attempts to dress me down. Gallaway's outclassed, and I don't care.

"He did. Why would I have anything to do with someone like you?" I throw back in an idle voice.

Gallaway's face purples.

Message received.

"You think I don't have enough to do with corralling overprivileged students here?" he seethes, pushing his chair away from his desk and fixing his belt.

I force my breaths to stay shallow and slow, as though I can't be bothered to do more, and raise my eyes to his face, wondering if he'll catch the slip when my hand fists at my side.

If he sees me as one of the cohort of the lazy and the spoiled my father is no doubt a part of in his mind, then perhaps he won't see the threat laid out before him.

Gallaway's lip pulls back to expose yellowed teeth. "I believe your girlfriend is in possession of a significant portion of the country's wealth."

My breath hitches without my permission.

I need a smoke.

Saliva pools in the back of my throat. "I don't much care." I study my nails. "We broke up weeks ago. School ski trip. Is there anything else?"

He stares at me. "If you cease to be helpful, my eyes will fall on Roxy. I'm sure she's free now, without your … protection."

Gallaway's knowing smile douses me head to toe in a cold deluge, my skin prickling every part of me, except for my scars.

His fingers rub small circles on the ruined desktop

in a patch of something I can't tear my eyes away from. The vision of Roxy in Faith's place dims my vision as my hands tremble. I'll do anything to protect her from this man.

He's unworthy of bearing the title.

I break posture for the first time.

Gallaway watches me with eager eyes as I circle his chair and begin massaging his shoulders.

"My father taught me many things." Tight muscles layered beneath the heavyset man's shirt bead with instant sweat. "How to read a man. He taught me how to understand their needs. Their ... fetishes. And..." I click my tongue near his ear. "All the worst things a man can do. Want. Need." I lean down, whispering. "Someone like you." I run my fingers along his vertebrae, counting soft enough for him to hear.

"What are you doing?"

I smile, still counting as I clasp my hands around the principal's thick throat, palms up, and flick sideways in a light, undamaging touch.

He flinches anyway.

I step around his chair, facing the dripping man with my back to his door. "My father taught me many skills, Mr. Gallaway. He also taught me how to negotiate."

Gifting the principal, whose neck I could have snapped with my bare hands but instead handed him back his worthless life in trade for keeping his hands off Roxy, a cold smile, I slip out of his office and turn my phone on.

Elen: **Is that—**

Zeke: **If he touches Roxy, I'll kill him.**

I scroll through the messages and hundreds of lines of comments, all the same ranty shit. I get it; the same stuff overpopulates my head. Nyx is absent.

Frowning, I switch chats. Heading to the other one that Roxy is in that she thinks she banned me from but hasn't. I scroll through that, starting at the top.

What a mess that fast became last night when I was off moping. My thumb brushes over Nyx's lullaby before his silent exodus. I should've started at the end.

I swear, my feet already moving as I head toward my room. Zeke beats me there. As predicted, his face is white with fury, scarred hands trembling as he crushes his phone between his palms. Breath hisses between his teeth, but nothing else comes out.

"I spoke with Gallaway," I start in an even voice, proud that it doesn't shake half as much as Zeke's hands, though mine tried to earlier.

"What punishment did you cook up?" My best friend's strides never falter as he keeps coming at me.

I don't move, holding his gaze.

"Castration?" Elen asks, as he rounds the corner, already talking.

My lips roll back to bare my teeth. "Incarceration. Maybe a little wet work."

"Always good to start at the top." Zeke doesn't miss a beat.

I nod as they fall into step beside me. "Tell me about Nyx."

JOSS PHOENIX

Chapter Twenty-Three

All Fall Together

Roxy

On Wednesday, a week after I confronted Aster, the cafeteria ran out of sushi. *Watercress and water chestnut salad it is, then.* I've become attached to first world problems in short order.

I should have known then it heralded a bad day/week, but as always, the boys and Rhani managed to distract me.

"Look at you, all cozy with the Elite." Amelia tilts her perfect, blonde head to one side as her gaze sweeps across the table. Rhani huffs, but the newcomer's gaze lands on ... me?

I shrug and toy with a pickle. "Cozy as can be." The stupid words fall out of my mouth.

Zeke stares at me, and he gets a shrug too, albeit a tiny one.

"Maybe you're sitting at the wrong table, then." Amelia twirls her hair and plucks out her cherry red phone that matches her cherry red Ferrari she arrived in on the first day and flipped me off from. She's also got a range of matching lollipops.

"Whatever, Melly. Don't you sit, you know, somewhere over there?" Elen leans back and waves at the corner of the room.

Rhani snickers, lining her phone up to film the whole thing live while I try to sink into my chair and disappear.

Zeke glances across at me and I freeze in place, the warning in his gaze evident. *Move and you're ash.*

I choose life.

"I thought you'd like an invite to somewhere

better, is all." Amelia flips her hair again, rubs matching lip gloss on her puffy lips that have to be enhanced with her middle finger aimed right at Rhani's phone, and smiles at me, kind of genuine, which is weird. "Let me know."

I blink after her as her cherry duckbutt departs, leaving us in silence.

Rhani stops filming and clicks her tongue. "That was so disappointing. I'll have to do an apology live later for whatever the duck that was," she mutters.

"That felt … weird," I mutter, still staring after Amelia.

"Or right," Elen adds, holding up two fingers for an air high-five.

I pretend to tap his fingers with a watery grin. "Uh, sure?" I mean, how many times can my world change in a semester? The thought of losing the group around me leaves me as chilled as my salad. Never have I missed sushi so much in my life.

"Have you heard from Agent Dick?" Zeke asks, ignoring the drama llamas and digging into his burger.

I swear the boy eats nothing else. Maybe some onion rings.

"I thought you were on a duck ban." I flick him with a piece of watercress from my salad that I'm not going to eat anyway.

"I did say duck." The watercress, a little worse for wear, floats back in my direction.

"Liar."

He shrugs off my accusation and turns his attention to Elen, speaking through a mouthful of food. "Hear from your stalker fans again?"

Rhani shakes her head in disgust. "Glad you're my brother. I'd hate to have to try to weed you out of the potential gene pool."

He flips her off without looking.

"Have you heard from Adam?" I ask Rhani as the boys break up, arguing about something on Elen's phone. I glance over at him, smiling, but he catches my eyes and ducks his head, avoiding me. My smile turns down to a frown.

What's up with that?

"He's messaged a few times. I need you to make sure Zeke is busy tomorrow," Rhani murmurs under her breath, sending a sunny smile and a one-fingered salute her brother's way when he glances up.

I glance between them, my stomach clenching. I'm all for backing my girl up, but lying straight to Zeke's face doesn't sit well with me. Still...

Hope fills Rhani's pretty face. *Duck it.*

"Okay, I'll cover," I say around a mouthful of my salad that sticks in my throat when I try to swallow.

"Thanks," she mumbles, already on her phone and she dings messages off.

I bite my lip and study my plate. The salad refuses to go down. Pushing myself up from the table, I throw my bag over my shoulder where it catches a nerve or something that pinches. The wince that follows is the insuppressible sort, and Zeke is on his feet in a second.

"What'd you say to her?" he barks at Rhani, one hand extended to halt my progress.

She snaps back at him with some sassy remark that infuriates him further, making it that much easier for me to dodge his lunge. He swears, no ducks harmed this time, as I dart out of the cafeteria doors.

Short pants leave my chest as I make it around the next corner and find an empty corridor. My back presses to the cold wall. I close my eyes, taking a precious second. If Zeke finds out whatever I agreed to, he'll shave me in my sleep.

Or not in my sleep.

"Roxanna Queel?"

I wince and crack an eyelid at the disgruntled looking senior who stares at me, a blue and black card extended between his fingers like he doesn't want to touch it.

"What's this?" I make no move to take the card that feels like impending doom on an already duck filled day, and I'm fresh out of quackers.

"Your appointment." He thrusts the card at my chest when I refuse to take it and walks away.

I stare at the dark card that tumbles to my stomach without trying to catch it, the whole situation too reminiscent of the graveyard the day of my aunt's funeral and the FBI agent's card.

Didn't Zeke bring this up?

Gravity takes hold, and the card slips to the floor. Two long, slim fingers pick it up.

"You've been summoned." Elen twirls the card in his hands, and it disappears from sight. A strained smile, not his usual, flirtatious rockstar one, decorates his aquiline face. "You don't have to go."

"Go where?" I frown at him. "What's going on?"

He shrugs, rolling his neck. It's a very Zeke movement, and I'm more than suspicious. I also know from past experience that the rockstar won't tell me anything until he's ready. Sighing, I poke an elbow into his ribs for recompense. Hey, a girl has to get her ducks somewhere, right?

Elen doubles over, but it's all farce as he pokes me back and it's *on*. Fingers, giggles, and a little saliva flies as we attack each other, ending with his long arms wrapped around me, and my back pressed to his front.

Breathless, I struggle for a second, but I've got nowhere to go. "Mercy?" I plead, as his fingers settle on my waist.

Instead of digging in, they squeeze. "Maybe," he murmurs in my ear, letting me go.

I blink, sliding my arms around my middle in a one-person hug to replace the warmth I lose when he backs off. "Okay?"

He sends me a lopsided grin that's more my Elen and toys with his tongue ring. "You, Roxy girl, have an appointment to keep. It's cool. You've got company."

I bite back a million questions and go for the most toddler-esque one that suits my mood best. "Why?"

Again, I'm on the receiving end of one of those enigmatic looks I can't decipher.

"You shouldn't be alone."

The penny drops. "Aster," I snap, whirling away.

I make it a full four steps before I realize Elen isn't beside me. The corners of my lips curve up in a stupid smile. Maybe I've broken through his facade? I turn back to find him standing in the middle of the corridor, watching me relaxed as all get out, hands tucked into his pockets. His uniform is rumpled in a casual-but-not-intentional way, and he looks all rockstar sexy, like he woke up that way.

The smallest smile graces his lips. "This way, Roxy."

I huff and pivot on the spot, marching back the way I came. As I pass, he leans down to whisper, though the corridor is as deserted as when I turned into it except for us.

"Still an eleven."

I have no idea how much I'll need those words in the next minutes, but they make me inordinately happy—enough to forget Aster's intrusion on my peace for now.

It's a moment that lasts as long as my short walk to the principal's office.

"What did I do?" I whisper as I press my hand to the door, then pull it away, unsure what I'll find on the other side. I roll my lips inward, but no amount of biting quells—*ha*—the nausea building in my stomach. Skipping the salad was a mistake.

"I don't think it's what *you* did, so much," Elen murmurs, pressing his fingertips to the back of my hand and pushing the door open with me. "We've got this."

I'm not sure if he's convincing himself, or me.

Across the hazy room sits a large, balding man I recognize from the school's website as Principal Gallaway. I offer him a tight smile and press my hands that decide to sweat on the spot to my thighs.

"You wanted to see me? Sir?"

"Ah. Miss Queel." The school head mangles my name the same as the prefect who handed me the note.

In my periphery, Elen winces on my behalf, but I don't care. I want out of this constricting office, absent of all light and air. It hasn't hit me until this moment that I'm claustrophobic, but I know right now with absolute certainty that I am.

"Quell," Elen corrects him, and I kind of wish he hadn't.

Gallaway's attention redirects to my support crew of one. "Mister Vash. My resident rockstar. The invitation was for Miss *Quell* alone. You may go." He dismisses Elen with a wave of his hand, but I back up a step, and run into a wall of K-pop solidarity.

"He's my moral support," I blurt, heat slamming into my face when they both stare at me, a different variety of amusement written across both their faces.

"He's not required."

"I'll stay." Elen's fingers rise to play with my hair.

Gallaway makes an exasperated sound with his

tongue. "Fine. Sit down, and try not to interrupt. I know you're given free reign here, but…" He shakes his head as if he's had enough of Elen's antics already.

The Korean rockstar tilts his head back as he settles in the seat to my right and gives me a quick wink.

Some of the pressure building around my chest eases, and I suck in air. It's not fresh, but at least I can breathe.

"What do you need me for?" I'm proud my voice comes out loud and clear in the small office. The more I look around, the more I see that seems out of place.

The scarred desk, the worn patches on the back of the old leather chair the principal sits at. The smoky looking glass that isn't the crystal-clear stuff that lets in light like in the cafeteria and our dorm rooms. I turn to look at Elen and find him studying the principal with an open look of dislike on his face.

The bald emotion is so unusual on him that I start, knocking him out of whatever headspace he lost himself in. He gives me a quick wink as I try to pay attention to Gallaway, who has been talking the entire time. I've missed the first part.

"And after your aunt's passing, I believe you've inherited quite the estate?" he finishes, looking quite pleased with himself.

I open my mouth to say *you can have it*, but a discreet shake of Elen's head stops me. "Yes," I say in my sweetest voice.

This isn't a dance I'm familiar with, but I trust my boys, and they know the steps intimately.

"Indeed." Gallaway leans forward on pudgy arms, his eager face pinked and glistening with sweat. I lean as far away in my rickety chair as I'm able without scooting backward. "I wondered if you might think of supporting the school in some way? For taking you in on short notice. Provide a package, so to speak." His gaze drops from my face to the rest of me.

Revulsion ripples over me as I press into my seat back. The room returns to its shrinking state. "I don't think—" I choke on the words, not knowing what needs to come next.

Aster, I need you.

Now.

Tears prickle the backs of my eyes. I need out. Like, now. Breath lodges in my throat while Elen bores a hole through the principal's head with his eyes, and Mr. Gallaway continues his practiced spiel.

Elen shifts his attention to me. One look is all it takes, and he's there.

"—that everything has settled, yet. She met with her lawyer last week," he butts in. "It might be a while before the transfer is … reorganized. It's messy," he adds with a smile worthy of every band poster he's ever graced.

The celebrity motion is belied by the smallest tick around his lips. I *know* he's dying to play with his lip rings. Suddenly, I'm glad he stayed and didn't abandon me to my fate. The way Gallaway looks like I'm some object he's had a long-standing fascination with leaves me sick on the inside and repulsed on the outer. When I leave his office, no amount of scrubbing will make me feel clean again.

"Hmph. Yes, these things can be delayed. But still. You must have access to some … funds." The principal's eyes get greedy as he leans closer, his fingers stretching across the desk.

I curl my hands away, tucking them into my stomach. Vomiting is out of the question, right?

Elen's hand curls in my hair, at the back of my seat where Gallaway can't see. His touch grounds me.

"I'll donate something. A music award, or program, yes? Something to encourage … participation." Elen's fingers flex on the back of my neck, belying his own tension before he resumes his massage.

Somehow, knowing he is as affected as me by this situation makes me feel less alone.

Gallaway's eyes light up like it's New Year's midnight stroke as he misses all the innuendos laid out in plain sight. "You'd let me use the band name for promotional purposes?" he breathes.

Elen laughs, a self-deprecating sound I hate because he feels he has to do this on my behalf. "No. It's better," he purrs, laying honey on his trap in a dose the headmaster can't decline. "Use my name. I'm going solo."

With that pronouncement, he rises, his hand gripped firm around the back of my neck as Gallaway gabbles something incomprehensible in the wake of Elen's offer. I scurry at his side and slip out the door he closes behind me, letting out his breath in a whoosh.

I face him, ready to do battle, but he shakes his head and catches my hand, towing me down the hall and making a sharp turn. I don't know where we're headed and after a few more turns, I'm not sure he is, either. Maybe as far away as possible.

I'm good with this plan.

After an eon, his steps slow. Elen slumps against the wall at his side, staring out the window, though he doesn't release my hand.

"Were you serious in there? You're dropping the band?" I asked, awed.

I can't imagine how that will affect his career. Or rather, I can. It means no backups, no contingencies. From here on in, every success—or failure—sits on his shoulders alone.

Elen faces me, the lines of his mouth drawn tight. "Yeah. Wasn't how I wanted to announce it, but … yeah. I am."

"Have you talked about this before?" I frown ât him. "Do they know?" His band would be the most important, or his infamous agent.

He shrugs. "I've told Nyx."

"Not the boys?"

"Which ones?" He grins impishly at me.

I punch his shoulder, letting out some of my angst. "Our boys. Zeke and … Aster." I huff out a breath.

"Hey, you said his name without sounding like you want to kill him. Proud of you, Roxy girl." His eyes shutter and he hums.

I stare at him. "What are you doing?"

"Planning your song."

"My what?"

He stops humming and cracks an eye. "Your. Song," he says. "I need a headliner. Roxy Girl will be it."

My stomach swoops. I give a nervous laugh, backing up a step, palms raised. "You can't be serious."

Elen stills, his entire body leaning toward mine. A fraction of a second later he launches back around the corner and returns a different person, laughing along with an entourage of five girls I've never seen before.

"So," he says, when they all stop laughing at something I missed while I fold my arms and stare at him, nonplussed. "Roxy here says I can't use her for my first solo song. Whaddya think?" He waggles his eyebrows in their direction, and they all burst into a fresh round of giggles.

I roll my eyes and, because I'm that mature, I stick out my tongue, too.

"Ooh, lick me," he purrs.

The sound is so guttural, so raw, I startle and pull

my tongue back in my mouth, blushing hot to the roots of my hair. I'm surprised the cherry red doesn't turn to true flame.

"Stop that." I frown at Elen and the girls who gaze at him, their eyes glazed with all things fangirling.

Much the way I did that first morning before I set foot on Alchem Academy grounds. Before I walked through the gates, when the Elite were rating everyone. Before Elen gave me my *eleven*.

My stomach cramps. I turn away, heading along the corridor he left me in to go find his little harem without any sense of direction or destination. It doesn't matter. I need to get away from him, from Gallaway, and everyone.

Elen's footsteps echo in front and around me as he chases me down, and the urge to sprint away from him leaves me tripping over my own toes. Running won't matter; his much longer legs means he catches me within seconds though I turn down another hallway I don't know.

He grips my sleeve with no intent of letting me go though I tug away.

"Hey, stop," he mutters. "I didn't mean to scare you."

"No. But you did mean to make me feel like an object." All the good he did back in Gallaway's office has been tarnished with the display in front of his fanclub. "That sucked, Elen."

I stop when he tugs on me again, and find him looking down at me, his expression tight. Not his usual face at all, more like back at the table in the cafeteria before. The urge to ask what he was doing on his phone that made him so annoyed then hovers in my mouth, but he sweeps it away, surprising me as always as he steps in closer.

"I'm sorry, Roxy. I shouldn't have—"

"No, you shouldn't," I interrupt, still angry despite his efforts at an apology. "Don't treat me like a *thing*. I'm not a—a—toy." I swallow back Aster's painful words.

"No, you're not," he says in his usual soft voice, and I'm relieved to have him back. "I shouldn't have treated you like that."

"No, you shouldn't have," I agree, but there's no heat in my voice this time. My anger wanes. I sigh and reach up to tap the lip ring he's still not playing with. "I hate that you used your rockstar-ness to get me out of trouble in Gallaway's office. I hate that I don't understand the—the intricacies of this world yet and can't seem to look after myself. I love that you're going solo. And I hate that you used me as a diversion for your own freak out."

I wonder if I've lost him, knowing how gentle he is under all the costuming and makeup and facade he puts on.

Elen hums again, but this time, there's words. His music is so different to Nyx's. That boy is pure soul. But Elen … he's all heart.

"We're tied together
On this never ending
Ever turning
Heart numbing
Roller coaster with you."

I stare as he serenades me in a whisper, knowing this is part of the song. My song, and that he didn't pull that out of his duck butt. Or maybe he did, but I don't think so. His lyrics give him away.

He offers me a softer smile, one more like him. "Not all of us found family after leaving the one we had custom-made. And the one we thought we did—" he

swallows hard and I think he's talking about his band "—
sometimes it doesn't work out." He catches my hand
when I retract my touch from his piercing and brings the
tip of my finger to his lip. "Forgive me. Please?"

Something vulnerable I've never seen in his eyes
before flares beneath the colored contacts I love on him. I
nod, and don't pull my hand away.

"Okay. But no more licking. It made it sound like
I— Like we had done—" I stumble over my words,
unsure how to finish, but I know he gets the gist.

Hey, he *said* it.

Elen has the grace to look a little crestfallen.
"Okay. I promise there will be no untrue innuendos in
your song." He sneaks a glance at me through long lashes
that are all his. "But I'm still writing it."

I huff a laugh. *Like you haven't already done that.*
But I let it slide. "Of course you are."

He grins, loping along beside me when I start
walking again. Still with no idea where I'm headed, but
that doesn't matter so much anymore with Elen by my
side. He holds my hand the entire time, all the way back
to the dorms, while he hums the same tune from before.

My song.

JOSS PHOENIX

Chapter Twenty-Four

Beauty in Silence

Nyx

Ignoring the fights over brunch is too much. I can't deal with the constant bickering and *noise*, so I slip away from the table while Elen and Zeke are still fighting after Roxy leaves. Part of me aches to follow her, walk along her wherever she heads, but I don't want to be in her space when she needs to be alone.

Instead, I aim for the woods, the spot I saw her last there, and hope she might follow the breadcrumb trail back to where we sat that night.

But it isn't Roxy I find.

The hard line of Aster's shoulders speak of a constant anger seen more often in Zeke, but as I settle beside him it's clear his anger isn't aimed at the world around him—his loathing is directed inward.

"Is she safe?" He doesn't look at me, flicking up the cuff of his shirt to display fresh bandages beneath.

I shrug and tap the material.

Aster sighs and hangs his head.

For a moment I think he will reject me, but then his head rises and his jaw sets. Long fingers I've seen work a tattoo gun with a degree of finesse I lack sometimes folds back his sleeve to expose four new sections amongst his scars. I knew he had them. I just hadn't seen them.

Listening has its perks.

Aster blows out a breath. "She's hurting."

I nod, reaching out and looking up at him. He nods his permission. My fingers graze the bandages I know he's done himself where they're askew at one end. "Zeke?" I murmur.

"He doesn't know." His voice is like whiplash, but there's little emphasis in it, like he's tired of fighting an enemy he can't see. "If he saw..."

"You're hurting." I whisper this as I fold his sleeve back and let my fingers drift away. It's too much contact, like how the cafeteria provided an excess of noise earlier. The forest is quieter.

It's the same as the difference between Elen's music and mine. His is beautiful, loud and noisy, but there are too many words for my taste. Mine is more ... sounds, moving together. Alongside each other.

Aster fixes his cuff, hiding the marks. "Every time I hurt her," he admits hoarsely. "Not me. Her."

I bite my lip. It's harder to hate what he does to her if I know he suffers for it, too. "She won't cry."

He laughs, and it's a broken sound. I like it. "Not in front of us. I might." His confession hangs beneath the forest's canopy, away from the school's clustered buildings, a known secret given.

On impulse, I lean across and press my lips to his cheek.

Aster starts, but turns his head and meets my mouth with his. The contact is soft, fleeting. Something there passes between us. A breath, and it's done.

"Is she safe with you?" He searches my eyes when he pulls back, breathing a little harder.

I shrug, my noncommittal answer earning a quirk of his lips.

He laughs again. This time the sound is darker. "I like your lullaby. It suits her."

Aster pushes up to stand over me, dusting leaves from his slacks before he strides away without another word.

I lean back against the boulder and close my eyes, smiling into the silence that follows, no longer needing to chase after anyone. Maybe she'll come to me.

Maybe I'll find her later.

I flick my phone to a song none of them have heard yet, darker and quieter and nothing she'll like.

It doesn't matter.

****

When my body stings with cold, I push up from the forest floor and wind my way back around the buildings with their soft glow, retracing the steps I think Roxy will have taken, but I can't find her anywhere. I open my phone to message her, but the group chat is gone, and the one left has Aster in it.

I close that down, not wanting to talk to anyone else because they'll want to chatter on without thought. Roxy can do that too, but her words are softer and they mean something. Unlike her, I didn't come from a home where I couldn't afford anything, but I did come from a home where everyone in it hated the person in the next room.

That was so often me.

So I learned to retreat, hide in my music, find peace in quiet sounds away from everyone else. Words mean something and nothing at the same time. I use them when I have something to say to someone I like.

Fighting freaks me out. I still run and hide, maybe not as fast anymore. Sometimes in plain sight, when I retreat inside. That way no one can reach me.

Except her, and sometimes Zeke and Elen and Aster.

I end up so lost in my head, walking in circles, that I don't see Roxy until I almost run right over her.

"Hey." She peers up at me, her face lit with curiosity. Two chocolate bars are clutched in her hands, held to her chest like she thinks I might snatch them away from her.

I reach out, press her hands into her chest, and smile.

Roxy purses her lips. "I was hungry, okay? That salad was gross. It didn't do anything. And I kind of missed dinner. Blame Elen."

I raise an eyebrow at her feast.

She offers a nervous laugh. "Stop that. I know it's not healthy, okay? But the kitchen's closed. I didn't know what else to do."

I glance around and check my phone. She's right. It *is* late enough for the kitchen to be closed. I hadn't noticed either. I bite my lip and look at her through my lashes. Deliberate in my step, I turn away, walking slow.

Roxy falls in at my side. "What do you know that I don't?"

I smile and offer her an earbud. She takes it without another word and trades me for one of the chocolate bars. I stash it for later. The back of her hand brushes mine as we walk. I retract, folding into myself, but she won't have it, gripping my sleeve and linking our pinkies together.

When I won't look at her, she peeks under my hoodie I wear beneath my leather jacket until I smile. Then she gives me back my space and I can breathe.

But I don't release our joined hands.

Roxy lets me lead her to the fence that borders on the town side of the school, away from the main gates. Gilt in gold, they're ugly as can be. I avoid those at all costs. Here, away from cameras, closer to one of the corners of the school's boundaries, it's easier to move around unobserved.

Elen and I figured that out months ago.

I grab the fence and hoist myself up, straddling the top between the pointed bars that are wide enough for me to wedge my narrow ass between and hold out my hand.

Roxy stares up at me. "This better be worth more than two chocolate bars," she mutters.

I flick my fingers and she grabs my hand, letting me pull her up. She weighs next to nothing as I swing her past me and over to the other side without much effort, slipping down onto the balls of my feet and landing catlike.

She stares. "Boy has skills." I start walking again, but she halts me, interlinking our pinkies and holding them up. "I'm not losing you out here in the dark, okay?"

I glance around. It is darker here, and for someone who has never walked into Yuleton after the sun has set—jokes—it might be a bit daunting, but I get the impression she's playing it up. Or...

"Aster?" I rasp, giving her time to answer.

The temperature around us drops, the night air turning chill with the scent of damp earth and dew.

"Gallaway," she answers cryptically after a tense minute, slipping her entire hand into mine.

I don't mind the contact. Her's isn't as loud as others, even Aster or Elen. A memory twigs of the boys talking about the head's tendencies with students, and I stop walking to look into her face. "Hurt you?"

She shakes her head, frowning. "No. But ... creepy as all get out, you know?"

I nod, pulling her away from the school and toward the tiny town. Its glow grows brighter with every step, and soon we're walking behind a row of shops, each eliciting a different scent.

"Oh, my God. This one?" Roxy stops behind a small, Italian cafe and looks at me, hope lighting her eyes. I hold the door for her and she steps inside, grabbing a menu from the counter. "Show me what you like," she demands.

Twenty minutes later, we're back over the gates, hauling enough garlic bread and boxes of pasta and sauces to feed a small army with leftovers as we return to campus. We split the bags and return to holding pinkies, though she walks a lot closer to me, the backs of our arms brushing with each step.

"The song, Nyx," Roxy says as we reach the bottom of her building. "It's—" She pauses as a hulking shadow emerges from a nearby doorway.

"Wanna tell me where you've been?" Zeke asks dangerously, glaring at her, but not me.

I know he's mad at me for leaving the chat, but I couldn't stay after I shared the song. It was meant for her.

"Nope." Roxy tosses the bag toward him and extracts the container of gnocchi. "Calzone's yours. Night!" She leans in and kisses my cheek like I kissed Aster earlier.

I freeze, my breath stalling at the playfulness in front of Zeke, but manage to twist and press my mouth to the corner of hers. "Listen to your lullaby," I whisper, just for her.

Roxy's pretty eyes widen as she backs up with her late-night snack and her secret, clutching everything to her chest, including the chocolate bar I manage to push back into her hands before she turns and dashes into her building.

I wait until her light flicks on over her bed and she waves at me before I turn and walk away.

Zeke rumbles by my side, but I don't mind because it turns out I was wrong earlier.

We found each other, and it did matter, after all.

Chapter Twenty-Five

Beggars and Choosers

Roxy

I should be overloaded after everything that's happened, but spending time with both Elen and Nyx makes me realize what's missing from my life, and it's not that I'm avoiding dealing with everything aunt-related.

Or at least, it's not only that.

I still don't feel like I belong.

Hanging out with Nyx yesterday left me feeling like the newb I still am in all things Alchem related, and Elen's easy overconfidence display is yet another marker of a world I am part of but where I don't fit. Which is how I end up at Aster's door at six in the morning, banging on it with as much discretion as my growing anxiety allows in a bid to locate Zeke *and* manage not to raise the entire dorm.

See? Totally considerate.

His door creaks open as he leans into the corridor, bemusement written across his still dozy face as he swipes sleep from his eyes. His hair is ruffled in all directions, and he's shirtless, though he still wears his chains.

I bite my lip as he keeps looking at me and says nothing, though he gives me the smallest, secret smile that leaves my stomach in freefall. Forcing my attention where it needs to go, I look past him and speak to the person who can give me what I need.

"I want to go home." I blurt this with all the grace of a toddler finding her big girl voice.

Zeke raises his head from his hands where he sits with his knees spread at the end of the bed, his face as drawn. "Now?"

I nod, and it hits me. "You two share a bed?"

Zeke takes one exasperated look at me and glances at Aster's back. "Get her inside before she creates a bigger mess."

Aster huffs his agreement and catches my waist, pulling me inside as I squeak. The door shuts behind me, and then I'm stomach to stomach with the ex-who-hates-me who stares at me like I might be next on the breakfast menu.

A short glance across at Zeke tells me he's in his usual irritable state. I wriggle against Aster and push at his chest. "Let go."

He bares his teeth and does exactly that.

I stumble back into the shut door with a gasp and pretend my swimming vision is from the impact, not his rejection. That I asked for.

Damnit, this morning is all sorts of screwed up. Already.

"This wasn't a good idea," I mutter, pressing my palm to the door.

"No shit," Zeke answers, cracking his knuckles. "But you're here now."

"I couldn't sleep." I twist my fingers into a knot behind my back where they can't see.

"We could." Aster sends a meaningful glance at Zeke, one I know he wants me to see.

I close my eyes. "This is … not okay. I'm sorry. I shouldn't have come here."

"No. You shouldn't." A hand slaps the door I try to open, holding it shut. "I want to know what's got Roxy Quell so knotted up that she can't sleep." Aster's *right there* in my space. His arm extends over my head while the other pushes a mug of tea into my hand.

"What's this?" I ask stupidly.

"Tea," he replies, guiding me to the bed next to Zeke and perches on the corner, sandwiching me between them. "Now talk, Roxy."

"I—" I bite my lip.

Aster tracks the movement.

Zeke sighs. "You may as well stay," he says in that voice with the same razored edge that grows sharper by the minute. "Say what you gotta say in front of him. I'll tell him later anyway."

I bump his knee with mine. "Yeah, but you're not supposed to tell me that."

He laughs, shaking his head. "Roxy, Roxy. I swear I was having a good dream."

"And?" I raise an eyebrow, ready for a fight.

"Then you showed up. It got better." He steals my mug and takes a gulp of steaming liquid that heats my hands to almost scalding temperature and gets up to refill it for me, passing it back. "You wanna go home. Why now?"

Another shrug. "I mean, I haven't been back. Since they... And there's been changes. Lots of them."

I look sideways through my lashes at Aster who sips his own tea and says nothing, watching me, absorbing everything. I hate him. I love that he's so close, but the moment he hurts me again I'll shatter.

This was such a bad idea.

After a sleepless, tense night when all I could see were double sixes on a pair of dice, my father's face, and the hellhole I called home waking Zeke to take me back seemed like such a good idea. I don't want to go. I *need* to be back there, like the place calls me.

I still don't know why. I guess I'll figure it out when I get there. When we get there.

"Maybe I had a dream about it." I echo Zeke's words in a cruddy lie neither of them buy. "But mine didn't get better."

He snorts. "We all get those, girl. All right. I'll take you, but you're driving."

I blink at him. "No. No way." I know how precious he is about his Jeep. "I like living."

He laughs outright and steals my tea again. I give up on having any at all. "You wanna go home, you drive. I'll be there to make sure nothing happens. Deal?"

"I'm coming, too," Aster puts in, yawning.

I stare between them and shake my head. "This is not how this played out when I left my room this morning."

"We don't all get what we want, Roxy," Aster purrs in my ear.

I elbow him in the stomach and come close to wearing his tea, but it's worth it for the answering groan I earn in response. "Fine. But I'm not responsible for any damage."

Zeke stares at me for a long moment and shakes his head. "It hasn't sunk in that you can buy the entire company that makes them, has it?"

A sound escapes me that seems out of place, but it's too late to take it back. "Um, no. And I don't want to because, perspective."

He studies me. "I don't want that for you either. Let's go."

"Now?"

"Yeah, now. You woke us up. We're caffeinated. So let's do it." Both he and Aster rise.

I'm left sitting on Aster's bed for the first time in my life, and I haven't even taken a chance to look around his room. A quick scan shows all dark furniture and the biggest four poster, heavy wooden bed I've ever seen with a midnight canopy that blocks out all light.

"Ah—" I stare between them in their boxer shorts

and inked chests on display … including Aster's scars, wrapped in clean bandages. *There's a conversation for another fight.* "Did you guys sleep together last night? Like…" I frown, unsure how to put it.

"Did we duck?" Zeke asks baldly.

I wince. "No, that's not what I meant. Well, it is, but I didn't want to say it." I try to dig myself out of the hole I've created, but from the amusement stretching both their mouths I'm making my personal Roxy shaped divot deeper.

Aster leans in and presses his lips to my ear, caging me in with his arms, though no other part of us touches. "Are you jealous I might be getting a little action? Or do you wish you were him, hmm?" He grazes his mouth along my cheek in a motion so familiar my body overheats even as I shiver.

"Stop." Zeke's voice whiplashes out as he shoves Aster away from me. He glares at my ex, then turns that same look on me. "You bust in here at unbelievable o'clock. What do you expect you'll find? No, we don't screw around, Roxy. Not that it's your problem if we do. Now get your duck butt up for your first driving lesson."

I rise on shaking legs. "How do you know it's my first?" I say, but it's all bluster and bravado.

He throws me a typical exasperated Zeke look, though I know it's Aster he's angry with, not me. Mostly. "Because you couldn't afford new shoes back then, let alone a car or driving lessons. Your dad wasn't around, and your mom was an addict. That you survived at all speaks of how tough you were before this shit started in your life."

I stare at him, then Aster. "How?"

Zeke snaps his fingers in my face. "Look at me, not him. This is what I do, Roxy. What my family does. Digital ducking espionage. Security. However you want to frame it. Looking you up?" He tips those offensive fingers beneath my chin and draws my wide eyes to lock onto his fiery ones. "That was a fun little job. The girl who came from nowhere and became someone."

He breathes hard by the time he finishes the longest speech I've ever heard him give, but I'm panting a little too. I know I should be angry—furious, even—at the invasion of my privacy, but this is Zeke, and … I'm not.

"Okay. Home and driving lesson?" Right now, that seems the lesser of the two evils standing before me.

His face fills with a blinding smile that knocks me back a step as he tosses me his keys. "Good girl," he mutters as he leads the way out of Aster's room.

I follow half a step behind, praying I haven't agreed to a deal I can't afford.

****

Twenty minutes and fifteen unintentional bunny hops down the road, I know I've overinvested in my goodwill.

Aster sits in the backseat laughing to himself every time I screw up, and my new life goal is to make him vomit with every turn.

I want to go home.

Never had those words seem so pathetic, or prophetic. Or maybe that's my driving.

Aster continues laughing himself to death, though I don't miss the way his fingers dig into the leather of Zeke's back seat, or the resulting huff as we make it across one state and into the next.

After a while, Zeke's stupid, broad hand releases his death grip on the console, and he brushes his knuckles across my knee. "I don't think I've been out this way before," he comments, staring at the passing desert.

I snort, unable to drag my eyes off the road

because of things like you know, death. "I don't doubt it."

Aster laid down sometime in the last half hour, stretching out across the back seat, tossing something in the air that's distracting as all get out.

I shake my head as the whatever-it-is flashes across my eyes in the rear vision mirror. "Stop it," I mutter on repeat, like a child's toy with the button stuck down.

Rough fingers clamp around my thigh.

The sudden pressure brings me back an inch, and I inhale a full breath. "I'm okay, I'm okay."

"We're not." This comes from the backseat.

"It's fine." I put an end to the mindduck that's been doing my head in for the last fifty odd miles. "We're here."

I drive into the gutter and pull up the handbrake. The poor Jeep makes a horrendous sound. Zeke takes his anxiety out on my leg, squeezing hard enough to cut off all circulation. I did kinda deserve that.

As I turn a guilty look at him, I find both boys staring at me with their mouths hanging open.

"What?" I shrug, peeling my hand off the steering wheel, squeezing bloodless knuckles to encourage circulation.

"You. Are. Not. Driving. Home." Zeke glares at me.

The return to our customary social sphere is almost comforting. He gets out and slams the door before the decrepit, rundown cottage that seems to have fallen into further disrepair in the absence of anything living in it. There are a few extra rats, maybe.

I climb out of the car and shut the door, locking it. Aster follows me close behind, his presence undeniable even in my too-quiet old neighborhood that seems alien now, months after I left.

Like I never belonged here, either.

I wrap my arms around myself.

Zeke turns back to me, bracing his arms across the top of the Jeep and dwarfing the oversized vehicle in a way that shouldn't be possible. "Are you sure this is a good idea, Roxy?" he asks in a low voice.

I study stubble growing on his chin that he would've shaved off for a school day, and decide I like it.

I blink, catching myself staring at him. "I mean, we're here now." It's a non-answer.

He doesn't call me out on my duck … anything.

My stomach plummets, leaving the ground swaying beneath my feet. It gives a lie to my words as I step away from the security of the boys and the car, though they seem immune to my nausea.

Zeke extends one of his long arms across the top of the Jeep with an open palm in invitation. I walk past him with my head held high and my nails biting into my skin.

Hands in his pockets, Aster falls into step with Zeke behind me, the void of his presence palpable there.

If a rich bully falls in a poor neighborhood and no one's there to hear him...

I shake my head of image and focus on why I came here.

Closure. Or something else? Answers. But those wouldn't be here. They'd be at my aunt's place. My place. I stare at the door before we go in, knowing I'm at the wrong house.

"I'll be a minute," I mutter, unsure if I'm talking to myself, or the boys flanking me.

A cool hand wraps around my elbow in a gentle squeeze. Aster jolts like the contact burns and retracts the touch.

I don't miss them glancing at each other out of the corner of my eye before the three of us parade up the front steps. I skip to one side and miss the rotten part.

Aster steps straight through it and curses colorfully.

I giggle, and that earns me a reproving Zeke-nudge to my ribs. "Be nice, babygirl."

I shoot him a glance backward. "Are you kidding? He laughed at me for the first hour and annoyed me for the rest of the drive."

Zeke raises one large shoulder, huffing at the air. I turn back to the screen door that's covered in moths and cobwebs. The house seems to be vacant, though I'm surprised it hasn't acquired squatters.

Who knows, maybe it has.

I push on the rusted hinges that stick that much worse than they did before. Thick arms slam over my head and the door swings open. I duck under Zeke's arm and into the hall filled with dust motes designed for a variety of sneezes.

This isn't my home. It wasn't ever a home.

"We need a soundtrack for this," Zeke comments to my back.

"I'm gonna stay right here," Aster mutters from the front door as we venture deeper into the house, the last place I saw Mom.

I breathe in and choke on an astringent scent of someone else's ghost—not one of mine—and back up, bumping into Zeke in my haste. His gentle prod to my lower back keeps me moving forward into the cloud of memory I force myself to push through. The souls of innocence collected and destroyed here. The boys fit in, their youth matching the age of the *guests* Mom used to entertain in order to get her hit. Some of her friends might have looked like them, too.

Vomit rises in my throat. I choke, pressing my hand to my mouth as the shivers start and don't stop.

A really, really, bad ducking idea.

"Roxy." Zeke rubs my back in soothing motions as I soak in his warmth, the single *alive* thing in this hellhole. "Breathe slow."

"I shouldn't have asked to come here."

"Yeah? But we made it. Let's look around."

I nod, taking shallow breaths, and lean into him. I shouldn't have done that, either.

His arms wrap around me. "Give it five minutes, Roxy. Then when you want to leave... Remember what I said at your aunt's?"

I face forward, not looking at him, or I might fold to the temptation on offer.

"Burn it to the ground?" I echo his words in my own way.

"Whenever you're ready." His lips brush my ear.

My shivers stop.

I take a step forward down the hall. The tiny kitchen looks as I left it. A chair, its once neon bright, now melon pale orange and back split, sits beside a chipped table that doesn't match. Tacky, multi-colored linoleum squares make up the flooring, the random pieces replaced in a broad enough selection that the haphazard patterns almost appear intentional. Something flickers in the light that shimmers through the back door beside the pair of tiny bedrooms there. The two that we crammed into.

I take a step toward them as Zeke's hand lands on my hip, gripping tight enough to pull me out of my daze.

"Behind me, Roxy. Go to Aster." He pinches me harder when I don't move, the motion so un-Zeke like that I *do* move. "Someone's here."

I freeze instead of doing what I'm told—not that

I've ever been good at that anyway—peering through the shadows that turn eerie as they shift around a familiar form.

"Aster," I mutter, throwing shade.

So much for *I'll stay here* at the front of the house.

But it's not the boy who can't who steps into my old kitchen, but a man with dark hair, his shoulders set in a hard line I recognize as a certain brand of determination. Dark jeans are covered by a glossy leather jacket that isn't as long as the one that Nyx wears, and in his hand, he grips a matte black weapon I can't take my eyes off.

"Who are you?" My lips form the words that come out in a faint sound that's not a sentence.

"The hell are you doing here?" My arms are yanked backward by one set of hands as another arm wraps around my waist. Cool hands catch me against a hard surface. "Get her into the car, get it started," Zeke snaps the order over my head.

"Wait, I need to see someth—" I object, forcing my way between them to the man opposite us.

He stills, staring at us all, and Zeke's words register.

I'm not the only one who knows his face.

"Roxy, get out of here *now*."

I look into his eyes, and the world stops revolving for a fraction of a second. "I know you," I whisper.

"Roxanna." The boys stop fighting either side of me as the man's lips split in a blinding white display of too many teeth, so rare in my neighborhood. "Do you, now? You must've been young. I wondered if you would."

I blink. "My mother … always had yellow teeth. Yours look like something from a movie. You were

259

wrong for this place. So wrong," I say, forcing the sounds out through numb lips, my head filled with a dizzying roar as I sway between Aster and Zeke. Their hands grip my arms tight enough to mark, but I barely feel it.

My gaze sinks to the tattoos inked around his thumb and forefinger where they twitch at his side. For his next hit, perhaps. I'm not sure yet. My focus settles on the pair of dice imprinted there. Two sixes, face up.

Alarms ring, all the red flags flutter.

"Six Dice." The name slips out.

His eyes narrow and refocus away from watching the boys, back to me. "She figures it out."

But I haven't. Not yet, anyway. But I'm so close. I was right to come. All my answers are here.

"All those nights. Dad. He was with you, wasn't he? Not *playing* dice. He was…" My mouth dries as I back into Aster, sliding my hand along his thigh, aiming for the knife I know he keeps there. "And then with my Mom. You came here with drugs." Bad drugs. That was the reason I had to take her shifts at the diner. Because she was so out of it after that she couldn't function at all.

"Roxy," Aster mutters in my ear, his hand closing around my wrist, intent on stopping me.

But I'm faster. More desperate.

My father wasn't playing dice when he quit his usual legal job and went to work as a guard at the prison. He was meeting *this man*. Or connecting with him. Or…

Finding a way inside my tiny, meager family. A family that Aster and Zeke knew about. An intruder in my family home who Zeke recognizes.

My mind blanks as the one piece of information slides into place that I know with absolute, utter certainty.

"You murdered my aunt."

This time, it's Aster who curses, his arm attempting to close across my chest, but it's too late as I rip the knife from its place on his belt, slipping the blade into my hand like Zeke taught me.

It doesn't matter if there's little light. Six Dice reaches for his matte black weapon, but he never quite gets there. Because the blade leaves my hand in a clean underhand throw, the same one I practiced with Zeke. I don't blink, and then the handle protrudes from the man's lower stomach, beside his hip. He doubles over with a shout, before Zeke's fist collects him straight in the face.

Six Dice's body flies backward, the knife ripping upwards in an inked fist I know well.

I don't get to see the rest because the hand wrapped around my wrist yanks me out of the house.

"Come on, Roxy." Aster pulls me forward and when that doesn't work so well, he pushes me past him and onward, cursing under his breath. "Move, dammit." He lifts me off my feet, hustling us back toward the door we entered through.

His foot goes through that same stupid step, and I giggle again as he kicks his way through rotten timber on his way to the Jeep. *Inappropriate, inappropriate...* His hands don't shake once as he buckles me into the passenger seat and reaches across to start the car.

Zeke pours out of the house on a run and snatches the key, shoving Aster into the back. "We have to go," he hisses, his arms trembling as he slams the door and revs the engine hard.

"What's that smell?" I stare at the dark spots that decorate his shirt, the astringent scent I recognize from the house that fills the inside of the car.

"Gasoline." Aster grips my shoulder, leaning between the two front seats, staring at the house, checking my seatbelt.

I shove him back and point at his own.

Cold eyes hold mine, unwavering.

"What did you do?" I demand, switching my attention to our fuel permeated driver.

"Count, Roxy," Zeke orders, ignoring my outburst as he pulls out from the curb without looking. "Now," he barks when I don't start, and he floors it.

"One," I whisper. "Two—"

Aster joins me.

"Three," we all say together in a hushed voice.

The rear vision mirror flashes with the explosion that sends a cloud of black soot into the air followed by a wave of flame as my rickety house lights up.

"I made you a promise." Zeke gives my shoulder a hard squeeze, glancing into the back.

"Where did you find gasoline?" I breathe.

Zeke shrugs, facing forward as we speed away from the burning pile of matchsticks that represents the cumulative total of my previous life. "He already doused the place. Looks like he was intending to do the work anyway." Zeke holds my gaze without flinching as his hand finds mine. I expect no less of him.

I swallow hard, the image of Aster's knife leaving my hand to bury into the man's gut, knowing he was responsible for the three deaths that left me alone in this world.

"He can burn with it."

****

The world blurs by the time Alchem's golden gates—I swear I'll never get used to those things—pass the Jeep's hood in long shadows. Aster hasn't spoken for a while, and Zeke is busy murdering the steering wheel, like he—

Bile creeps up the back of my throat. Nope. Not doing it. He said my house was doused in gasoline. That accounts for the odd, sharp scent I couldn't place when we walked in. My head was so busy not cataloging everything in sight and refusing to process what I couldn't at the time in the ultimate overwhelm that I failed to note the obvious.

He hadn't though, and I didn't think Aster missed it either.

Just me.

Prime survival instincts right there.

I shiver at the thought of what could have happened if I turned up at the house alone, without the boys as back up. If I opened my mouth and spat out the truth I hadn't connected before. Because it's obvious as pie that the man in the kitchen of my childhood home, decrepit as it had been before Zeke turned it to ash, isn't a stranger to any one of us.

I recognize him from his interactions with my mother. One of the many men she entertained while she and my father were separated seeking hit after hit, whether it was for drugs or alcohol, sex, or to alleviate loneliness. Each addiction seemed to run one into the next.

And on my father's side, Six Dice. The man he gambled with. Or maybe he *was* the dice, and something bigger is at play. Neither Aster nor Zeke seemed shocked to see him, though they were wary. Threatened, as though they sensed danger greater than skin deep.

Because they know him.

Knew him.

The shivers don't stop.

Zeke swears some more, no ducks involved, and pulls up with the abruptness of an FBI agent who's run out of questions. It isn't until I look up that I realize we're parked beneath the shadow of my dorm.

"Thanks for the driving lesson," I whisper, gripping my seatbelt with both hands and not making a move.

"Roxy," Aster starts in a strained voice, leaning forward in his seat.

I blink at him and my mouth opens, but Zeke beats me to it. "I thought it was you," he grates out.

All movement stops inside the Jeep. All air.

Aster turns to his best friend—I *think* they're still best friends—and laces his hands on his lap. "Is that so?" he responds, like he's earned a distinction instead of a pass on a test.

Zeke's mouth snaps shut.

Mine doesn't.

"Me, too." My confession falls flat.

Aster flinches like I've hit him, rocking sideways in the backseat. His eyes slide my way. For a second, I think he'll lash out. Then he's outside, the rear passenger door slamming in his wake.

"Aster," Zeke grates, gripping my wrist tight for a brief moment, making direct eye contact. It's reassuring, and terrifying, like staring into a void with no safety net. He pulls me closer across the leather bench seat, as though he needs contact, uncertainty swimming behind his fathomless charcoal gaze.

"He's not going to stop walking," I say, knowing this side of Aster because he's a mirror of me in this.

I would run, and him walking away is the same thing even if he says otherwise. He's lying to himself, and we both know it.

Zeke releases my hand and follows. I wait a whole second before my door catches my hip as I tumble out, bumping straight into his still form, like he knew I wouldn't do as I was told anyway.

"Roxy…" His sigh lances through me.

Ignoring that too, I trip around him. "Aster," I call.

He stills, a silhouette that makes heroin-chic look

fat, and half turns. "I'm so glad of the trust you all have in me."

Elen and Nyx emerge from the shadows near my dorm, like they were waiting there.

Nyx carries his phone, though for once he isn't looking at it.

Elen frowns. "What did we miss?"

Aster swings toward them and I can bet my night's well needed sleep he's smiling, a big, fake front from the way the rockstar backs up in a hurry. "They've figured out I didn't murder dear old Aunty Sloan on Roxy's behalf." His words are brief, ending in sharp intervals that hang in the fading afternoon.

The air remains pensive, tension rising as each of us step closer, penning in the wild animal he's becoming.

Aster's spine tenses as he loses it. "Was this your fine opinion of me, too?"

Considering I knifed a man and Zeke finished the job, we have a distinct excess of glass houses for this conversation right now.

Elen's eyes widen as he backs up another step, hands held out in supplication. "Whoa, not my fight."

Aster stops laughing. "Coward."

"Fine. I did, all right? We all thought it. Because it's Roxy, right? We know what you'd do for her. Hell, we all would," Elen snaps. His eyes shutter as the wind picks up, blowing his blue and black hair around his face. Regret etches lines around his mouth. "Aster–"

"It's fine." Aster slips his hands into his pockets and wanders between them, Nyx making space though his brow furrows. One hand reaches out, but Aster bats the tentative touch away without looking. "I said it's fine, Nyx."

Nyx shudders, wrapping his arms around himself. I risk a look at Zeke's thunderous face, decide he can take care of himself, and run to Nyx's side. He lets me slide an arm though his, gripping his wrist. Cotton-covered fingers rub mine through his hoodie, no direct skin contact, but the pressure is there as we cling to each other, weathering the unpredictable storm of the best and the worst of us.

"Don't walk away," Zeke says. "We have to fix this."

Aster shrugs. "Maybe it can fix itself."

"Not with your father involved."

"What does that mean?" I whisper, but the wind steals my words and makes them louder than I ever intended.

Aster twists on the spot, offering an enigmatic smile. "Shall you tell her, or should I?"

Zeke glares back at him, leaving us all in a stalemate where no one dares to breathe.

It's Aster who breaks the tension with a too-easy shrug I know is deceptive because it's him. He walks toward the forest without another word, Zeke heading in the opposite direction. Even Nyx disengages, sidling away.

One by one, they all move off, heading to different corners of Alchem, leaving me alone with a heavy dose of guilt I can't bear alone, without the answers I crave.

Chapter Twenty-Six

What I Won't Let Hurt Her
Aster

Droplets of blood and sweat that isn't mine sail past my ear followed by Zeke's fist. That next blow comes after one of my own that doesn't land its mark. We've sparred for too many years for either to present an easy target, which makes landing a blow that much sweeter.

Zeke and I share a language of violence, though he, alone, of our group is speaking to me. Elen and Nyx are still in their avoidance phase, and Roxy has made herself scarce. The guilt written across all their faces that evening came too close to being too much to bear, but at least the man in the ring opposite me has the balls to face me after fessing up to his sins.

I can respect that, even if I'll still take his penance in salt and blood.

My thigh screams as I lower into a crouch and aim for a body shot that hits its mark. Zeke *oofs* above my head. I bounce back up onto the balls of my feet with a shit eating grin on my face. Even so I'm not fast enough to avoid the scarred knuckles flying toward my jaw.

The blow knocks me back a step as I shake my head for clarity, catching the sassy wink he throws my way.

"Body shot got nothing on a facial shot, motherducker," he mutters, still holding to the ridiculous vow he made to Roxy that's held up against all odds.

Rather like her.

"Peace." I swipe my hands across my jaw, registering the fresh tender spot. *Double dose to Zeke.* A roll of my shoulders and I'm ready to go again, my blood pumping with my own brand of fury.

Anything to wear through adrenaline after the catastrophe at Roxy's old house.

They don't think I saw their moment when I left the car yesterday, but it was hard to miss the intimacy between them. What used to be between us, even though what I see I know is because of my order—our agreement—months ago. Or maybe it's because it's her, and it's something that much more.

He reached for her when he thought I wasn't looking, and she didn't push him away. I knew then I'd lost her forever. And it *hurts*. My heart shredded on the spot, like it's still shredding now.

It was the job, right? What I asked him to do at my father's house months ago. Now ... regret is the order of the day. My personal pity party. I shake my head to dispel the memory, and the distraction costs me. I miss the foot that sweeps behind my ankles, knocking me flat onto my back.

The warehouse's utilitarian ceiling with its enormous industrial sized fan dances with black stars as I try regaining my feet, and fail.

Zeke peers over me, one hand extended. "That's enough for the day."

I knock his hand away. "I tell you when it's done."

He doesn't move. "We're done." The hand remains.

I take the offer, letting him pull me up. Everything hurts. My thighs. My back. My head.

Hell, the room still spins.

Dipping out from the ring, letting the ropes slap my back, I slug back water more than is sensible, then tip the rest over my head. My vision blurs for a second.

When I straighten, Zeke jerks his head toward the showers, though he lets me lead the way. Scalding hot water is a relief and a penance both, soothing aches while unearthing new ones. I bare my teeth to the twisted reflection in the pristine, tiled wall that's no more than a disjointed mass of a monster already made.

"Don't take too long, princess." Zeke raps his knuckles on the door of my cubicle.

Unlike any other school with their communal showers, Alchem offers a degree of privacy with individual cubicles, oversize compared to anywhere else. I towel off, dressing in my pants and leaving my shirt hanging open. When I emerge with water still dripping down my spine, Zeke holds my tray with the chains I laid on it earlier, the silver reflecting on the black velvet in an old-fashioned comfort, or an arrogance.

The corner of my mouth quirks. I know how Roxy would view the tradition, throw it back in my face.

It doesn't matter how many times I've asked Zeke not to do it; he refuses to break with his habits. Rather than insult the man, I offer him respect. Lowering my head I take the chains, linking the cold metal behind my neck and crossing each one over the other so they can't be untangled.

I feel his eyes on me as he watches the process in fascination. He's never asked. I've never offered to discuss my reasons.

When the tray is empty, he slides it away into his pigeonhole and pockets the key. "Can we agree to beat the shit out of each other at the same time next week?"

I work the opposite shoulder from before and something cracks. "Why not."

My hair dries on the walk across campus. I keep an eye out for Elen, Nyx, and Roxy, but the three are conspicuous in their absence. I suspect they're holed up in one of the dorm rooms. I don't resent their closeness; I envy them the ability to hide away together.

What happened at Roxy's dorm building strays to the edge of my mind. She is becoming one of us, having taken everything that's been thrown at her. Resilient, a survivor... She's the stuff Alchem legends are made of, even if she doesn't recognize it herself.

But what happened in that house won't go unnoticed, for obvious reasons. I'm waiting for the FBI to make another appearance when they connect the dots. If there's one thing I've noticed about law keepers, it's that they like to make arrests as their key measure of success. Rarely does it matter *who,* or if the person wearing silver bracelets is the person responsible for the crime committed, but I won't let them touch Roxy.

Neither will Zeke. Nyx is starting out in this world. He has so much potential *if* Elen can convince him to pick his music-filled butt off the ground. The Korean's solo career will tell its own story.

As for me... I need to check on her. Deciding to cut through the admin building is the shortest way to her. I dart between the foyer doors and take a left past the medical bay, giving a wave to Kellen Matriarch who is there with his attending father. Another left takes me past the head's office. The door at the end of the corridor will spit me out one building away from Roxy. Of course, it's when I'm so close to my goal that all literal hell breaks loose.

Like the devil himself has been sitting at my shoulder this entire time and decides to announce himself on cue.

My father emerges from Gallaway's office, his buggy eyes running over my still sweaty form from my brisk walk across campus. "The person I wanted to see next."

Since when have I been a person to you?

I give him the same, brief scan. "Be quick. I'm on my way to do something."

"You can wait a moment for your old man." He parks his Italian suit in my path until I have to stop. My father looks me up and down and sighs.

"Are we doing this here, Alonso?" I murmur, itching to fish my smokes out of my pocket.

The corners of his mouth flatten at my disrespect. "I hear you've been … busy. I also gave you an order."

My expression blanks. *I thought I'd have more time.*

But why should I have more than a few hours before he came down on me.

not Roxy not Roxy not Roxy—

If he steps in, whatever control I have over her fate is beyond whatever ducks are left on campus.

I make a noise in my throat, try to clear, it and settle on not choking myself or him. "You know I like to play with my food."

That flat mouth of his turns into something akin to a smile, and I know my mask isn't as complete as I wish. "What a pity Gallaway is occupied. Otherwise, this would be a nice little meeting, don't you think?" My father slips his hands into his pockets like this is a day jaunt.

My mouth dries. "What do you mean, 'otherwise occupied'?"

His smile widens. "Why don't you look for yourself?" He nudges the door open with his toe.

I tip my head to one side, enough to peer in to find Roxy standing beside Gallaway's desk, his hand trailing along her back and heading toward her skirt.

Stomach acid rises in my throat. "Don't you dare—" I hiss.

My father's hand smashes into my chest, pushing my back against the opposite wall with a show of strength I underestimated. "It appears she's moved on to other pastures, wouldn't you say?" Alonso shuts the door, laughing so hard his body joggles like he's produced the finest joke in all of history. He stops on a dime. "You should share this reward with him."

My mind takes over as the world spins around me. "My reward's in there." I tip my head to one side, cracking my neck as I brush his hand off my chest like it's nothing. "Don't give away the prize."

My father smirks. "Then get it back. If you can."

I stare at my father for a second too long though my feet and body are already lunging toward Gallaway's closed door. It might be my imagination, but I swear I can hear Roxy's voice on the other side. More than her voice.

Alonso's laugh obliterates her soft tones as I stumble into the principal's office with its tacky carpets and dim lighting.

Gallaway's hand halts inches from its destination, and a relieved breath leaves me that the contact I feared hasn't occurred yet.

The perceived horror whitening her eyes tells a different story, however.

"What do you want, Craven?" Gallaway glances at me in annoyance, not so fine lines creasing around his eyes that match my father's.

I reach back out the door and pray for a miracle. My hand closes around a thin wrist. A sideways glance confirms the presence of the other girl I'd seen in this office before. I don't bother to beg for forgiveness. I want Roxy safe, and I'll do anything to achieve that. The boys were right to worry about my intentions after all. Perhaps they should have focused that concern in a different place.

Gritting my teeth, and not taking my eyes off Roxy for a second, I pull the other girl into the office before either can object and wind my other hand around Roxy's wrist. Tugging her into my chest, I throw the sacrificial lamb into her place.

Roxy's pretty mouth opens, but I'm not in the mood to fight her. My hand catching her jaw and squeezing gives her a hint of what I need from her, though it doesn't conceal her objection. Nor do I give her time.

"This is more your lane, principal." I throw him a smirk. "I believe I earned my reward."

I tighten my hand on Roxy's jaw when she starts to object. Sending a wayward prayer to the heavens, I release her and find her hand instead when she closes her mouth, though her eyes narrow. I'll cop a mouthful from her soon, and I'll have earned it, but right now I need to get us both the hell out of here.

"Your name doesn't hold as much weight as you expect, Mr. Craven." Gallaway's mouth pinches in a parody of a pout.

I want to remove a body part and shove it in there, but that would get me expelled. That's a crap idea, because then I wouldn't be able to look after Roxy. My father's twisted sense of amusement rolls over the entire situation, but he's not in the hallway when I pull her clear of the principal's office. My heart slams hard in my chest as she clings onto my hand, sometimes digging her nails in as I walk fast, others trying to tug free, but I refuse to let her go.

When we hit the outside of the building, I release her, giving her the freedom she seeks. "You're welcome."

She rubs her wrist and watches me with the

whites around her dark eyes still showing. "I thought you'd be happy to see me brought low."

My throat contracts and my arms ache as I stand still, parted from her. "I'm glad you think so little of me."

"You've given me no reason to believe otherwise," she lashes back, fear making her voice tremble, but it's the wrong sort of fear. Not the sort I inflicted.

The chains around my neck constrict. I tug at those and when they provide no measure of pain, I opt for digging my nails into the back of my scalp where she can't see. The sharp sensation allows freedom from the building cacophony between my ears. The brief insanity backs off and like the blades in my room that allow me silence in sleepless hours, I can breathe, if only for now.

"Well. Not much choice there." What question did she ask?

A small frown decorates her brow. "Aster?" She takes a step toward me, breaking inside my personal space.

Stay back, gotta stay away—

My fingers itch to reach for her, but I keep them rigid at my side, watching her with predatory eyes. "Stop moving."

She edges another inch forward. "Why?" she banters.

Shouldn't she be the one cowed after that? But Roxy Quell has always done things in reverse. When I bullied her, she stood up to me, even fought back. Instead of being afraid, or running away, she rises to the challenge, like now.

It's intoxicating. I can't get the scent of her, the image of her, out of my head.

"Because—" I snap my mouth shut, stare at a point over her head, and try to reduce my hammering pulse.

Because I'm not in control of myself right now.

Because I can't stand to see another's hands on you, even when I ordered it.

because because because—

Because I still love you.

My fingers flex at my side, the movement less than voluntary. "Go back to your room, Roxy. You're not safe here." The words tumble from my lips, all too practiced after the months of torment and heartbreak.

She tips her head up, staring right through me. "Were you born this way?"

It's my turn to be on the back foot. "I beg your pardon."

"Were you born broken, is that the problem?"

I give her a hint of a smile, leaning into her space, sharing her air that slips from her lips to mine, and halt a fraction of a millimeter above her. Then I drag myself back before the contact I crave can occur.

Her eyes flare wide with the renewed need that slices through both of us, replacing the anticipated contact that's ruined when her hand raises, slapping across my face. I relish the sting, the mark that raises in her wake. A trophy of her burning rage.

"Don't ever touch me again."

Her voice is cold and detached. Dark eyes pierce me, staring down at me despite our reversed height differences. Perhaps she's learned something else from Alchem.

How to be like me.

Roxy stalks away, rounding the corner as my lips twitch.

She might hate me, but I've never been prouder of her.

JOSS PHOENIX

Chapter Twenty-Seven

Run and Hide

Roxy

It seems an age since I've spent time in the dorm. The simple hours laughing here with Rhani, planning the ski trip, painting…

Anything from *before* is an alien concept. I can't fathom the freedom that allowed me to laugh, or flirt, or create. The one thing I can think of is to lock myself in the bathroom and fill it full of steam to hide in.

Unlimited hot water is another fresh luxury I'm still not used to and one I'm sure I'll covet forever.

But the bathroom is occupied. Rhani sings at the top of her lungs.

My bed offers a secondary haven. I curl under the covers, facing the wall, the lights on my half of the room off.

Noise ceases when my roomie emerges from the bathroom, and the light flickers off. Some of the heat ekes out that the bed doesn't provide, though I burrow deeper, wishing for tonight I can have my room back to myself.

The moment the thought crosses my mind I banish it in case it comes true by accident.

"Are you awake?" Rhani hisses with little showmanship, though there's a note of uncertainty underlying her question.

"Trying not to be," I grump noncommittally.

"But you are!" She bounces on my bed and decorates my quilt with droplets that seem to sink straight through to my skin.

I scissor my legs, knocking her off the bed and smile when there's a soft whump and she lands on the floor.

What? I'm broken tonight.

"Ow," she mutters. "Message received."

I roll over, all contradictions. "Sorry?"

She peers up at me. "Are not."

I smile for the first time in hours. "You sound like Zeke."

"I can slap like him, too."

A laugh escapes me at that. The thought of Zeke slapping anyone is laughable. Hence the sound. But then I remember what he did, and why we all fought with Aster and why I feel this way.

Scared of what we did. Afraid for what comes next.

Guilty.

We hurt him. No matter what Aster did to any of us, I know he's devastated by the way we all reacted. That he pulled me out of Gallaway's office says he still cares, but his parting words belie the damage done by our conglomerate mistrust. And then my reaction to him.

I don't know if I can fix that. I'm not sure how.

Rhani's off the cuff comment triggers a plethora of images swarming across my vision. I shake my head, aware of how mad I look but maybe a little insanity is the order of the night.

"Are you going to tell me what happened?" Rhani nibbles on a hangnail, staring up at me.

Except this girl is never guileless.

I slip one foot out from the covers and poke her shoulder with my little toe. "Your brother happened."

"He does," she says. "But it's more than that, isn't it?"

Despite that I have the campus gossip mill as my roomie and shouldn't open my mouth and tell her anything, I nod, burrowing lower in my covers. I'm one step from throwing the whole lot over my head and wailing. The pressure building around my chest coils too tight, a spring on the edge of letting go.

"I went home."

The words burst out, freeing air space in my lungs. I gulp air while Rhani's face creases in concern.

"That traumatic, huh?" she whispers, her mouth turning down in sympathy.

"I think we killed someone."

I know we did.

Rhani grins. "Zeke does that." She echoes my earlier sentiment. I shake my head, and her smile becomes a frown. "You mean it?"

I nod, unable to force anything else out for a moment. Waiting for the tears to manifest, I'm shocked to find my eyes remain dry.

"What happened?" She leans forward, her elbows on her knees, looking up at me.

I hesitate.

"Are you okay? When did this happen?" She grabs my hand and squeezes. "Did you get hurt?"

The flood gates open. Still no tears, but the moment there's a show of compassion, all the words tumble out. From turning up at Zeke and then Aster's room early in the morning, to begging for a lift. I include the horrendous driving lesson that has Rhani in tears but leave out the part about the boys in bed together.

I figure some things should remain private and whatever their relationship, neither deserve to have that broadcast all over Alchem.

It's bad enough that I'm telling her secrets that could end with all of us in serious trouble. Rhani's hilarity reduces when I get to the incendiary part of the tale, and I finish at the car.

No point going further than that.

She stares at me through luminous, reflective eyes for a long moment and nods. "You're free, then."

"What?"

"Of the FBI."

"I don't follow."

She makes an exasperated noise. "You said this man—Six Dice." She says it like a title. "He murdered your aunt? Then it's done. They can close the case and leave you alone now."

I shrug. "It's not like they've been following me around."

She blinks. "Are you blind? There's been a car out the front of the Academy every day for the past three weeks. If they aren't in the grounds questioning students, then they're watching us."

It's my turn to stare. "How do I not know this?"

"Because you've had a whole lot of stuff to process?" She nibbles the hangnail that no longer needs attention and looks away.

I set my jaw. "Does everyone know?"

One shoulder hunches in admission. "Pretty much."

My lips purse. And no one told me. I slide my hand under my quilt and find my phone, gripping the device tight.

"I'm sure they were going to?" she offers.

"I'm not," I grit out.

No longer wanting to hide, I grab my last clean canvas and my supplies, heading for the door.

"Where are you going?" Rhani calls, though she doesn't get up.

Somewhere where I don't have to worry about people telling me lies to my face. Even ones by omission.

Because not telling me was the same as lying to me. And they're all guilty of that, including her.

"Keep what we talked about to yourself, if you can," I say through clenched teeth as I kick the door open and shoulder my way through with my art supplies.

The door stutters closed, pausing long enough to let me glimpse the hurt on her face before it creates a solid barrier between us.

****

The dorm's rooftop offers the silence I need to work and find peace in my mind. Rather than hide in the bathroom cloistered away, the open, chill night air allows a freedom I hide from but need anyway.

I have no idea what I intend to paint when I start, but instead of hitting the blacks and reds I tend to favor in these sort of self-destructive moods that are one degree away from self-harming, I fill the canvas with pale shades of gray, glinting silvers, and pearlescent whites. After my arms ache and my fingers are numb I realize it's Aster looking back at me. Not Aster like when I painted his other portrait, the one he slashed.

This one is a close up of him in flight, the moment he whisked me from the house with Zeke on our heels. Here, his hair whips around his face as he looks back at me, his eyes drawn tight. His mouth, too. Everything about his expression is angular, though his features are still in the angelic class. That hasn't changed.

Beneath his sharp jaw, hints of silver glint upward in a reverse, a fallen halo where his chains twist in an endless noose wrapped around his throat.

I stare at the canvas so long that I can't differentiate fallacy from reality.

"You must be numb."

I jump on my impromptu seat made from an upturned janitor's bucket and stare past my canvas, half rising on trembling legs that have indeed gone to sleep though I refuse to admit it to the object of tonight's painting obsession.

"Stalker. What are you doing up here?"

"Rhani said you ran off in a huff."

I glare at him, unsurprised at his renewed obsessive tendencies that mirror mine. "She did not."

His mouth softens, unlike the version on my canvas. "She's worried about you."

"And she called you?" I make a disparaging noise.

"Well, no one can wake Zeke once he's done for the night unless it's an emergency. Even then he's unpredictable. And ragey." Aster rolls his neck and a few things pop.

I wince. "What's going on between you two?"

"Would you believe we're lovers?" Aster raises a challenging eyebrow.

"Believe it? Yes." I consider and nod, though he looks surprised at the admission, and I hold a finger in caveat. "But you're not."

"Are you an expert in male dorm relationships, Roxy? I promise you there are plenty who share beds and leave before the sun rises each morning." Aster prowls closer, donning his predatory persona.

I refused to be cowed by him anymore. "Zeke didn't leave in the morning. You love each other, yes, but not as lovers. He did for you what you once did for me. Stayed with you so you wouldn't hurt yourself." I consider, tilting my head to the side. "More."

"Is that what you think?" He reaches the corner of my canvas, dangling his fingers above it. Where I would otherwise stop him, I let him turn the wet paint, marring the corner so he can look into his own face. "Roxy…" he breathes.

"Yes. It's what you do," I say, confident in my assessment. Unashamed of my art. Of myself laid out raw before him.

"You've changed." It's not a question.

I hold his gaze. "Lots of things have."

This year. From before.

The corners of his mouth flicker. "I like this version of you. It's … fierce."

"I'm so glad you approve." I gather my things and turn away, heading for the back staircase I discovered in my search for a quiet space hours earlier.

"You forgot something." He calls me back.

I glance over my shoulder where he gestures to the portrait, more than life sized next to the real thing.

Loose hair whips my face as I stare him down. "No. I didn't."

I leave Aster Craven on the rooftop alone with my interpretation of the best version of himself and wonder if he can live up to it.

JOSS PHOENIX

Chapter Twenty-Eight

House of Cards

Roxy

Six Dice's name was Marvin Heath, and he was employed by Aster's father to ensure my aunt's fortune fell into line with Craven Enterprises. I learned that fact courtesy of my favorite FBI agent, and not from the people who should have told me. He's the reason Aster ended up with that stupid silver locket that freaked me out for months. The easiest way for a hit man to keep his targets in line was to have them in his pocket in a literal sense.

But this particular job seemed to have longer term connotations. Ruin the family, member by member. When Alonso Craven couldn't find his way into Willa Sloan's fortress home, they resorted to other methods. Hence Aster's initial love/hate relationship with me that became an obsession. That blew out into something no one ever expected, or could control.

A lie by another name still smells like duck feces.

"Can you repeat that last please, ma'am." Agent Brown looks pissy that I never did call him after our tissue moment in the graveyard, but I'm so out of ducks I don't care.

The way he looks at me, that speculative gleam in his eye, however, reminds me of the triad of agents at my aunt's house, and *that* puts me on edge.

"She's done here." Albert Whitman pulled out all the stops and hauled himself down the west coast on the grueling ten-hour drive to Alchem the moment my goodwill ran out and my name turned up on a plain white card delivered to my calc class.

Aster's confidence never wavers. For everything

he's done I don't doubt his honesty in this moment. He's not a part of this, and I'm glad, for all the pain it caused, that we fought over his *did I/didn't he* story earlier.

Because now, I know who to trust, even amongst the liars.

The boys flat out refused to let me go alone and escorted me until Albert turned up, shaking Aster's hand with ill-concealed suspicion and a small dose of relief that mingled on his lined face.

Gallaway made his presence known, brown nosing for all he was worth with the agents who wanted less of his attention than any of us. Elen and Zeke employed themselves in creating a *them-and-us* wall that let us all breathe while Aster, Albert, and I battled the FBI on different fronts.

Which achieved little, except for gaining the information I didn't know and telling the same, pre-programmed story we all agreed to tell beforehand. We prepped hard in the last weeks, despite fluctuating levels of animosity between us, and it paid off, until this moment where Albert made himself known, and we stand at an impasse.

"I'm sure your *client* doesn't want her arrest on the six o'clock news." Agent Brown decides to play hardball at the eleventh hour.

Albert draws himself up in his rumpled suit. "My client has lost her entire family. She's been displaced. The house she was born in burned down last month. And in all that time, agent," he said, stressing the title with a small 'a', "you haven't done the job I'm sure someone employed you to do once."

I bite my lip and give Albert a mental thumbs up and a rise. I've seen how much my aunt paid him, and it's a ludicrous amount. He's undercharging, and he's about to be told that.

Aster lounges against the door to the plain office the agents seconded for their use. Brown's partner stands beside him, hands clasped in front of himself. I study their forms, noting the differences in their stances. The way the other agent's shoulders remain stiff beneath his cheaper suit jacket, while Aster wears his like they're pajamas, reclining into the wall that props him up like it's a privilege to serve him.

He sends me a wink I feel to my toes. "Agent Brown." Aster looks at me, checking, though I know he didn't forget. I nod, wondering what he's planning. "Is Roxanna clear of charges, and the investigation surrounding Willa Sloan's death concluded now?" Aster keeps his voice light, though his eyes could smoke that carpet at less than twenty paces with their intensity.

Agent Brown's lips purse. "Most—yes." He changes his mind when Aster pins him with a look.

"And my father?"

"Will not receive charges, of course, Mister Craven." Agent Whatever at Aster's side changes the tempo in the room.

Agent Brown stiffens, meeting Aster's eyes for a moment, as though understanding something his counterpart misses.

Aster nods, his next word clipped. "I believe Mister Whitman is correct. You are done here."

Albert beams at my ex, and I get the impression his opinion of the Craven portfolio is about to change, or at least, its heir.

Brown turns his head on his thick neck and stares at Aster like he can't believe the wealthy offspring dares interrupt his interrogation. "Go, Craven, or you'll be escorted out." He dismisses the most dangerous person in the room, and that's the single mistake he'll make today.

Aster's phone is in his hand, flipping over, the

case slapping his palm with each turn. "There are so many ways to thwart an investigation," he says in a deliberate undertone. "You say you can't be bribed, but what does it take? A million in your bank account? Five? Unnamed, unnumbered. Enough to cover your daughter's chemo treatments..." He lets the words hang as he paces around the room, as though he's lost in thought.

I look down at my lap and study my hands. Leaving him with his phone was a mistake. Aster has spent the last hours planning this approach, gathering all the information he needed to break the man in front of him, turning strengths to weaknesses. It's what he does, even without Zeke's assistance. The bigger man is a creeper of a different level that's impressive to watch. Aster is ... dangerous.

"You—" Agent Brown lunges, and I rise.

"Stop," I snap. "This isn't the way you want to end your career, laying a hand on the son of one of the most powerful men in the country."

Agent Brown looks right at me and seems to realize who he's talking to for the first time. Another strategy the boys and I brainstormed on the drive home from my burned out house in Nevada. He thinks I'm a grieving, bratty schoolgirl. Leave that facade in place. Blow it up when it's needed. Not a second before. It didn't matter who the target was. It would work on plenty of people. Zeke and Aster had a few tailored approaches for specific agents they deemed threats thanks to the information Zeke pulled from his father's intel systems later on.

Agent Brown didn't make the list.

"Sit down, Miss Queel." Like the school head, he mangles my name.

Albert opens his mouth to correct him, but I hold out a single finger.

"It's Quell." Aster answers for me.

Another power play. I learned my lessons well.

Don't answer when others will for you. Make us look like your lackeys, your strength.

Your silence will be unnerving. Let him wonder what else he's missed.

Walk away with your head held high.

Agent brown whiplashes back to Aster. "I know that."

"Do you?" His slow smile raises *my* hackles, and he's not trying to irritate me.

Albert shuffles papers at my side, packing up without discretion. Clearly, he's seen this play in action before. I wonder if she ever used it, my Aunt. What I might have learned from her.

"Come on, Roxy. It's time to go."

Zeke's hand closes around my upper arm, lifting me upward, and with little effort I find myself on my feet and outside the airless room.

"Thanks." I reach out two hands and grip the ones offered at waist height, one cold, one hot that both squeeze back. The cold one lets go too fast. I frown at Aster's back, hating myself for the pang that slaps my heart at his absence as he approaches Brown and his partner, dipping his head to speak to the shorter man in a lower tone. "The bullying can stop now," I snark, giving Albert a hug and a quick *thanks* as he dives for the nearest bathroom.

"He's refusing not to pay for the child's chemo." Zeke's hand remains clasped firm around mine.

I look up into coal black eyes lit from within. "So, not a bribe after all," I murmur, unable to keep the pride from my voice.

The corner of his mouth quirks. "Not quite. Come on. He can catch us up."

I let him lead me out of the building. When I expect us to head toward the forest, Zeke surprises me, turning around the back of the admin hub to a grassy area around one side of the sports field. Often full of cheering students on game days, right now it's empty, except for us.

He pulls me down on one side of the sunny hillock. I land on my butt and curse.

A finger pokes my forehead.

"No ducks harmed, remember," he murmurs, wrapping an arm around my shoulders and arcing his body over mine.

My heart hammers while the rest of me freezes. Torn halfway between the flight and fright response, I do nothing but stare up at the behemoth leaning over me. "What are you doing?"

Zeke lowers the arm behind me until it touches the ground, keeping me encapsulated against his chest. "Wanna try this again, Roxy?" His eyes search my face, a rare sign of his uncertainty.

Relief he's not barging through me again clashes with an instant hate of the expression on his face. "I don't want you to be afraid of anything with me," I whisper back. I don't know why. It's not like there's anyone else around us.

"I'm not afraid." He lies straight to my face, dipping his head until his mouth brushes mine.

My breath stutters and I nod once. "Okay?"

"Yeah?" His mouth settles against mine on a sweet breath.

"Yeah?" I can't not make my answer a question.

It doesn't matter because this time he goes slow, erasing all the fear of last time, seeking permission for every sweet touch. If Aster taught me how to kiss, Zeke teaches me how to stop. *Everything*. Thinking, worrying, panicking. My eyes shutter as I sink back into his arm, letting him hold me up, letting him in.

And breathe.

Sometime later, the sun disappears.

"Is this the way you thank everyone for helping you? Albert will be excited," Aster drawls, slapping his too-perfect behind into a patch of grass beside our heads.

"Duckhole," Zeke mumbles, pulling away a fraction.

My heart should be pounding, but it beats slow. Even my eyes struggle to open, and when I manage there's a dual, sharp intake. Zeke's arm tightens around me as a cool hand finds mine, then releases, as before.

Tears prick the corners of my eyes, but when I look for him again, Aster is gone.

"Let him go." Zeke rearranges me in the fading afternoon sun so we catch the last of it on the hillside.

My back presses to his chest, his legs making vee shapes either side of me where I snuggle between them. Long arms wrap around my stomach, inked fingers interlocked.

"He runs more often than I do." I trace the patterns along his wrists as he rests his chin on the crook of his shoulder. "More than I used to."

"Nah, you're still a runner." Zeke kisses my cheek as I lean back into him, closing my eyes. "You okay after everything in there? They were brutal."

I consider and shake my head. "I've had worse."

He huffs a laugh. "Thanks."

"Not you," I poke him. "Ego trip, much?"

"A bit." He falls quiet, his breaths settling while my brain starts turning over.

"Back at the boxing gym..."

He groans into my shoulder. "I'll apologize as many times as you need, babygirl. I'm so f– ducking sorry for that."

"No, you egotist." I slap his hand. "The tray with the chains, and things. Why do you do it? Serve him, I mean." The sentiment tumbles from my lips.

Zeke tucks hair behind my ears. "He's not … the easiest. But he doesn't have it easy either, Roxy. His father … it's all sorts of ducked up. Beyond ducked." He squeezes me tight.

"So, you're what, babysitting him?" I frown.

"More than that. You're right, what you said when you found us together that morning. I do love him," he says simply. "Like a brother, or a lover. If he wanted that, I'd do it. Whatever he needs. What you need. Does that help?"

I swallow hard. "You mean it?"

He nudges his cheek to mine. "'Course. You might not get it, Roxy, but we all feel that way for you, too. Each other. We're a family. Weird one, maybe, but who cares. It's us."

Simple words for a not so simple declaration.

"I love that about you." I twine my fingers through his, my throat thickening as I force words out before I choke on them. "You don't sugar coat anything." His knuckles tighten on mine. "That's the second longest speech I've ever heard you give."

He huffs against my neck as the sun drops the horizon.

"Yeah. Me, too."

Chapter Twenty-Nine

Dance Like Everyone's Watching

Roxy

The end of school year dance arrives super fast. Decorations cover almost every surface, and every single day, Elen is accosted by giggling fangirls begging him to have Failure Asylum play. His plan to go solo isn't public knowledge yet. I'm not even sure if he's told the rest of his band. He wards eager fans off with an endless supply of patience and endless pockets full of signed merch.

The rest of Alchem Academy is as crazed over other things. Finals are a week away, and after that Rhani has planned a shopping trip. My stomach plummets remembering how our *last* shopping trip panned out. Both Zeke and Aster have been absent from my life for the last weeks, providing a slice of sanity and breathing space, like I'd forgotten how with them around.

Nyx and Elen have been on a music writing spree that leaves me at Rhani's disposal and she's *all* about the dance. The theme is desert—not to be confused with dessert which is what Elen first tried to convince me to dress like. Rhani's fully in her element, immersing in socials lives I dodge at every opportunity.

But I can't avoid her planning forever. Finals aren't a week away; they're almost done.

"When's your last exam?" She bats eyelash extensions at me.

"This afternoon. Calc." I wince, knowing I'm going to fail in outlandish style, though I doubt my efforts will be appreciated.

"Ooh, same, of course. So, shopping after. I'll get our usual chauffeur—"

"Nope."

I hold fast to my denial and stare her down.

Rhani raises a manicured and dyed eyebrow. "No?" she repeats, like I'm the most offensive creature on the planet.

"Nope." I shrug. "I mean, someone had to say no to you sometime. May as well be me."

She stares at me with an open mouth. "Okay, Roxy. What's your plan for dressing for the dance then?"

My plan is to not go at all and avoid the nature of the endeavor, but I don't think I'll get away with that.

"What about Yuleton?" I remember the night Nyx took me to get takeout at the little Italian restaurant in the town below the school. For the life of me I can't remember what else was in the street. "Gotta be a dress shop there."

Rhani taps her phone against her chest. "That's brilliant. I bet no one goes down there. If there's a shop, it's a quick walk, and there's no chance that we'll double up with anyone else."

I don't much care about that last part, but the idea of not being cached away with Zeke in close quarters for hours at a time and trying on clothes in front of him again lifts me into my comfort zone a fraction. Sitting with him on the hill was perfect. Too perfect. Now I'm scared of anything that might shatter that memory, like the ones I had with Aster that have never mended quite right.

Happy in her planning, Rhani lets me cram for our last exam while she doesn't bother studying at all.

****

Despite proclaiming how much she sucked at calc when she arrived, I can't help but envy Rhani when she waltzes out of the exam forty minutes before anyone else. I straggle out last, frazzled and brain dead. I'm trying to locate my phone in my bag when she hugs me from behind and strangles me. Again.

"We're done!" Her squeal lights up my brain. "You survived your first year at Alchem Academy. Well done, Roxy." She beams at me like a proud mother hen.

I roll my eyes as I detangle myself from her embrace. "I mean at least *you* passed—" My throat dries as I find Zeke staring at me from over her shoulder.

At least he isn't glaring, this time.

The clasp of my bag bends under my feral grip as I edge around him. "Uh, howdyougo," I mumble, staring at the ground.

"Look who insists on playing chaperone. *Again*," she mouths this last part.

I retreat a step. "I need to get something from the dorm—"

"Nope. No backing out," Rhani announces. "This was your idea and it's a brilliant one. Now, come on." Her hand wraps around my arm, and she tows me forward.

I make the mistake of looking over my shoulder as she leads me toward the gates.

Zeke follows at a distance, but his eyes lock onto mine the moment I turn back. A knowing smile twists the corner of his mouth as his gaze coasts over my body. I flush hot and cold all at once.

Twisting back to face forward, I tune into Rhani's chatter on color choice while my brain is still trying to solve test problem sixteen part b and ignore Zeke's incessant presence.

Fail the second right there.

The walk releases tension I didn't know I stored during finals week. My stresses over whether I flunked or passed are lesser now, and I join in Rhani's one sided conversation in full. We reach the short row of shops without incident.

I take in the town during daylight hours that looks

so different without shadows hiding the edges of the tall, narrow buildings with their quaint scalloped architraves and bow window displays. I'm also checking over my shoulder to see if someone noticed our escape from campus. This time, at least I *know* we're being followed. Rather than freaking me out, Zeke's presence is somewhat ... reassuring.

Rhani pauses in front of a haberdashery and wrinkles her nose. "I'm reassessing your life choices." She grimaces at the shop front's pink and green candy-striped towers.

I want to object, but even I can't deal with the amount of pink and pomp going on in that window frontage. I edge back a step and run into a wall of solid heat.

"Maybe that one would suit you better." Zeke doesn't bother to step back like a regular person, nudging me forward like a wayward puppy who lost its path.

I stare at the gap between two buildings where he points over my shoulder with his chin to what looks like an actual freaking cobblestone lane. Inside the corner sits a filigree framed window display showcasing a gold dress that looks like it's made of mermaid scales.

"That's perfect," I breathe. If I hadn't been sold on the idea of the shopping trip, I am now. It might be a mad dash to see who gets that dress first.

I don't need to turn around to know Zeke's wearing a smug expression. I'll have to do something to bring him down a peg, after I thank him. But later. Maybe.

"'Bout time you developed some taste," Rhani says with approval, crossing the road in long strides.

I follow, bemused at her new mission as Zeke falls into step at my side.

"I've got some things to do, so if you don't need

me hanging over your shoulder this time…" He drifts off both in voice and step, veering away, though he shoots a narrow-eyed glance at his sister.

I sneak a look sideways. "I think you're safe. She's into one store owner." His eyes darken at the mention of Adam, and I wish I'd kept my mouth shut. "We're okay. Go." I offer him encouragement, wondering why I'm reassuring the hulk of a man who invited himself along on our shopping trip. Though to be fair, he did find the shop.

Zeke keeps wandering away with a little more oomph in his step than before as I hurry to catch up with Rhani and sling my arm through hers.

"Did you drop me in it again?" she asks in a mild tone.

I flush and release her arm. "Maybe? Unintentional."

"Uh huh. Dibs." She reaches the shop door first and calls it, pushing inward to the soft ring of a dainty bell that dangles over the threshold, sweet talking the assistant before I can physically locate one.

Moments later, I'm stashed in a changing room with an armful of appropriate desert theme colored dresses that dazzle my eyes. Picking at the first layer of fabric I didn't pick out, I trail my fingers along the golden material that does indeed resemble Saharan sands, if with a bit more glitz.

"You got the mermaid scale, right?" I call over the heavy velvet barrier where Rhani rustles about on the other side.

"Uh huh."

Most of my selection is all sheath-like and skin tight, nothing I could have picked for myself. "I think I got the body con. Wanna swap?" I cross my fingers.

"Not a chance, baby."

Damnit.

I sigh and pick up the first dress, mangling the zip. Unable to work it, I go for the next with the same result. This will be a disaster if nothing even opens for me and I can't even try it on.

A confection of old gold lace sails over the velvet curtain of my cubicle. I catch the puffy pillow, picking at the delicate scalloped edges that look handmade. Not heavy enough to resemble a tablecloth, the deep bronzed lace looks sophisticated enough to grace a red carpet.

"Uh, thank you," I called to the faceless assistant who must have heard my plea.

This one has buttons, and I manage to wiggle my way into the dress, even manage to do a few up. Discarding my bra that won't go with the strapless top, I reach around for the tiny buttons at the back with no hope.

"Rhani, swap do up?" I call out, crossing my fingers.

Silence.

I poke my head out and wiggle her curtain. "Rhani?"

The curtain opens to reveal … nothing. She's already done and has left me.

I sigh and emerge into the dressing room in full, fluffing the floor length gown around me like a lace bell. Holding the back together with one hand, lest the sales person get an eyeful they don't need when they come to find me, I reach back, but I need to be a contortionist to make this work.

Maybe there's a handy tool… I suppose I should check the price tag on the item, as it both looks and *feels* like it's worth a fortune, but as everyone keeps reminding me, I don't have to do that anymore.

The excess still seems wasteful, and I can't get

used to that feeling. Nor do I want to get used to that. Some part of me needs to cling to the girl from Providence with dirt stuck under her nails.

Lost in my head, I don't notice the other occupant in the dressing room until he speaks.

"That one." Zeke's deep voice sends a shiver along my spine.

I swallow hard and turn my back to him, pulling my hair out of the way with one hand. "Could you do me up, please? I didn't get a chance to look, and…"

Deft, albeit rough, fingers graze my bare back in a gentle touch as he works on each button. "Perfect. Wear your hair up?" He makes it a question rather than a demand, and I smile.

How far we've come.

Not that we've talked much since the house. Or the funeral. Or the day he kissed me and I ran away. Our splintered history ripples around us, shattered pieces never meant to go together, though we keep trying to force them to fit, anyway.

Until one of us is hurt.

Or both of us.

I swallow again, my smile slipping as I turn back to face him. "Do I have you to thank for finding this?"

He nods, a barest movement. His eyes flick from my face for a fraction of a second. "Yeah."

"Thank you."

"Consider it an apology for everything I ruined for you." Zeke swallows hard. His thumb grazes the inside of my hip through the lace before he whips about on his heel, stalking to the other end of the dressing room in a typical Zeke-esque escape.

"Wait." *Now who's the demanding one?*

He turns side on to me, his silhouette thrown into sharp relief beneath the spotlights that focus on the middle of the room for the best effect, highlighting the domineering strength of him, the stoic set of his hard jawline.

"You don't need to apologize for anything." I take a step toward him. "Not anymore. We did that, remember? It was me who came to you, then. That's at least half my fault. Maybe all of it. And then…" I tilt my head back, my lips curving into a smile as I remember his mouth on mine in a different memory, one blanketed in sunshine and peace.

He utters a hollow laugh. "I was a coward. I fought you, and I never told you sorry. I should have been fighting *for* you. Yet you still forgive me. I'm not worthy of this." His voice breaks as his fingers flutter toward me and drop.

My Angry Boy and his ego. The smallest smile wants to break free, but I know he'll see it as me laughing at him, and I don't want to damage his pride further.

"You are," I whisper. "Or else we're all not worthy of each other, and where does that leave us?"

Zeke swears under his breath and blows out air. "Let me say sorry to you once," he pleads.

I take another step forward, into his space, and he shifts on his feet. This is another bad idea, here in the shop, but I can't stop. "Where did you go, when you left us?"

His eyes get shifty. "I had errands."

"Like what?"

"Are you always so nosy?"

"Just annoying."

A smile plays at the corner of his lips. "Wear your hair up for the dance, Roxy." It's an order, this time. He turns to face me in full.

I twist my hair up, lifting it above my shoulders. A few strands dangle over my face and I've run out of fingers to push them back. "Like this?"

He nods, his breaths short and shallow. "Yeah. Like that." Hesitant, as though seeking permission, he reaches out to push the strands back, tucking them behind my ears. His large palms cradle my face for a second, and his mouth contacts mine again. The kiss lasts a breath, but it's *everything*.

"I'm sorry," he whispers, his eyes deep and soul filled as he leans back, though we still share the same air for an instant. "I'm sorry I hurt you. Scared you. All the things I didn't do. Everything I did."

"It's okay," I breathe back and then he's kissing me again, and I forget to care about breathing at all.

"And you worry about *me* in dressing rooms." Rhani snorts, breaking into our quiet moment. "Nice dress though, Roxy."

Zeke's hands drop away. An indecipherable look bores deep inside me, and a moment later he strides out of the dressing room, the epitome of pensive silence.

I can't meet Rhani's eyes as she giggles away to herself, though she does free me from the dress. Changing back into my own clothes, I bundle the delicate lace up to find that it's already paid for—no freebies on who did that. I promise myself I'll buy him some lary, over bright, not black decorative thing for his Jeep in recompense—and lead the way back up the hill toward Alchem, though it's Rhani and me this time without him.

Zeke's absence is noted, but Rhani has other things on her mind, like makeup and socials lives to fill her schedule. My legs ache by the time we hit the dorms—the elevator is stalled at the base of the building *again*, and I'm happy to tumble onto my bed, kicking my shoes off after I hang the lace dress in its bag in my closet.

"You can't pike on me now." Rhani pouts after

she's completed her mandatory lives on socials, waving a bottle of salted caramel whiskey in front of my nose.

"Oh, God. No," I groan, covering my eyes. "Can I opt to not wake up with a hangover tomorrow? I thought we were doing dance stuff?"

"We did dance stuff. Now, we party. The boys built a bonfire. Come on." She grabs my hand and yanks a tired me from the dorm.

I pause long enough to flap about for my phone, my key, and to slug water. I know my roomie well enough that the sort of fluids she intends to imbibe are not the hydrating sort. Feeling semi-responsible, I follow her to the back of the library where campus dips into a hollow.

With the last of the exams for the year done, Alchem unites to blow off steam. We still have obligatory classes for the next week, but they're scheduled to hand in major projects, collect art, close off admin and things. Nothing serious. I suspect less than half the student body will attend the remainder of classes and socialize more often than not. The dance is coming up, and after that I suppose everyone will head off to their homes for the break.

I haven't thought about home or where I'll go, what I'll do with myself, but the thought of being without the boys or Rhani hits me in the stomach like a true sucker punch. The whiskey is a lot emptier when it makes it to my hand. I take a double slug that burns all the way down and leaves me coughing up a long-forgotten body organ.

Someone slaps my back. "There's my girl."

I glare at Elen as my eyes water. "I'm sure it's an attractive look," I splutter into the back of my hand.

He smirks. "Gotta get it up sometime, Roxy girl. May as well be tonight."

"Nah, she's the fun police. No fun being had here." Rhani's already in full swing, shaking her perfect booty around the bonfire. Smoke and haze filters around the area, thickening as I watch. A cloying scent hits my nose, and I cough a little harder.

Elen turns me around. "You've never smoked a joint, have you?" He watches me speculatively.

"Nope." I inhale a shallow breath and try not to choke. *Fail.*

"Let's move you over here, 'kay?" He slings an arm around my shoulders, leading me away from the sweet scent toward the bonfire that's too hot and too bright but somehow less smokey than the back of the library.

"Kay," I mutter, letting Rhani grab my hand and swing me around.

I dance with her until my feet ache to their bones.

After a few more shots of the salted caramel whiskey, my shoes disappear and I keep dancing. It isn't until my throat sticks, aching—for actual water—and my preparative sip before leaving the dorm fails me that I realize the boys are all huddled together by the library, talking way too seriously for my taste.

I sigh and look over at Rhani who sways on her feet even though she's leaning on a random dude who also sways. "Gonna go be the fun police," I call. Then I mouth, "*Adam.*"

She waves me off, and I manage to make my way barefoot across the grass to the boys.

Aster talks into his phone that's held out into the middle of their circle.

Zeke pokes him the moment he spots me and the phone disappears. All conversation ceases as I break up their confab.

"I'm pretty sure at least one of you is supposed to

be dancing with us." I tilt my head and frown when no one meets my eyes. "Or you could tell me what's going on."

"Nothing, Roxy. Go have fun." Aster blows me off.

I flip him the finger, turning my back to him. Eyeballing Zeke, who I know is trying to stay in my good books, I hold out my hand, but he doesn't budge, his back pressed flush to the bricked wall, staring out at some point over my head. So much for his, *'we're a family'* speech.

"Elen?" I shift my attention to the blue haired K-pop star, but even he shakes his head.

"Not tonight, Roxy Girl. I'll make it up to you another time, but…"

I shrug, pretending that them blocking me out doesn't hurt for the first time in months. Not since they used to do it on purpose, but this time it feels worse. It's not bullying, I'm just … not included.

"It's okay." I force a smile. "Let me know if I can help or anything. Gonna go find some water."

I pivot on my heel as someone swears, hoping my fake smile holds on, and head toward the girl's change room one building over. The library bathrooms will be locked tight, but the gym is often left open for late practices. Traipsing all the way across to the cafeteria for a vending machine water or back to the dorms both sound like a cruddy idea in the dark.

Away from the bonfire, the night air nips at my exposed arms. I wind my arms around myself and try to quicken my steps, but the dancing and alcohol hits me in one. My t-shirt and jeans might have seemed warm to walk in from the town to the school earlier, but it offers little protection now. Aware of a familiar gait following me, though I'm unsure if it's Zeke or Aster ready to herd me back, I tuck my elbows into my sides.

Hurrying around the side of the building that blocks out the last of the residential bonfire heat, I try the main door. Blessedly it opens, right onto a scene I never wanted to observe and hope never to again.

Less than two dozen feet away Principal Gallaway has his paws all over one of the female students, pulling her clothes off while she bats at him with her eyes squeezed shut. Tears coat her pale cheeks. My mind snapshots the whole scene, unable to connect what's happening in more than a series of disjointed polaroids I'll piece together later.

Worst is the gym teacher, Mr. Birkin, filming the entire encounter.

Part of a squeak leaves my lips, but that's all that comes out.

A cool, long fingered hand closes over my mouth, Aster's arms band around my body as he pulls me back into him.

I freeze at the contact, my scream lodged in my throat though I can't tear my eyes away from the abuse unfolding before us.

My body decides it's time to react in a bleated, way too late reaction. I twist in his arms, clawing and fighting.

Aster growls in my ear, pulling me into the shadows, back along the hall. His breath is hot on my ear. "If you don't stop right now, everything I've spent weeks setting up will be for nothing, Roxy. I have to catch him in the act, or his reign of terror will *never stop.*"

He spins me around so my back is to the cold painted cement wall, his hands slapping either side of my head, caging me in. Aster's face is filled with rage, but tonight, it isn't directed at me.

I blink at him, processing at a much slower speed.

"You knew?"

His teeth are bared as he leans in, pressing his forehead to mine, his eyes fierce. "I knew that was almost you that day I pulled you out of his office. I did the best thing I could to save you," he says, voice cracking, and then with a burst of clarity, I understand.

The other girl. *Faith.*

Shaking my head, I shove at his chest. "No. You didn't— *No,"* I whisper, my gut churning.

"Are you coming?" Zeke barks from farther down the hall, accompanied by two men in suits I know as Agent C and Agent A from after the graveyard.

I stare at Aster. "That's what they were after?"

He nods, his jaw working without sound for a moment. "I think my father is involved. I want that to end, too."

The implications hit me a second time. "Aster." It's my turn to plead, reaching for his sleeve, but he walks away without a glance backward, following Zeke into the room where Gallaway, the girl, and Mr. Birkin are...

I lunge sideways in time to vomit into a corner of the hallway, straightening to wipe my mouth on the back of my hand a minute later to find Nyx holding my hair away from my face and stroking my back.

He leads me to a fountain outside the gym building where the party has broken up. Red and blue lights flicker through the hazy night air. I follow as he helps me wash my face and passes his hoodie over. I stare at the soft offering that smells of leather and forest and snow, and a tear breaks free. He nods, still silent, and presses the warm material into my hands.

Letting out a shaky breath, I pat my face dry and cling to the hoodie like it's a lifeline.

His presence is calming. We find a tree and sit

with our backs against it, leaning side by side as he places both his earphones in my ears, blocking out the world with his music.

I watch the scene unfold, hiding in his hoodie pulled over my head. Understanding why they didn't include me in this conversation, tears blur the colored lights until smoke, suits, and bonfire meld into one visual cacophony overlaid with Nyx's sounds.

Students scatter, though some like Rhani hang around. Doing more lives, I suppose, getting word out about the principal's arrest, though I can't bring myself to care what happens to him at all.

Ignoring everyone else, I lean my head on Nyx's shoulder, sucking in the comfort he offers in his brand of silence. He lets me purge my emotion, resting the back of his bare arm to my denim-covered knee.

The boys give statements and keep the FBI away while I steal a few more hours of disjointed peace. I know it can't last, but I'll take it anyway. I understand what they tried to do on my behalf. And I'm so freaking grateful it wasn't me.

But it shouldn't have had to be her.

JOSS PHOENIX

Chapter Thirty

Bippity Boppity

Roxy

Alchem Academy refuses to be cowed by a small thing like a sex trafficking scandal.

That's what Gallaway's indiscretion with Faith turned out to be; the head of a filthy snake that infected a solid twenty percent of his staff, reaching far greater than a simple filming and a sexual assault case, if such a heinous act could ever be consider simple.

Faith's best friend, Donovan, rode with her to the police station, refusing to let her out of his sight when she agreed to a rape kit, and that's the last any of us saw of her.

Rhani broadcast the news far and wide, her reach increasing with every word. There's no chance that Gallaway will walk from this event unscathed thanks to her prodigious, albeit rabid audience.

My boys slunk back into the shadows and pretended they had nothing to do with anything, turning the spotlight away from themselves, and me. They've refused to let me walk anywhere alone since. For once, I'm not arguing, though I still haven't worked out where I'm headed after the dance.

The week blurs past me in a rush of emotions and collected artworks that remained unslashed, though the portrait I painted of Aster on the rooftop was delivered to my room in the wake of the Gallaway debacle.

I stow it back behind the bathroom door, though at least I can stand to look at this one each time I shower. It's a weird kind of comfort that he's here, and not creepy at   all.

Or maybe it is creepy and I'm more broken than ever.

Standing in the graveyard saying goodbye to my parents seems an eon ago. So much has changed since then. Zeke is still angry, but not at the world. He's more targeted now. Aster fights his father. I understand a little more of their hate/hate relationship, though he still hasn't spoken to me since that night. Elen is taking control of his own destiny rather than going along with the crowd, and even Nyx stands straighter and talks more.

Which leaves ... me.

I feel like I've marked time for months, unsure of myself, the boys, everything, bumping from one catastrophe to the next. The one thing I have become spoiled about is the amount of hot water. Clean, endless hot water will forever be my Achilles heel. I'm shameless about it. And I suppose the acceptance of finding myself at Alchem is part of this new version of Roxy Quell, orphan and business owner.

Once, I thought I might sell Pyric Industries. I wanted nothing to do with the inheritance my aunt intended for me. Now, I wonder if I might not look into understanding her legacy, learn it inch by inch no matter how long it takes. Maybe I can make a part of it mine one day.

I suppose we all have a destined path, but not all of us have to take the one laid out before us. The girl who left Providence never expected to have friends, find love, or own clean, new clothes. She wanted food that wasn't out of date and a night's sleep before the *rinse and repeat* cycle started all over again.

That's not my path, and Six Dice isn't at the end of my lane.

But four boys I fell for somewhere over the last year are, and my chest itches with the secret that lies within. Not that I have much of a chance to keep that secret when I have less than a moment to myself at any point.

After my final art class, Elen lopes along beside me, as usual. His knuckles brush the back of my hand, and before I can say anything, he speaks first.

"Come on tour with me."

I snort. "Yeah, right." He doesn't say anything else, walking at my side. "What is this, a rockstar friends-with-benefits type offer?" I laugh again.

Elen shoots me a sideways smile. "You're so freaking cute."

My nose twitches. "I'm not cute."

"Are too."

"Not." I won't put up with the charade, and he refuses not to walk with me the way he has since the day Aster insisted one of them had to be by my side after each class. Even after the ski trip and Aster's commands no longer mattered, Elen persisted. My heart shatters fresh. I rub the spot over my chest like it can erase the pain, but of course it can't. "Why," I whisper, not expecting an answer.

Elen grabs the door at the end of the hall and holds it for me. I take the hint and walk ahead of him, feeling his presence even though he doesn't touch me as I pass by.

"Maybe I want to spend time with you, Roxy," he murmurs. "Go on tour with me when I go solo."

"Why would I go with you?" I interrupt. "How long would that be, anyway?"

His lopsided grin is back. "Dunno. Three months. Six?"

I halt and turn to face him, my mouth hanging open. He closes it with two fingers and leaves them pressed against my jaw.

I push his hand away, ignoring the fact that I like his easy touch, could get used to this. "You're asking me to go away with you for *six months*."

Elen shrugs. "Yeah."

His tongue plays with his lip ring, then the pointed barbell, the transparent one that nobody is supposed to see but I know is there. I study the movement over his pale, arched lip and drag my gaze back to his eyes. His lashes flicker, and I know I'm busted.

I push through my blush that's got to match my hair and toss the length that's grown out over my shoulder, fixing him with a reality check stare because my rock star bestie needs one.

"You can't ask me to go with you for six months," I say, all logic today.

He rakes his fingers through his black and blue hair. "Why not?"

I blink back at him. *"Because—"* I can't find a reason to save myself. *This is a ridiculous conversation.* I stamp my foot. "Because."

He flicks my nose. "Cute as hell, Roxy girl."

I don't dignify that with an answer. "You can't ask girls to go on tour with you to fill an empty space, okay?" I edge forward into his space a little when he doesn't answer. "Elen? Promise me. You can't do that. Someone will take advantage of you." I bite my lip. Childhood fame has skewed his sense of reality.

He watches me with hooded eyes, his tongue still playing with his lip ring, and it's distracting.

"Do we need to have a serious talk about what's appropriate?"

His gray eyes—no blue contacts today—brighten a little and his nose wiggles.

I lean closer. Yep, it wiggles.

Like a bunny.

"Okay," he says, back to being cool and bored Elen, and a little too close as he leans in until there isn't an inch between us. "I *can* ask you to come to the school dance with me? That's appropriate, right?"

I try to back up, but his hand is there on the back of my neck and I don't go anywhere. A tiny noise escapes me, and he smiles while my eyes narrow.

"The school dance?" My voice comes out all breathy and short.

"That's what I said." He stares at me smugly while I gape and grasp about for words that fail me right at the wrong time. He rears back and laughs. "My Roxy is starved for words. Who would've thought." His fingers massage my nape as he laughs at me, but it's not in a bad way.

More a *make-your-tummy-flip-because-I'm-a-shit-hot-rockstar-flirting-with-you* sort of way.

Oh, my God. Elen is flirting with me. Real flirting. Not harmless, cafeteria grade, hold-my-kimchi level flirting.

Then he closes the space he gave back, all the confidence in the world resuming as he towers over me. "Will you come to the dance with me, Roxy?"

I'm still looking at the shape of his pale lips, the way his tongue plays with those damn piercings when my mouth replies all on its own.

"Yes."

****

"If you sit still, I'll be able to get this finished, you know, then we can keep partying." Rhani shimmies, but it's an act she's putting on, like she can't stop.

No one can, each of us pushing through this last week like it's something we all have to do, students and remaining staff alike. A compulsion.

"Have you heard from her?" I address the non-elephant in the room, guilt overwhelming me.

Rhani pauses, mid-glitter swipe. "Faith?" She

winces at the name like it's taboo. "No," she says in a hushed voice. "But I think one of her boys went with her and hasn't come back, either. They're in a weird group thing, like you and…" She waves a hand to encompass my absentee boy—*friends, maybe?*—who are supposed to also be getting ready for the dance, though I'm not sure I'll see all of them tonight.

Elen promised to collect me soon. I turned my phone over at least half an hour earlier to prevent myself from checking the time. I reach for it again, and Rhani slaps my hand with her makeup powder brush.

"Ow," I complain, squeezing my stinging knuckles. "That thing is a weapon."

"Damn right." We both freeze as the door vibrates on its hinges. "Coming," she sings, then shoves me forward. "Go get it," she hisses, far too noisy.

I glance at her and shake my head, my lower half locked in place. "I can't."

Rhani sends me an exasperated look and pushes at my back. "Of course you can. You know this boy. He adores you. Now *go*."

"No. I mean…" My throat constricts. "I mean I shouldn't be having fun when she's not here." *When she can't.*

"Oh, Roxy." Rhani kneels before me in a vision of golden mermaid scales. "I know you've got survivor guilt. But you can't let that stop you from living. It's one night. We all need this." Her eyes plead with a heady dose of her own, and I get it.

But that doesn't stop my own deluge.

I bite my lip. "Yes, I can."

"Nope." She hauls me up and pushes me toward the door, yanking it open. "Ta-da."

Elen stands on the other side dressed in a pale suit that matches everything about him to perfection. His usual blue contacts have been swapped out to deep gold ones the same hue as my dress, and his lip rings are an array of blues and bronzes that contrast with his deep blue eye liner. In short, he's breathtaking.

My mind wipes as I stare at him, trying not to drool.

"Hey," I whisper as my words jam in my throat.

"Zeke was right," he murmurs reverently, clearing his throat after a moment. Elen sucks in a long breath and steps inside the room, kicking the door shut behind him.

I have a vision of another boy, paler, doing the same thing on a different night. One far less happy, that night all about pain, betrayal, and heartache. Banishing Aster's shade from my room, I focus on the boy—man—before me.

"These are for you." Elen presses a bundle of gifts into my hands. "Top one is mine. Do that first," he adds with a shy smile.

Elen, shy?

I check a second time and know I'll remember that smile forever.

His fingers shake as he helps me tie the feather corsage to my wrist, fluffing it up and fussing until I stop him, my touch gentle.

"It's beautiful. Like you," I say softly.

Oops. That kinda slipped out.

He blinks at me and that shy smile turns devastating and cocky.

Not the effect I was aiming for, but it seems to work for him.

"Aster's next," he mutters, fixing a gold, glitter-tipped dahlia in my hair. More fussing, but his touch is gentle and Rhani helps him with some hairpins.

"This is a lot." I stare down at the small collection of gifts left.

A pair of gold crystal snowflake earrings is next. I know who those are from as Elen lifts them to my ears.

"That happens when you're dating four men at once," he murmurs. "Glad they've all got good taste."

"Is that what we're doing?" I hiccup a laugh, that overwhelming feeling hitting me hard as I rock on my heels. "How come you're alone?"

He shrugs, grazing his fingertips over my cheek. "Seems to work for us. Screw everyone else."

"Rockstar rules, right?"

"That's right." He pauses, then places the last gift, a stencil, in my palm. "Nyx said you get to pick where it goes."

I swallow as I stare at my introvert musician's creation. All of us are intertwined in the tattoo he's designed, our names linked within the flow of the image that depicts us all.

"Don't you dare cry and ruin that makeup I've spent hours applying, Roxanna Quell," Rhani threatens, waving the powder brush in my face.

A tear trickles free and she sighs in defeat, but it's Elen who grabs her tools and attacks my face. "I got this, Roxy. I've left plenty of salt on stage. Got tricks of my own." He presses a kiss to my temple when he's finished scant seconds later. "Better?"

I raise my chin. "I think so?"

Rhani gasps and bows to Elen. "You're my favorite forever." She hugs him, flicking her forefinger between them. "We need to do socials work."

He laughs and gathers me under one arm. "Ready to go, Roxy?"

The same doubts as before slam into me. I shake my head.

"Not again," Rhani whispers, grabbing tissues.

Elen shoos her away, cupping my face. His eyes

narrow, and he nods. "It's okay, I get it."

I sniffle. "You do?"

"Yeah. I do." He pauses. "I left a tiny village of starving kids. Half a country of starving kids. I can't feed them all, but I try, Roxy. Every damn day. Right now, I have to split what I earn five ways. If I go solo, I can do what I like with my money. Maybe that's a good reason for you to take on that business of your aunt's that scares you."

Put my narcissistic aunt's money to better use, cleaning up schools and protecting girls from trafficking. She'd hate my reasoning. It's perfect.

I stare at him in wonder. "I didn't know that."

His crooked smile does things to my stomach. Good things. "Now you do."

"I just … you all give me so much. What did I give you to deserve this level of…?" I run my fingers through the feathers he tied to my wrist.

I swear his eyes glow as he entwines our hands and squeezes.

"Roxy, I need you to hear me," he says, loud and clear.

I blink and look up at his serious tone, right into his eyes and get lost there for a moment.

"You don't cower from Aster. No one does that. Not even Zeke. And, Angry Boy? You don't back down from him. You face Zeke head on. That's courage, Roxy girl. You've earned their respect, and their love. You're my muse, and you listen to Nyx, make him feel important for once when everyone else ignores the weird kid who doesn't speak. But you *hear him*. You can't buy that. In a world full of power and wealth, you give us what no one else can. It's why we're all in love with you." He squeezes my fingers as my heart stills. "In case you didn't know."

"I— I—"

He laughs, but not in a mean way. In an Elen way. "That's twice I've stolen your words. Come on. Don't wanna be late and a bad date."

"There's a song in that," I mutter as my heart starts again, leaving me flushed all over.

Elen casts me an amused glance. "See? My muse. Never letting you go, Roxy girl." His lips press to the top of my head as he escorts me to the door. "My Roxy."

My traitorous pulse ricochets around inside me, bouncing off into a thousand beats while I stare at him, still speechless.

"Have fun, lovebirds," Rhani calls, but I'm so lost in his words I almost forget to wave.

****

Alchem's dining hall has been transformed into a glittering sea of sand. Gold and bronze hues reflect off every surface thanks to a giant aureate disco ball suspended from the center of the room.

But in true Alchem style, and gold kind of being their thing with those stupid gates and all, this is no regular disco ball. Suspended from the mirror shards are hundreds of tiny glittering crystals, each shaped like a miniscule grain of sand that refracts the shattered light into a dizzy centrifuge until a galaxy of stars revolves around us.

Even Elen seems taken aback at Alchem's combined decorative skills. "Impressive." He squeezes my hand as we enter the room, tracing the band he wrapped around my wrist.

"Possessive little rockstar, aren't you?" I mutter out the side of my mouth.

"Oh, Roxy girl. You have no idea."

I shiver at the promise in his voice and scan the room for familiar faces. Rhani will be the last to appear in her personal style. I wonder if Adam will make an appearance. Tonight is supposed to be for students, but, somehow, I doubt she cares about rules.

Elen's thumb brushes the back of my hand. "Drinks first, or dance with me?"

My mouth starts to say *dance, of course*, but I catch sight of Nyx doing a quiet little boogie on his own off to one side. His eyes are closed as he sways to his own personal beat, his earphones in, regardless of what music plays around him.

Several fangirls attack from our side. Elen gives me a small grin, squeezing my fingers. "I'll be a moment?" His eyes search mine. "Or I can say no tonight."

I shrug, not minding his insta-entourage. He'll need to maintain the wave of popularity to make it on his own. Who am I to stand in the way of his dream? Plus, he called me his muse earlier, and I'm still a little dizzy from that.

"I'm gonna go say hi." I spot Aster and Zeke propping up a piece of wall, their arms folded, standing side-by-side, one wearing a white suit, one in black. No free guesses on who is who.

Elen gifts me with one of those shy smiles I'll never have enough of. Ever. "I'll meet you there."

I smile back, and my attention drifts to the pair overseeing Nyx. I kind of like that they're watching, keeping him safe while he does his own thing. Being part of the Elite might provide a certain measure of security, but it doesn't prevent animosity thrown their way, and Nyx, ever lost in his head, makes for an easy target.

Abandoning Elen to his fangirl club and feeling a little guilty, I weave my way between dancers and pick up a jelly cup off one of the long tables decorated as mini sand dunes, hoping it's not spiked. My last attempt at alcohol happened the night Gallaway was arrested. I'm far from prepared for a repeat of hurling my stomach up.

Not in this dress.

Like the rest of our Academy students and remaining staff, I intend to make tonight the perfect night. Tonight is a party night, not to get blitzed off my face, but to remember Faith's sacrifice. What she gave up so I didn't have to.

My stomach tightens. I push back bile with effort, raising my chin high. Aster's unyielding eyes sweep over me, but it's Zeke's small smile that lights me up inside.

Unable to face either of them, I chicken out at the last moment, sliding in behind Nyx and lifting one of his headphones. "Where did you have in mind?"

It's a dangerous question. He left the location of his present, the tattoo stencil, open to me, but it's his design and he should have a say.

His hazel eyes open as he revolves on the spot and catches my hand. Turning my wrist palm up, Nyx traces the shape of the stencil on the inside.

I follow the pattern of his finger, mesmerized as he stares down at me, his lips moving on a single word. "Here."

"Perfect," I breathe back. *Like tonight.*

He smiles happily and opens his arms.

I fall into the first true hug Nyx has given to me. Resting my cheek to his shoulder, I realize how tall he is. He offers me comfort when we're sitting down and I'm crying, or I'm numb, or cold, or unfeeling. Somehow, that's when we always connect. Music is our bridge.

This time it's something else—all of us. My arms surround his waist beneath his usual leather jacket.

Everybody else might get dressed up, but he dressed down for the occasion. Like the boys in their pale and dark getups watching us, the distressed leather suits him.

Snuggling into his embrace, I inhale a deep breath of the woods, Nyx, and leather. The scents swirl around my head as I close my eyes and sway with him, letting everything drift away. Fingers brush my ear beneath the flower Aster gave me that Elen and Rhani attached to my hair.

A sprinkling of the golden glitter from petals decorates my fingers as I press to Nyx's warmth. I suspect Aster dipped the petals himself. God alone knows what sort of mess he made, but my thoughts are distracted as Nyx presses his headphones into my ear.

Forest noises fill my head. I forget everything else as his music takes over. The stream, night bugs, the silences in between. Everything he creates is magic. It's so different from anything I've ever heard. I move with him, safe in the circle of his arms, lost in the rhythm he's created.

"So beautiful." I risk shattering the illusion of our solitude to press my lips to the corner of his mouth.

As in the car on the way home from the ski trip, Nyx turns into the kiss to brush his mouth across mine.

It's all I get, and it's enough.

One kiss every six months. One hug.

The rare contact is enough to bring tears to my eyes. I'm a regular Blubbering Betty today. Tonight. The hug finishes as Nyx drops his arms and returns to his solo dancing. Unwilling to intrude on his peace any longer, I pass the headphones back, repeating the action in reverse.

He gives me a little head bob, his eyes shuttering to block out the world. He finds serenity in the face of chaos and everything going on around him as he draws his usual curtain around himself, closing everyone else out, including me and his keepers. But for a moment, however brief, he let me inside.

My heart glows with the secret I'll never release.

Hands close at my hips, thumbs brushing my waist. "Can I claim that dance now?"

I raise my eyes to meet Aster's stare head on, his gaze still unforgiving, unflinching. It's the same one I've been clashing with since the first day I set foot at Alchem Academy. He won't back down and neither will I.

But it's Elen at my back, and it's his hands wrapped around mine.

That's what happens when you're dating four men.

Is that what I'm doing?

Elen answered that question with a simple shrug. *It does for us.*

But as I stare at Aster where he leans against the wall, watching us, I'm not sure it does.

Elen seems to accept us as we are. Nyx in his way, too. Even Zeke watches us with a small smile, his shoulders relaxing a fraction. But Aster is lost in a torment of his own making. I'm not sure who he hates more right now—me or Elen.

I want to act out and blow him a kiss or do something outlandish, but I can't bring myself to hurt him any further. He's already suffering. He doesn't need me to add to his self-torture. But I don't need to hurt anymore, either.

I squeeze Elen's fingers and twist in his embrace, turning my back to everyone else in the room, giving my answer to his earlier question when he's waited with more patience than I ever give him credit for.

"I'd love to."

He leads me across the room, sliding his hands across my bare back and drawing me into his chest as a familiar beat starts to play.

I freeze for a moment and a huff falls from my

lips. "You planned this," I mutter as one of his own Failure Asylum songs plays.

Elen laughs, though it's the rumble of his chest I hear. "Rockstar rules remember, Roxy Girl?"

Around us, girls scream and rush to fill the dance floor while Elen and I sway to a song neither of us can hear, but we dance to the music anyway. He leads and I try to follow, sinking into the shape of him until his lips are a whisper of a breath away.

Tiny jolts zing across my spine as he trails his thumb along the open space of my dress and back up, leaving me breathless. I feel his smile, and that he knows the effect he has annoys me a little.

The feel of him, lean and tall, is so different from Nyx's thicker chest or Zeke's bulk that it sets me on edge. I scramble to find my balance, and he ends up laughing at me again.

I roll my eyes. "Cocky much?"

His answer is a sort of crooked smile that twists his lips as he moves us around the dance floor. A few steps, and I forget about being self-conscious, the boys watching, Rhani making her appearance, or the rest of the Academy, and sink into the easy circle of Elen's arms.

He leads me, not to the complicated dance I saw on his video but something simpler, swaying and turning, dipping me and falling into the music like the beat lives through us together. When the sound slows, his fingers curve around my nape to settle against my pulse, tapping there. He draws me closer, and I can't breathe. The corners of his lips still curve up in that strange smile, but his eyes send a different message.

Elen drifts closer while everyone else around us moves farther away, drawing me in as his mouth settles over mine. The way the boys kissed me in the car on the way home from the snow trip, those were fun, a distraction. We all knew that. Even a kind of comfort. For all the playfulness in his dance, I know something has changed. This is Elen, all of him, and he's serious.

This kiss is nothing like my first with him.

Aster dominated, teaching me all the things he wanted. Nyx is peace. Zeke—he stops the world. But Elen seeks to explore, hesitant before requesting entry … and then I fall.

It's okay, because he falls too. We tumble together into a delicious abyss. We drift together in a way I don't think either of us quite understand, or maybe he does, and I don't.

Aster Craven has proven that I'm naive, that I understand little about all the boys who refuse to leave me alone and seek to protect me from everything out there including myself, but he's the farthest thing from my mind right now. Elen encompasses everything. Long, cool fingers close around my throat in the gentlest touch, almost connecting, pressing in time over my pulse with the increased beats beneath my palm against his chest.

His kisses never end, and I never want to stop. Some immeasurable amount of time later we part, and I'm not sure who breaks the kiss first. My eyes feel heavy and lazy as I gaze up at him and the way he looks back at me sets off a fizz that sinks right down to my toes where they're still connected to the ground.

The dance hall returns, but it's disconnected. Music pounds inside my head. I jerk, a little disjointed like a marionette with cut strings, leaning into his chest for balance.

Elen's hand tightens on my lower back, pressing me flush against his body. The headiness of his kisses still riots through my body. Dizzy and swaying, I trace the lines of ink that peek from inside his open shirt collar and wonder if they go all the way to his stomach. His tongue plays with his lip rings and I smile, matching the movement in a mirror image, tracing the small indent in my own lip that his pointed barbell made when he kissed me.

It didn't hurt, though I felt the sensation, savoring it, but it wasn't painful. I rise up on my toes, trying to read the indecipherable look in his golden eyes I've been obsessed with since my first day at Academy when I met him before I even walked through those hideous front gates. Back when those eyes were blue to match his hair and directed at me.

Right now, they aren't, and they're filled with victory and triumph as he stares over my head at Aster Craven. The fizzing in my toes develops into something so much worse.

I yank away from him, but Elen presses his hand to my lower back, refusing to let me budge.

"Stay," he murmurs, cool fingers catching my jaw to hold me in place. "Don't run, Roxy girl. Not from me."

"Don't fight him." I let out a shuddering breath, my head still swimming as he rocks us in a slow dance that's at odds to the music blaring through speakers that are way too close.

Bodies jostle us as the dance floor grows crowded. He might be used to everyone's eyes on him, but it's not a sensation I like or want to become accustomed to experiencing. Elen brushes his cheek against mine, changing our dance to music he guides us to against the rhythm of the rest of the room. I kind of like that.

"I don't know this song," I whisper, unsure if he's able to hear me.

He smiles against my cheek. "I wrote something for you. Maybe one day I'll have the balls to play it." He hesitates a moment then hums, low in his throat.

I strain to catch the melody amongst all the cacophony filling the room, trying to block everything else out, catching some of the notes as I press closer to him. He makes another sound, this one of approval.

His mouth turns to catch mine again and the fizz returns all over. The rest of the room could implode for all I know as he presses me impossibly closer until we fit together like two jigsaw pieces that should never have been taken apart.

My peace lasts right up until his knee presses on a sensitive spot my dress fails to hide, ripping me out of my reverie.

"Elen—" I mumble against his lips, or at least, I think I do. His thigh pulses, the action invisible to everyone amongst my voluminous skirts while the effect on my body is ridiculous. Waves of sensation swamp me, and it's overwhelming. "Too much."

His forehead rests against mine, his arms supporting me, holding me up. "I know. It's okay." The music around us swells to something upbeat. No one else can hear the conversation that's just for us.

All the same my cheeks burn, and I shiver in his arms, locking my fingers into his shirt and knotting the material. "We shouldn't—"

He pushes my hair behind my ear and cups the back of my head. "I'm a rockstar, Roxy. I can do whatever I like."

The tip of his pinky skims the lower curve of my back through the lace of my dress deliberately. The billowing material conceals everything even though we're standing right in the middle of the dance floor. It's still not enough for anyone else to see, but I know what will happen if our bodies press together the way they are. I can't do anything to stop it because it's Elen, and I'm clinging to him, too.

"Oh, my God," I breathe, my skin prickling all over, the sensations uncontrollable. Uncomfortable. I don't stop him, but I *can't* stop him either, jammed in a loop as my body takes over.

Heat and cold wash through me in wave, leaving me panicking as my body reacts to the pressure he knows where to apply. Elen understands what he's doing, and I...

I don't.

His fingers tip my chin up, and this time his eyes are narrowed, focusing on mine. "Roxy," he whispers as our mouths brush.

Heat engulfs me. I squeeze my eyes shut, willing myself not to pass out as I let him hold me to him murmuring things I can't hear for the white noise that fills my ears.

And all the while, Aster Craven's hateful gaze bores into my back. I can't bring myself to move though I know I'll pay for what he's witness to at Alchem's end of year dance.

With a boy I love, and the boy I love to hate.

And the boy who hates me back.

JOSS PHOENIX

Chapter Thirty-One

Numb

Aster

All her firsts should have been mine.

A small thing, not even mine to claim since I gave her up at my father's behest, but I hadn't wanted to rush her. *Us.* Even when I had the chance. Roxy was—is—something special to cherish. Maybe we were stupid, thinking we were saving ourselves for after school, like marriage. An outdated ideal, perhaps, and one we never spoke about. A few short weeks is all I got with her before everything I craved was blown to hell.

And now what I want is something that I can never have, thanks to the man who sired me. Not with his vendetta or my obsession, and what I did to her. *For her.*

I storm out of the hall past all the cheap, garish decorations, across the threshold and into the shadowed corridor beyond.

"Mr. Craven, you know smoking isn't permitted—" starts one of the remaining teachers before I've taken my second step into the shadows.

I flip him off and keep walking. It'll cost me a favor to keep him in my pocket next year and a five-figure check, but I don't care. I can't remain in that crowded space any longer, staring at Roxy and Elen like a creeper. Her blazing hair looped down her back is so goddamn beautiful, and with his arms around her they look like some anime couple come true. What does that make me—the antihero, or something lesser?

I scuff my Italian leather loafers against a locker, hard enough to dent the metal and ruin the polish on my shoes.

It doesn't make me feel any better.

"Want me to get a young kid so you can beat him up, too?" Zeke mutters as he appears at my side.

"Keep that thought in reserve for later." I don't look at him, finishing my smoke and pulling a fresh one from the pack.

Zeke grabs the lot and the lighter, stuffing them into his own jacket.

I look at him, surprise hiking my eyebrows. "The hell?"

"You'll smoke yourself to death." He leans back against the locker I attacked and closes his eyes.

Because I have so many glorious years remaining in this world.

I hold out my hand, flicking my fingers upward. "Now will do, thanks."

His head shakes once. "No chance."

I consider planting my fist in the ass monkey's gut, but I know he'll punch me back, and then I'll be bruised and will still have to face my father after having Gallaway arrested, my evidence insufficient to tie him to Faith's abuse to my everlasting irritation.

For once, what I've achieved will have to be enough. The arrests, that is. In terms of defeating Zeke, I have other avenues. I'm smarter than him, and quicker, but he's stronger, plus he trains harder. He'll put me on my backside, and there's a degree of respect I have to give him for that.

No more than my ego can afford right now, bruised and battered creature that it is already.

I thrust my hands into my pockets and glower at the hall door that mutes the music shuttered away behind it instead. "Why are you keeping me company?"

"So you don't do something stupid."

"Involving death?"

"Something like that."

We fall into silence for a few minutes before he cracks. "Brought you a present." He reaches into his back pocket and tosses me a bottle of cheap vodka.

I turn the bottle over, inspecting the label. A grin breaks out on my face. "Shipped by one of my father's biggest rivals."

Zeke nods and closes his eyes again. "I know. It's not enough to get duckfaced, but…"

It's not, but it's a damn fine idea from where I'm standing. Hell, if I get him drunk enough, maybe I'll get my smokes back.

"I'm in."

****

Drinking with Zeke does nothing to quell my rage. Fury still brews at my father for asking me to give up the one thing I love in this life. Loathing at myself for giving into what he asked, for destroying her. Disgust that I still want her and that, after everything, I still can't deal with the sight of another's hands on her knowing I can't be one of them, too.

Maybe that makes it worse because at the back of my heart I don't mind. What hurts is that I want to be a part of what they're creating around her. That I'm *not* a part of their intimacy is what stings so damn much.

And so I hate them as much as I hate myself.

I lean against Alchem's golden gates, leaving Zeke to punch up inanimate objects in the gym, neither of us as drunk as we want to be. An unlit cigarette dangles from my numbed fingers, the paper damp from the drizzle that coats my hair and drips into my eyes.

All sensation has long since departed, leaving me without the onset of the cold ache. The empty stillness of the night and the cheap vodka combined spreads through me until I may as well be a gargoyle standing sentinel at the gate to a school of debauchery. The sins of our fathers come into the light.

There's something in that. Maybe Elen should write a song about it.

"Aster?"

I don't hear her approach because when she comes to me she's barefoot, her glitter heels dangling from her fingers. They drop into a puddle on her side of the gate, still on the school grounds while I slide down the gilded metal to sit on the other side, watching down the long drive, toward the town. The glitter dulls with mud as it soaks into the shoes, ruining the delicate slippers.

I don't give her footwear a second glance as she kicks up water that sprays my back. It's more than I deserve.

"Roxy. Go back inside."

She tsks at me. "Don't tell me what to do."

I huff back. "Nothing's changed."

"Did you expect anything to change? Is that what this is about?" Fine, cold fingers work their way along my back in a tentative touch.

A shiver follows her fingers, and I stiffen. "Now, Roxy. Or…"

"Or, what?" she asks, curious.

"Or I'll…" I bite my lip, drawing blood.

I'll destroy you out of the pure spite bred into my veins.

I'll love you the way I want and taint every part of you with the darkness within me. Would you like that?

Sometimes I don't know who I am. Do you?

"I don't think even you know, Aster Craven," she whispers her answer to my plea that falls from my lips even though I didn't grant my permission.

But it's Roxy. She's seen the worst of me.

I shrug, letting my melancholy settle back over

my shoulders, weighing me against the gate. "Sure."

She laughs, settling in the rainwater at my back. Her skirt flares out, flicking fresh drops up as her weight leans against me through the golden bars. "Did you agree with me?" Her voice fades as she points her face in the opposite direction to mine toward the school.

Her back is my single point of warmth as I focus on pressing my spine to hers, lining us up without an inch of wasted air.

She's too close. Too much. I tip my head back, letting out a shallow breath as I try not to breathe her in.

"Yeah."

I let my hands drop to my sides, my cigarette tumbling free from unfeeling fingers to sink into the puddle. The backs of my fingers brush some of that fluffy material of her damp, golden gown. I frown, still staring down Alchem's circular drive that leads to the town beyond where I once watched her chase her underwear across the smooth surface and stole a locket from her suitcase that now sits in my bedside drawer.

Rain water trails from her dress to my hand, wicking up my shirt sleeve.

"How long have you been out here? You'll get sick."

She snorts, and it's a cute as hell noise. "Yes, Dad." She stares in the opposite direction, like she's waiting for me to taunt her.

It's the standard I've set between us. Love and hate, pull and take. *Never again.*

My lips form a sneer she can't see. "Don't do that. Don't play it off." My words come out sharper than I want, showing I care too much.

"Aster," she whispers, my name a caress on her lips, a promise, and it's so, so sweet. My heart aches one second and freezes in the next moment. "I know, all right? He told me. Zeke. About your dad. What he does. Hurting you. Everything."

This last comes out on a half-breath and I know she's crying.

Over me.

Fuck.

I'm not afflicted with Zeke's feathered obsession, or bound by his promise.

My fingers fold around the ruined fabric of her dress, winding the material tight around my fist. So much for the boons of cheap vodka. "Did he."

Remind me to slap him later.

"Don't punish him." *Please.* She doesn't need to say that last. We both hear her unspoken plea.

Him, not me.

"That stings, little Roxy." My voice holds a tone so familiar to us. She stills at my back as I don the persona we both recognize. Not at my father's behest this time, but at my own. *See who I am, who you think you love and hate all at once.* "Why do you care about what my father does, what he is? Elen— He did that to you on the dancefloor—"

My throat constricts, and I'm done.

"You saw," she whispers, sounding both horrified and breathless.

"Yeah, I saw. I was watching you because I can't not watch you. That should have been *me*." A growl rips at my throat.

I clamp my teeth together before I reach through the gilt bars and pull her to me. She's not mine to claim, not anymore. I shove my numbed hand into my pocket and fumble for my lighter. The damn thing falls into a small puddle, sinking to the bottom of the clear pool. I swear, flicking the ruined cigarette down the drive. It skitters away, rolling in concentric, dizzying circles.

Nowhere near enough vodka.

She reaches back between the gap in the bars, taking the chance I ignored. Her cold hand closes around my knuckles over her ripped dress. "It's okay. You can destroy me all you like, but I won't stop coming back. I love you."

My heart squeezes on that pithy emotion I can't trust. *Hope.* The fallacy bred into us.

"After everything I've done, you come back. Why?" I stare into the darkness, trying to pick out the town's lights, but it's too late, and there's nothing there but shadows on shadows. "Why does anyone want me?"

That last admission isn't for anyone's ears but hers. A child's fear, whispered to the night. The rain sweeps my words away on an icy breeze and a fresh scattering of sleet that pelts us. She presses back into me, shivering and seeking warmth, but never pulling away no matter what I do.

"You came to my room, when she—your ex—" Roxy falters for the first time after all we've been through.

This girl with the beautiful heart and the beautiful eyes is so damn perfect. Proving she's human after all, and that she's telling the truth by her presence alone.

She won't leave, and she wants me.

I'm enough for her as I am.

My heart shreds in my chest at the concept.

"I remember." I trace Alchem's drive with my eyes alone. My lighter and my cigarette lie forgotten in their puddles beside her ruined shoes, the gate a barrier between them. I reverse my hand, managing to unclench my fingers from her dress and find her warmth instead. Lacing our fingers together too tight, I cling to her as my lifeline, my anchor. "I remember a girl lost to a toxic friend she trusted. And understanding because that toxic friend used to be a girl I loved who tried to break me, too. I remember you with those damn bands on your wrist, flicking them and flicking them and flicking them so that it hurt. Then when the numbness went away, you'd do it again and again and again. I remember being so scared that when the nothingness stopped and you couldn't make it hurt anymore, you'd turn to something worse." I flick the buttons open on my shirt sleeves with my free hand and fumble to place her hands over my scars, the even marks from mutilating myself every time my father hurt me. Higher, on the fresh ones I made from when I hurt her. "I was scared that maybe you would do this, and that maybe you wouldn't be able to stop."

That I wouldn't be there to stop you when you couldn't.

She presses her back harder against mine, her fingers arching backward around my wrist. Cold water runs in rivulets from her hair into my collar and down my back, warming where her skin touches to mine through her dress. The fine barrier of our clothes might as well not be there at all. Fingertips trace the landscape of my scars, memorizing them. I suppose she has.

"You're right. It felt insurmountable."

I cover her hand over my scars. "I know, Roxy."

Salt mingles with rainwater at the corners of my lips while we sit there, letting the night eat away the pain that bridges the scars that bind us. By the time I stand, our hands still linked through the gate's meager openings, the rain has lightened.

Roxy faces me, her make up running down her cheeks, and she's never been more beautiful. I reach through the bars, catching her chin and drawing her close enough to kiss, but I don't. Not yet.

"So beautiful."

She smiles and reaches back, away from me.

Three bodies merge out of the gloom that surrounds Alchem's buildings in the quiet hours while the school is silent. The dance has long ended, staff and students finding other occupations for these silent hours. Misting rain keeps everyone else at bay while we alone haunt the school's boundary like so many wraiths. My lips break their frozen shape. It suits us.

Zeke strides forward to flick the lock on the gate, uncaring as the hideous thing flies back and bounces against one of the brick towers we used to sit on, grading everyone as they walked through. Some of the golden paint flakes off to reveal the rusty black beneath. Tarnished and tainted within, like the rest of us.

He grips my shoulder hard through my shirt and hauls my soggy ass back inside the grounds. "Both of you get back inside before you die of something stupid like a chill," he grouses. His usual fury wars behind his eyes though it's directed inward, for now. Undaunted, he grabs Roxy, too. She stumbles barefoot into a puddle next to her glittery shoes, ruined and mud-splattered, forgotten.

"Easy," Elen murmurs, stepping up to wrap an arm around her waist, his lips pressing to her ear. "I told you to come on tour with me, princess," he says in what should be soft enough for the two of them alone.

But out here, we all hear it.

"Is that an open invitation for everyone?" I catch Roxy's other wrist, unwilling to let her go now I've found her again.

Zeke manhandles my shoulder like I'll collapse on him. He might have part of that right, as my knees wobble with the combination of cold and vodka. I thread Roxy's hand through mine on the right side of the fence. She looks up at me, what could be a flare of hope in her eyes for the first time as she holds onto Elen for a moment, then steps a little closer to me.

Elen watches her for a long moment, and drops his hand, giving in with his usual easy grace. I envy him that. "Might be, if he signs with the agent I've lined up." He jerks a free thumb toward Nyx, trailing his fingers through Roxy's damp dress in lieu of touching her skin.

She turns a sweet smile on him that sends blood heading lower than my stomach.

"That's never gonna happen," Zeke snorts, and I have to agree with him.

Nyx looks up from his phone and holds the screen up, luminous side facing out. A contract with his signature fills it.

"Motherducker." Zeke stares, his mouth agape.

Roxy reaches up and closes his jaw and he *lets* her touch him before she turns to Nyx, linking her arms behind his neck and whispers something in his ear. His arms wind around her and he kisses her like none of us are standing right here, watching the whole thing.

"Damn," Elen murmurs. He slips the phone from Nyx's outstretched hand and scrolls through, though I don't think he's talking about the contract.

Nyx and Roxy part ways. He feathers his fingers over her cheek in the tenderest gesture I've ever seen him make. My heart jolts at the simple contact, whispering a single phrase I can't bear to face right now.

She raises on her toes, her lips framing the same words she said to me minutes before.

"I've got a jet," I blurt.

I can't tear my eyes off my friends knitted together by the impossible girl with the beautiful smile who somehow wants us all despite our scars and flaws, and the horrors we made her suffer.

What I made her suffer, and yet she still loves me. Us.

Elen huffs beside me, handing Nyx's phone back.

"I've got a tour."

I catch Roxy's waist as she scoots past me before Zeke can make a grab for her. That can happen later. He grumps at me but says nothing else. We have all the time in the world if we're getting on that plane over the break. Months with her, and no one to tell us otherwise.

She nestles into me, not pulling away as I draw the words she said to me before along her arm. Her whole body stills before she presses into me a little harder and damn if my eyes don't flood again.

Uncaring who sees the emotion in me, I rest my chin on top of her head. Roxy feels good, a forbidden fruit like she shouldn't be here, but here she is. Her arms wind around me as she clings to my body and looks at each of us in turn, then back to me.

"And I have all of you."

Elen grins. "Thank God. I hated the idea of going on tour alone. Now I've got a warm up act *and* an entourage."

I snort and flip him off. "Never thought what going solo meant, huh? You tell them yet?"

He shrugs. "Guess I need to, now."

Roxy squeezes my back and holds out her hand. "Not alone you don't," she says. "Not anymore."

The shock on his face reflects something inside each of us as her fingers wind through his, certain I'm a mirror to him as well.

The girl I've loved and hated and fallen for a dozen times since then. My bully. My girl.

My Roxy. She can't hide from us anymore.

Never again.

JOSS PHOENIX

Epilogue

Let It Burn

Aster

An hour before we're due at the jet to join Roxy, Elen, and Nyx, I stand before my father's desk, Zeke beside me. Alonso Craven stares at me through slitted eyes that stray to the whip wound in Zeke's hand, and the gun in mine, then to the door open at our backs like he expects his lackeys to come running.

Spoiler: they won't.

Unknown to him, my mother's lawyers found a happy loophole that allowed me to collect on that trust fund before the allotted term. The expression *money speaks* is deafening in the mansion's silence.

The empty palatial house with its sole inhabitant can burn to ash afterward for all I care. I won't be coming back. Not with Roxy waiting for me.

My father licks his fleshy lips. "Do you think you could waltz into this house and bring your dog with you without recompense?" He jerks his chin at Zeke, who doesn't bother looking at him.

His scarred fingers toy with the barbs he's added to the whip. "I should have made a leash. And a collar. It would have been fun to make him crawl. Something for another time, maybe."

"You let him speak to me like that?" Alonso roars, shoving up from his desk.

I clamp a hand to his shoulder and shove him forward. Zeke grabs his other wrist and yanks Alonso across the width of the desk while I lean over his bulbous, sweaty body.

"Did you think they would look after you forever? If they didn't kill you after you killed me, it would be a miracle. I'm surprised you lasted this long." I spit. Saliva rolls down his cheek like the tear I know he can't shed.

"I will destroy you." Alonso shoves his substantial bodyweight backward, but he has nothing to give and I have a girl to get back to.

"Don't bother," Zeke says, scoring his name into the French polish with a corner of barbed wire. "You can't win. Lie there and take it."

I smile at my father's back, recalling the words he once said to me one punishment, but I can't remember for what. "I'll do you a favor. The police are on their way with video evidence of my mother's murder at your hands, pulled from the feed in your bedroom. You remember Nyx, don't you? He's the 'loser friend' I think you mentioned once. He was kind enough to extract the video and touch it up along with Zeke, here. You are familiar with the term deep fake, right?" I place a cloth wrapped package beside his head and press his hand on it.

He gasps when his fingers touch cold metal. "This is—"

"Your way out." My voice doesn't shake. "This is a nice loaded gun registered to your name. You're going to need this if you don't want my other loser friend, Zeke the Dog, here, to flay all the flesh off your back in the six minutes it's going to take for the police to arrive, and then shoot your balls off."

Zeke raises his eyebrows at that last part, and I shrug. What can I say, I'm anxious to get back to our girl.

"You can't do that," my father snaps. "This is ridiculous. Let me up."

"Like hell." I strip my shirt off and display my scars—all of them, including the ones inflicted at his command. His *lessons* in this room. "Remember these?"

"Fine. Do it," he blusters. "I can take it."

I throw my shirt back on unbuttoned, turning back in time to see Zeke lean over the desk and smile in my father's face, making eye contact with my sire for the first time.

"No," he says softly. "You can't."

He turns and heads for the door, winding the whip in his grip, counting with each step. I follow, my paces measured. We're not over the threshold before the gun goes off.

"Happy Birthday," Zeke murmurs at my side. "I should have gotten you something better."

I finger the black-on-black gloss invitation in my pocket for a club with no title bearing Roxy's name. "I have everything I need."

Neither of us look back as we leave the house bathed in blue and red lights.

JOSS PHOENIX

Epilogue Two

Play Her Song

Elen

Yu-Jun: **Found out through fangirls. Not cool.**

In-Su: **You're leaving us?**

Chul: **Who's leaving?**

Taeyang: **Elen's ditching us. Broke the girlfriend clause.**

Chul: **Sad.**

Yu-Jun: **No words.**

Taeyang: **Why bother with contracts. Thanks for that.**

Taeyang has left the chat.

Chul: **We'll miss you.**

Yu-Jun: **Got a plan?**

In-Su: **Don't stop writing. Got the gift.**

I stare at the chat that blows up the moment they find out, thanks to a leaked announcement after the dance, because I was too much of a coward to fess up when I should have. Losing Tae hurts, but I thought it would be more. I expected to be blocked by everyone within minutes.

Elen: **Going solo. Not stopping.**

Chul: **Wish you the best.**

In-Su: **Still insulted. Good luck though. Don't be a stranger.**

Elen: **Cross my heart. Steal my inspo.**

Yu-Jun: **Got my own.**

Chul: **Can we get laid, now?**

Tears prick the corners of my eyes as the chat devolves into our usual chatter, sans one. My thumbs are sore when time zones click over and they drift off, one by one. The friendship we thought had dissolved years ago reinstated in a second. Tonight is simply formalizing the end process. Thanks to Sonya, my legal side is complete and my solo life is in effect.

But not without the company of those I love.

My duckbutt went numb hours ago, and my battery is close to flat by the time I put my phone on the ground beside me, tears glazing my face where I hide behind the library, my feet propping me up.

Nyx settles beside me, sliding in like he's always been there. I suppose in a way, he has. His shoulder presses to mine. I'm surprised when he doesn't offer me an earbud, but brushes my tears away, concern lighting his eyes as he pays attention to each one.

As much as I'm used to stylists fussing over me before going on stage, having someone closer to me is … different. Not uncomfortable. But I know he's there.

"It's gonna be a lot of this over the next months," I warn him, keeping my words kind and sweet, unwilling to scare him. I remember this part. The excitement. The all encompassing, crushing fear. "For both of us, okay? Lot of emotion. Lot of pressure. Keep it in here." I tap his forehead. "And here." I press my hand over his heart and leave it there.

Nyx watches me for a second, and the fingers brushing away my tears become a light caress. His hand cups my cheek, and he leans in to cover my mouth with his. My breath stops though his heart pounds a little harder beneath my hand. Letting my eyes close, I tip my head back against the building, bringing him with me and kiss him back until the tears stop flowing and the ache in my heart eases.

I might have lost a family, but I've gained one, too. Closer, and so much more than before.

Nyx pulls away, crouching before me.

"You've done that before?" I ask, breathless.

Usually, it's Roxy who's out of words, but now, here, it's me.

He nods. "Aster," he says, drawing the letters on my shoulder.

"Huh." I tap his heart where my hand still rests over his shirt, and it's comfortable. "Remember what I said. Here, okay?" I swallow, Nyx's leather scent swirling around my head, his sense of music imbibed into my blood.

Zeke's cursing precedes his path as he rounds the corner of the building. "You two done snogging? We gotta go. Pilot's getting antsy."

I find Nyx's hand and squeeze.

He squeezes back.

"Yeah. We're ready now." I pocket my flat phone, no longer needing to check the messages to see who answers or doesn't, or what they think. The people in this circle matter, and maybe two others. Then I stop. "Who'd you leave Roxy with?"

Zeke's slow smile gets my feet started.

The End

JOSS PHOENIX

ABOUT THE AUTHOR

JOSS PHOENIX is a young adult Australian author who had way too many crushes through high school and never told anyone about any of them. She writes sassy characters, loves rainy days, has a secret stuffie collection, and swears she never has enough coffee, black or otherwise.

JOSS PHOENIX

Evernight Teen

www.evernightteen.com